Meltdown

The story of a tragic
psychological collapse

Geoff A. Wilson

kindle direct publishing

First published 2021
Kindle Direct Publishing (UK Office)
44 Ashbourne Drive
Coxhoe
DH6 4SW

Edited by Olivia J. Wilson
Cover design software by Pixabay and Canva

About the author

Born in London to a British father and a French mother, *Geoff A. Wilson* grew up in southern Germany where he went to primary and secondary school. He is trilingual in German, French and English. He studied for his MA in Geography, Cultural Anthropology and Archaeology at the University of Freiburg (southern Germany), before completing his PhD in Geography at the University of Otago in Dunedin, New Zealand. From 1992-2003 he worked as a Geography Lecturer/Senior lecturer at King's College London, and from 2004-2019 as Professor of Geography (Emeritus Professor since 2019) at the University of Plymouth (south-west UK). Geoff became a world-renowned academic expert on questions about the resilience of human communities, more specifically about how rural communities cope with, and adapt to, change, disturbances and disasters. He has published over 100 academic articles on the subject and has written several books including *Environmental management: new directions for the 21st century* (with Raymond L. Bryant; UCL Press, 1997), *Multifunctional agriculture: a transition theory perspective* (CABI International, 2007) and *Community resilience and environmental transitions* (Routledge, 2012). Married and with one son, he lives in a small village on the south coast of Devon, UK. Geoff retired in 2019 to become a full-time writer. He specialises in psychological thrillers, young adult fantasy books and dystopian novels. *Meltdown* is his sixth novel.

Books by Geoff A. Wilson:

The 'Lllobillo Children's fantasy series':

Lllobillo: The Secret Portal (Austin Macauley, 2017)

The Viking Curse (KDP Publishing, 2020)

Psychological thrillers/Psychological fantasy:

Depravity: A Story About the Darkness of the Human Soul (KDP Publishing, 2020)

Meltdown: The Story of a Tragic Psychological Collapse (KDP Publishing, 2021)

The Dream (KDP Publishing, 2021)

Dystopian fiction:

Pandemic (KDP Publishing, 2020)

Short stories:

The Machine (KDP Publishing, 2021)

Check out Geoff's YouTube channel (you can find it under 'Geoff A. Wilson') where he talks in short videos about his book writing strategy and each of his books

Foreword

This is a tough story and will not be an easy read for many readers. And yet it should resonate with most as it is about friendship (which we all experience in some form or another in our lives), about kids at school and their often brutal, strange and uncompromising worlds (which we all have been part of), about the complex and often difficult relationship between children and their parents (again, all of us can relate to this whatever relationship we have had with our parents), about difficult changes in people's relationships with each other (which we all experience during our lives, some more painful than others), and about jealousy and envy between friends (again, most of us can relate to this). Most importantly, this is a story about the tragic psychological collapse of a person who seemed quite normal as a teenager but who, for various reasons, broke down mentally as an adult and never recovered – a psychological meltdown many of us will have witnessed among people we know.

Although the story is set in former West Germany between the 1970s and the present, this is not a particularly 'German' story. Indeed, it could be set almost anywhere in the world, i.e. the US, France, the UK, Australia, or indeed in any of the burgeoning transition economies that are increasingly sharing the social, economic and cultural problems, pressures, traps and challenges that shape individuals' modern life pathways and that, at times, can severely affect individuals' psychological wellbeing. After all, we all go to school, we all make friends at school and beyond, and we are all dependent on the vicissitudes of life that may toss us one way or another and almost always in unpredictable ways. And we are all psychologically vulnerable to greater or lesser extent, whether we like to admit it or not. We all have our pain, troubles and secrets, and none of us gets through life unscathed.

May this story, therefore, be a warning to all those parents, daughters, brothers, friends, sisters, grandparents, sons and acquaintances of fragile personalities who do not realise that psychological meltdowns are frequently the result of a series of seemingly innocuous and unrelated events that can add up to immense psychological pressure and that may break a person's fragile disposition. As recounted here, it is often also the, in hindsight, unwise personal choices in life, when one reaches one of these important bifurcations in one's complex decision-making tree of life, that, ultimately, define the psychological fate of an individual, and which can cast her or him on a pathway of irretrievable psychological meltdown.

1

14th June 2019. Hans looked anxiously over the back rim of his sofa. There was the noise again! Sweat poured down his chubby face and he had to squint awkwardly as sweat trickled into his left eye. He nervously swiped the sweat from his forehead, but he was afraid to make any noise. Here it was again. That noise! Somebody was in his flat, he was sure of it. Hans thought he heard faint footsteps. *No, no, no!*, he thought, his fear rising and his throat tightening. Hans crouched again behind his sofa, kneeling and sobbing, his arms tightly holding his chest trying to stem the trembling of his body. *But I am safe here, I am safe behind this sofa!*, he thought while trying to placate his inner demons, this indescribable fear that pinned him helplessly to the ground.

After a few minutes of kneeling on the hard, wooden floor, not daring to move for fear of making any noise, Hans slowly rose again to peer over the rim of the sofa. He could swear that the noise was still audible, somewhere out there in his apartment. *But where are the intruders, why do they never show themselves?*, he thought angrily while picking a loose strip of skin at the side of his right middle finger, pulling and pulling until a dark line of blood threaded the edge of the nail. The skin around his finger, already mutilated by his teeth from previous occasions, felt hard and calloused, with bits of dried blood evident where he had gnawed off chunks of flesh in the past. Hans spat out the small chunk of half-dried skin, looking at his mangled finger and wiping his mouth in disgust. For what seemed like an eternity, Hans glanced again over the rim of his sofa. He could see his living room, part of the kitchen on the left, and a small section of the corridor leading to the front door of his flat. But there was nobody to be seen. The noise of shuffling footsteps, rattling plates and pans, the brushing of a body against furniture, heavy breathing coming out of a battered throat, and the swishing of gloved hands brushing over pictures on a wall, all these noises, audible so clearly a moment ago, had suddenly all dissipated.

For a few minutes now, Hans had heard nothing. And yet, just like over the past five days, Hans did not dare leave the safety of the den he had built behind his sofa. Discarded food and food wrappers were strewn everywhere, including empty bags of crisps, nuts and dried fruit, and crushed plastic bottles he had filled with water just before fleeing to his den. There were also two plates with rotting remains of vegetable lasagne and a meat and rice dish he had quickly snatched from his fridge, before barricading himself behind his sofa, and which he had gulped down cold over the past few days. Various wrappings of *Snickers*, *Mars* and *Milky Way* bars he had scoffed down, when hunger had overtaken him during these endless past five days, were also strewn at his feet.

In his confused and panicked state, Hans did not notice the vile stench coming from one corner of his den where he had relieved himself over the past days, with several turds lying in a large pool of piss that had seeped both under the sofa, into the pile of still unopened food, and into one end of the bedsheet he had hastily retrieved from his bedroom before escaping to the den. Hans' unwashed and soiled clothes, which he had not changed for at least five days and in which he also slept, were filthy, smelly and reeking from the fact that Hans could not properly wipe his bottom for lack of loo paper, which he had forgotten to stash during his escape from the threatening noises.

But Hans either did not notice or care about the smell coming from his body and surroundings, as he was entirely focused on listening out for the intruders, on working out where they were in his apartment, what things of his they were touching. Just the thought of these bastards rummaging around in his flat made him retch. For hours he would cling on to the rim of the sofa, concentrated, focused and listening out for the intruders and ready to duck if one of them came into his line of vision. Only when sleep overwhelmed him would he stoop down onto his soiled bedsheet to catch a few fitful hours of sleep, somehow feeling protected by the rough firmness and solidity of the back of his sofa. Although light came in from his large living room window, somewhere out there with the curtains unreachable from his den and seemingly miles away, Hans had developed his own rhythm of sleeping and waking. Sometimes he would doze for a few minutes, suddenly waking up with a start when he thought he had heard a noise, but sometimes he would sleep for a few hours which his increasingly exhausted body demanded, irrespective of whether it was light outside or not. At times, Hans was not sure whether he was asleep or awake, as his confused dreams seemed to merge with reality. Had he dreamt that he heard a noise, or was one of the intruders rummaging again in his kitchen? Had he dreamt that he woke up, or was he really peering from the rim of his sofa? In brief moments of lucidity Hans would pinch his arm to check whether he was awake. Or was he dreaming that he was pinching himself?

Hans again wiped the sweat from his brow. He was utterly exhausted. *Why are these bloody intruders not showing themselves?*, he asked himself over and over again. *Why are they taunting me? Why do they want to destroy me, these evil pricks!* He carefully glanced over the rim of the sofa again. There! Was that not the flicker of a shadow he had seen through the frosted glass panes of his bedroom door? And that faint noise? Was that not one of these bastards going through the bedroom drawer where he kept his underwear and socks? Hans' body convulsed at the thought of one of these bastards touching his underpants. He imagined rough, calloused fingers fondling his underwear, smelling it, spitting and pissing on it or even soiling it with their semen! How could he take this much longer? Utterly exhausted Hans lay down again on his soiled sheet and closed his eyes. As sleep quickly overtook him, his trembling body began to relax, his morbidly obese frame eased itself into a slightly more comfortable position on the hard floor, and he began to snore loudly, his mind drifting away into a place where, for a brief moment, he escaped his growing fear, angst and anxiety.

Part 1

Friendship

2

25th July 2019. Gregory looked out of the window of the large bungalow where he lived with his wife and son (who was now at university) in their small coastal village on the south coast of Devon in the UK, east of Plymouth. He was in a pensive mood. He had just come from the bathroom where he had looked at himself in the mirror and was surprised at the old man looking back at him, at the changes the years had made in him. Such moments could strike him without warning, betraying his belief that he was essentially unchanged.

Having recently retired from his job as an academic at the local university he found that he had more time to think, especially about the past, about people he knew and had known, about relationships, about … life itself. But this reminiscing about the past had also been brought about by one of his long-planned retirement projects, which involved scanning and sorting all his photos – old paper prints and slides and more recent mobile phone pictures – into a digital archive which could eventually be passed to his son and anybody else among his family and friends who would be interested in receiving copies of old and new photos of themselves and people they knew.

This was where Gregory had come across pictures of his old schoolfriend Hans. The pictures had been taken with Gregory's new camera at the time, during a school trip from their German school to London. It must have been 1978, in Year 12 at school when Gregory would have been 17 and Hans 18. In one picture, Hans glanced at the camera with a lost-puppy-eyed-look in his brown eyes and a sheepish grin that suggested that he had been caught unawares when the picture was taken. In another photo, a hint of jealousy was possibly perceptible in Hans' facial expression as he – again seemingly caught unawares of being photographed – stared askance at Gregory's other schoolfriend Bill who smiled at the camera with a confident, almost arrogant, look on his face.

Gregory had looked at both pictures with surprise as they had suddenly jolted back memories about Hans, like a sudden unexpected and uneasy call from a distant past. Over the past few years Gregory had not forgotten Hans, but, like many things in life, some old schoolfriends and former acquaintances had retreated into the background, had been pushed aside by other, more pressing events. These memories were always there somewhere, but, at times, needed some trigger, such as an old photo, to be brought back towards the front, to rekindle memories, to register again in Gregory's consciousness. Gregory was still regularly in touch with several of his old school and university friends, and indeed saw some of them, like Bill, frequently (although many lived in continental Europe and as far away as New Zealand where Gregory had studied for his PhD), but Hans had not been among those he had seen recently or regularly.

As he stood there, watching a flock of birds gliding into view through the large living room windows, Gregory thought back as to why he had lost contact with Hans. *After all, we were best friends for at least four or five intensive years, from about age 13 to 17 or 18, at a time when we were both most impressionable when it came to being influenced by friends and our school peer group*, Gregory thought while scratching his stubbly chin. It was still early in the morning and Gregory's wife Amelia was still in bed. The house was eerily still, and only the screeching of seagulls circling above the estuary could be heard outside. But then he reminded himself that he knew exactly why he had lost contact with Hans, and that it had not been a coincidence or because other things in Gregory's life had kept him too busy. It was because Hans had changed, because he had become this 'other' person that Gregory had no longer recognised, or accepted, as the friend he once was. So, which Hans had the photos Gregory saw conjured up? The current imagined one, struggling with life after several psychological breakdowns, or the flamboyant one from their childhood past? Gregory knew that there was never only one of anyone, everybody changed, of course, but few had changed as much as Hans. And, of course, history itself was only ever a story, told by the ones, like Gregory, who survived it.

In the end I am just a coward!, Gregory thought not for the first time while clenching his fist and biting his fingers nervously. He recalled the fact that, during his last visit to see Hans in 2010, he had not been able to cope with how Hans had changed, to handle the psychological transformation of his former friend, to face the emotional demands Hans had placed on him at the time. Just after seeing Hans in person for the last time in 2010, Gregory and his family had moved house and Gregory had not passed on their new phone number and address to Hans. He had also not given Hans his mobile phone number. *Do I regret having severed the contact with Hans?*, Gregory wondered while looking over to the posh houses on the other side of the estuary. *Do I feel guilty because I have 'abandoned' Hans? But then none of my other friends wanted anything to do with Hans over the past years either, even over the past decades. Everybody abandoned Hans, not wanting anything to do with someone who had gone mad ... nuts ... bonkers. I can't be too hard on myself here, as most people would struggle to cope with somebody who lost their mind.* But he also had to admit that he had not thought much about the possibility of visiting Hans again over the past nine years. Hans, and his whole sad story, had indeed been pushed into the background, relegated to the side-lines, and increasingly erased from memory. *And now these photos from our London trip that have suddenly brought it all back!*, Gregory thought irritated and angry. *Why can these ghosts of the past not leave me alone? But then it is human nature that we should care about our fellow human beings, especially about somebody we had classed as 'best friend' at one point in our lives. And what was I expecting anyway, scanning all these old photos? Of course, they are bound to bring up memories. Don't kid yourself!*

Gregory sat down at the living room table with a sigh. He knew that, from this moment onwards, he had to re-engage emotionally with Hans and his sad life story. The seed was planted, the ball was set in motion, the buried distant memories could no longer be ignored. Indeed, now that Hans' story had resurfaced in Gregory's mind, he knew that he could no longer avoid it or push it aside, especially as it must have lingered there somewhere in the background over the past years anyway, always ready to be rekindled, acknowledged and confronted with the flick of a photo album page or a scanned photo. Suddenly and unexpectedly, as several stark and painful memories about his last meetings with Hans came flooding back, Gregory started sobbing, gently placing his face in his hands and feeling the wet tears trickling down his cheeks.

Gregory cried because he knew that Hans' story was one of the saddest stories of all the people he knew, a story about a person's life pathway where questions had to be asked whether at any point in time another path could have been chosen that may have changed the way things turned out. In discussions with his students at university, where he had specialised in researching the resilience of small human communities, Gregory had often talked about people's 'path dependencies' and whether decision-making pathways were either inevitable and predestined or malleable and under a person's full control. Gregory often likened a person's life pathway to a tree, with childhood and youth most typically akin to the trunk of the tree, straight and unilinear, shaped by the decisions taken – in a 'normal' family at least – by the parents on behalf of the child, i.e. where to live, which school to go to, which people and relatives to associate with. But then a tree trunk branches off into a multitude of individual branches and twigs, each one possibly representing a crucial life choice, most typically in one's late teens or early twenties (at least among people growing up in advanced economies where children were usually not forced to make life-changing decisions early on in their lives). Key decisions included, for example, taking the final school exams or not, or a decision whether to study, to work as an apprentice, to travel for years, to go out with this girlfriend or boyfriend or another, or to stay on your own. The friends one makes, the foolish little decisions one takes naïvely, some working out, some not – all of these individual life choices influenced the future life branch one would be on. Of course, many choices were not set in stone and decisions could be amended, changed or rectified, branches intersected with other branches and one could, occasionally, jump from one large branch to another. Gregory had often thought that a more fitting analogy was perhaps a frayed rope where life choices were braided from individual strands. As with choices and opportunities in life, braids unravelled, strands split and new life opportunities emerged. But the problem for most people was that the life rope did not fray neatly, although filaments may criss-cross from braid to braid and, occasionally, two braids tangled to form a new braid altogether. But the more stuck on a branch or braid – or a life pathway – one was, the more difficult it was to veer off course, to change one's ways, to break through 'path dependencies', and to rectify mistakes of the past. If one's life choice had taken one a long way along a specific branch or braid – for better or worse – it became progressively more difficult to jump from one branch to another as the distance between them grew, making it increasingly difficult to change course. The conservatism (with a small 'c') of older people could often be explained by the fact that they were truly 'stuck' a long way up a life branch – i.e. path-dependent – with little or no way to think and act outside the life pathway they were on, and not able to reflexively accept viewpoints and ways of life of people on other life branches. Although life was full of examples of people changing the pathways of their lives even later on in life – i.e. tangled braids or intersecting branches – most life pathways were decided between the ages of about 18 to 30, and, once stuck on a branch, that was it for most people. You had to live with the choices you had made, again for better or worse, for richer and poorer, and it became increasingly difficult to step onto another life branch, to alter the course of your life.

Gregory thought about his own life pathway which had been, on the whole, a successful and happy one: a steady childhood, albeit marred by his parents' divorce; an excellent education at a German high school and a good German university, with his PhD completed in New Zealand; a fantastic wife and a nice son; a good university career for both him and his wife with a good double income; and a nice and solid pension which was the envy of many of his friends and acquaintances. Overall, Gregory knew that he had either been very lucky or that he had taken good life pathway choices (or both), the risky decision in the late 1980s to go from Germany to New Zealand to do his PhD being one of the examples which had worked out nicely in terms of opening many new opportunities in the English-speaking world and enriching his CV in very positive ways. And yet, in all honesty, it had been far from certain at the time whether this would turn out to be a good life pathway choice, both with regard to career options and personal development, although, in the end, it had all turned out very well.

Of course, you could never compare one life pathway with an alternative 'what if' scenario, as it was impossible to assess how another life pathway may have turned out. From a different perspective a seemingly successful life branch may indeed look rather bland and boring, while another possible life pathway may have led to complete disaster. But Gregory was also a firm believer that you could at least partly shape your life pathways – the branch of the tree you climbed on when you took key decisions aged between 18 and 30 – and that, as a German saying went, 'where the enthusiast stands is the top of the world'. In other words, through enthusiasm and even obsession about a specific goal you could at least partly shape your own destiny, although, for various and complex social, economic and cultural reasons, such options were not open to everyone.

All of the life pathway decisions were, of course, complicated by issues such as health and psychological wellbeing – those things in life upon which you may have less control and that were often shaped more by your genes and family history. After all, you had no control over who your parents and relatives were and what legacy they would bequeath to you in relation to your genes and propensity to illness, inherited wealth, intelligence, and the socio-cultural mores within which you grew up. So, being a relatively free agent with regard to life choices depended, of course, very much on being healthy. Ill people, especially those with a severe illness from childhood onwards, were often severely constrained in their choice of life pathways by their illness, although, again, there were plenty of examples where severely ill people had managed to embark on very fulfilling pathways. The late astro-physicist Stephen Hawking, pursuing a very successful academic career while suffering from highly debilitating motor-neuron disease, was one of the more famous cases in point; or indeed Gregory's very own father who, despite suffering from severe muscle loss from polio, had had a very successful career as a world-renowned optical engineer specialising in the development of lenses for large-scale telescopes.

Thinking again about his friend Hans and his life choices, Gregory wondered, not for the first time, how important Hans' initial psychological state had been in his decisions about which life pathways to choose. Gregory was not a psychologist and had no training in clinical psychology, but from the readings he had done as a layperson on the subject he knew that it often was a typical 'chicken-and-egg problem'. What came first: the chicken or the egg, i.e. the chosen life pathway and the ensuing psychological problems, or the psychological problems leading a person to choose a specific ill-suited life pathway? The case of Hans epitomised the complexity of the issue: on the one hand, Hans' life story could easily be interpreted as one where poor life choices and sheer bad luck had led to severe psychological problems, but it could also be seen as the story of a person with at the time undiagnosed severe psychological problems being allowed to make poor life pathway choices because of a pre-existing precarious psychological state. Of course, it probably was not that black-and-white. The way Gregory saw it from his current vantage point of being able to look back over several decades, in Hans' case it was probably poor life choices that exacerbated a problematic psychological disposition, more like a see-sawing pathway in which a person made a specific choice which slightly worsened their psychological well-being, which in turn affected the next life choice, and so on – in Hans' case all exacerbated by a problematic and difficult family set-up, especially with regard to Hans' father.

Gregory knew that everyone had their own pain and secrets, and that nobody went through life unscathed. But in no other person he knew, and whose lives he had observed (including his own family, friends and acquaintances), had the correlation between life choices and psychological breakdowns been so stark as in Hans' case. Hans' story, therefore, was a warning to all those parents, brothers, sisters, grandparents, sons, daughters, friends and acquaintances of fragile personalities who did not realise that psychological meltdowns are frequently the result of a series of seemingly innocuous and unrelated events that can add up to immense psychological pressure that, in turn, can break a person's fragile disposition. It was often also the – in hindsight – unwise personal choices in life, when one reached one of these important bifurcations in one's complex decision-making tree of life, that, ultimately, defined the psychological fate of an individual, and that could cast her or him on a pathway of irretrievable psychological meltdown.

3

25th July 2019. Gregory could not remember exactly when he had first met Hans. Spurred on by seeing Hans' picture from their school trip to London, Gregory had tried to find the earliest evidence of Hans' presence in his life. After digging through multiple photo albums he had inherited from his deceased mother, Gregory had come across a faint picture from a newspaper cutting his mother had labelled 'Primary School Class 1969'. This clearly showed Hans, aged about 9, in primary school sitting a few benches away from Gregory, but Gregory did not recollect having much interaction with Hans then. Obviously Hans was in the same primary school class as Gregory for several years, but his memories of Hans as one of his best friends started much later when Gregory was about 13 and Hans 14 years old. Judging from this early picture, Gregory and Hans had apparently always been in the same year group, first at primary school and then, from the age of 10 onwards, in secondary school.

Gregory and Hans grew up in south-west Germany, in the town of Heidenhausen an der Frenz (the latter denoting the location of the town on the river Frenz), a small town of about 50,000 inhabitants located in the eastern region of Baden-Württemberg, in a valley in the hill area of the *Schwäbische Alb* (Swabian Alb) close to the Bavarian border. Gregory's parents, Ron and Alice, had moved to

Heidenhausen in 1964 when he was 3 years old, as his father had taken up a job at the nearby *Karl-Schweiss Factory* which produced optical equipment (best known to the present day for its microscope lenses but also involved in telescope technology and military optical equipment). Before the Second World War, *Schweiss* had originally been solely located in Dresden in the eastern part of Germany, but after the closing-off of Eastern Germany behind the 'iron curtain' in the Soviet-influenced Eastern European sphere, a parallel factory was established near Heidenhausen. A key reason was that West Germany was interested in the continuation of production of high-quality optical equipment for West Germany, independent from a reliance on the original firm that was now in what had become the *German Democratic Republic*. A second reason was that the region of the eastern *Schwäbische Alb* around Heidenhausen offered a well-educated and highly skilled workforce in a region that was in dire need of an economic boost, especially after the post-1950s closure of most of its increasingly uncompetitive textile firms.

Gregory's British father, who for various reasons had been keen to leave the UK at the time, and who had just completed a PhD and research fellowship in optical engineering in London, had jumped at the opportunity offered by a well-paid position at *Schweiss*, and Gregory's French mother had also been happy for the family to move there. Although a French citizen, Gregory's mother had been brought up in *Alsace* in eastern France, which was as much German as French. As a result, the move to Heidenhausen was not much of a culture shock for her, as she spoke

German fluently. Gregory's brother Max was born in Heidenhausen in 1964, his German name testimony to their family's wish to integrate fully into German society (Gregory's dad had learned German relatively quickly and Gregory always remembered him being fluent in the language). Many families of those who had started work in the rapidly expanding *Schweiss* business lived in Heidenhausen, as the town offered cheaper housing than other towns further north, which were much more expensive as they were within commuter distance to the economically booming capital of Baden-Württemberg, Stuttgart. As a result, hundreds of *Schweisser* families (as the workers at *Schweiss* became to be known) had moved to Heidenhausen at the time when Gregory's parents moved there in 1964. The impact of the *Schweissers* on the town was evident through the labelling of one of the posher neighbourhoods as *Schweiss Siedlung* (*Schweiss* settlement) with most of their children – including Gregory – labelled as *Schweiss Kinder* (kids from parents working at *Schweiss*), who almost all went to the nearby newly built *Franz-Bosch-Gymnasium* (Franz-Bosch secondary school/high school).

Although not much aware of it at the time, Gregory was convinced that this label of *Schweiss Kinder* had led to a form of positive discrimination for him and his immediate peer group, and that this subsequently had played a key role in his relationship at school with non-*Schweisser*s like Hans. Although at *Franz-Bosch-Gymnasium* nobody talked openly about being part of the *Schweiss Kinder* in-group, they were seen from the outside as coming from families with better educational backgrounds than the non-*Schweisser*s and were, as a consequence, also often seen by many non-*Schweisser*s as aloof and, possibly, a bit arrogant. The differentiation between *Schweisser*s and non-*Schweisser*s was exacerbated by the fact that almost all *Schweisser*s came from families that either had an international background (like Gregory's family), or who had come from other parts of Germany. *Schweiss*-Kinder, thus, almost always were more knowledgeable about the rest of the world and other cultures than the kids who came from Heidenhausen and surroundings. Possibly, therefore, the segregation between *Schweisser*s and non-*Schweisser*s in their year group was always there 'in the background', and may have influenced peer-group formation, stability, and, most importantly, rejection. However, from Gregory's perspective at least, this segregation rarely played out in openly acknowledged taunts, jeering, heckling or, indeed, open fist fights. *But then, maybe, a different story would be told by someone from the non-Schweisser group?*, Gregory had to admit while thinking about Hans and the situation in his former school class.

Because Heidenhausen was one of the few towns that was economically struggling in otherwise relatively wealthy Baden-Württemberg, the contrast between peer groups from different economic backgrounds was possibly starker at schools such as *Franz-Bosch* than in many other German towns and cities, especially as *Schweiss* workers had relatively high salaries. Gregory remembered his impressions of Heidenhausen as a town when he grew up: although it was the centre of his childhood universe, it quickly became evident to him, even as a young kid – either through various trips and holidays his family undertook to other towns and other regions in Germany or through derogatory comments from his visiting relatives (which he did not always fully understand at the time) – that Heidenhausen was a relatively poor place. The closure of the textile industry in Heidenhausen, which had also ravaged many other geographically remote towns all over Europe, had left scarred remnants of industry in the form of dilapidated and empty warehouses, factories and workshops that were still visible in the townscape of the 1960s and 1970s, and that were testimony to the fact that no other industry had replaced them. The closure of industry had had a devastating ripple effect on the town's housing stock, and Gregory remembered well many empty buildings, especially at the bottom of the valley on the town outskirts where most industrial workers had lived in the past. He also still had vivid images of the relatively dilapidated town centre with rather bland and struggling local shops, the odd dilapidated pubs and cafes, and a few dishevelled chain stores with uninspiring displays that were testimony to the relative poverty of the town's inhabitants.

As a result, and during the 1960s and 1970s in particular, the regional council took the bold decision to 're-invent' Heidenhausen not as an industrial town but as an educational hub for the region of the eastern *Schwäbische Alb*. This led to the creation of two new secondary/high schools in addition to the already existing three schools, and provided, over the years, some much-needed additional income for the depleted town coffers. But even this could not stem the outflow of people from Heidenhausen to more vibrant centres nearby.

Indeed, Gregory had always been well aware of the fact that Heidenhausen was one of the few towns in prosperous Baden-Württemberg that had lost population since the 1950s, and, as far as Gregory knew, the problem persisted to the present day.

Gregory's secondary school, the *Franz-Bosch-Gymnasium*, was one of these newly established schools. From its first year of opening in 1971, the year when Gregory joined the school as a ten-year old (Germans start secondary school at a relatively early age after only four years of primary school), Gregory's school class contained a complex mix of *Schweiss*-Kinder, kids from Heidenhausen from various socio-economic backgrounds, and, linked to the new strategy of Heidenhausen as a regional school hub, children from many surrounding rural villages. The latter were usually bright (entry into German *Gymnasiums* requires the passing of a relatively tough entry exam), but were often seen by the other schoolkids as a bit 'backward' and 'peasanty'. They usually came from socially conservative families and were often Catholic. Indeed, the region around Heidenhausen had a complex mix of Catholics (*katholisch*) and Protestants (*evangelisch*), with some villages predominantly Catholic while the neighbouring village may be Protestant. This complex religious geography had meant that, inevitably, villages and towns had been at each other's throats during the 30-Years-War (1618-1648), and much animosity remained between the two groups to the present day. The division into *katholisch* and *evangelisch* was yet another of those socially constructed, artificial and utterly stupid barriers that separated kids within the same school class from each other. However, the most distinguishing feature of the school kids from surrounding villages was that they spoke with a broad *schwäbisch* accent – the distinctive and rather parochial dialect of the region. Thus, rather than saying "Ha nein, weisst du! Du bist halt ein Arsch!" (Well, you know! You are really an asshole!), they would say "Ha noe, woisch! Du bisch holt a Aaarsch!" Indeed, one of the rural children in their school class, Klaus Hintermaier, would come to play an important role in Hans' late teens, and played a key role in exacerbating Hans' evolving psychological problems.

Gregory was, therefore, convinced that this multiple and complex social, economic and cultural stratification of pupils in their year group had also played a role in explaining some of the social dynamics and peer group power tussles and antics that had worsened the psychological problems Hans was facing later on. It may have also exacerbated the ever-present brutal and Darwinian streak among rival factions in their school class, and may have led to outsiders feeling even more marginalised.

Yet, despite the relative poverty of Heidenhausen, Gregory was fully aware that, in comparison with most of the rest of Europe, and certainly with most of the rest of the world, the south of West Germany where they grew up was a bubble of wealth, still riding high on the back of the West German 'economic miracle' of the 1950s and 1960s. Although relatively poor in comparison to the booming urban centres near Stuttgart and the south and south-west of Baden-Württemberg, Heidenhausen was still a comparably well-off town with only few families living in poverty (and those were usually propped up by a generous social welfare system). It also had relatively few homeless people, although, like most European towns of its size, Heidenhausen did indeed contain some rather unsavoury and 'unsafe' districts located in the town centre behind the railway station.

But West German places such as Heidenhausen were also in a bubble of international protection through the post-second world war aftermath of Allied protective power and NATO. Gregory remembered vividly his parents – who had both lived through the atrocities of the second world war in Birmingham (father) and Strasbourg (mother) – talking about how safe they felt in this part of the world. Gregory recalled a trip with his bike with friends from primary school – they must have been aged about eight at the time – to a nearby forest where American soldiers were stationed on a military exercise. Gregory remembered being impressed by rows of tanks and military vehicles, the jocular and casual interaction of the American soldiers with the locals who had come to gawp at them, and his first taste ever of chewing gum handed down to him by one of the soldiers with a big smile on his ragged, tanned and sunglassed face. Indeed, if Gregory remembered rightly, this was also the first time that he had seen a black person (a black soldier sitting on top of one of the tanks), further testimony to the fact how remote and unglobalised Heidenhausen was at the time.

But places such as Heidenhausen could also not avoid being caught up in the West German obsession of trying as hard as they could to forget about the atrocities of the Nazi regime. This occurred mainly through a – in hindsight –

strange self-imposed lack of self-confidence (despite of Germany being a nascent global power), based on the guilt felt by most Germans about having allowed the atrocities of the Nazi regime to run their deadly and lethal course unchallenged. Although by the 1970s many West Germans, especially the younger generation, had begun to tear themselves off the shackles of the guilt felt by the previous generation, this German guilt and shame was nonetheless ever-present in day-to-day life in Heidenhausen's families, its public life, and its schools. Gregory and his friends were blissfully unaware of this when they were young, and Gregory – despite of his British citizenship – had never felt out-of-place, chastised or segregated in any way by his schoolmates because he was not German. If anything, and despite of having lived outside of Germany for several decades now, adult Gregory still felt more German than British himself and, indeed, very *schwäbisch*. As a result, his cultural and spiritual *Heimat* (home) had always been, and would always continue to be, Heidenhausen and the *Schwäbische Alb*.

And yet, the first time Gregory remembered feeling that something was not quite right about how West Germans at the time dealt with their Nazi past was during a history lesson, when they must have been about 14 or 15 years old. Rufus, another one of the *Schweiss*-Kinder and an increasingly good friend of Gregory's, had asked their stern history teacher why the Second World War was not on the school curriculum, to which the history teacher had no clear answer. Indeed, the teacher had bypassed the question by waffling on about how the school had no control over the regionally-set curriculum, and that the Second World War was still a too recent event to be covered in a history lesson. Gregory remembered the baffled look on the faces of some of his fellow pupils. After this episode, the history teacher was secretly labelled as a 'Nazi', a label that stuck based on the teacher's age (he would have been about 18 when the war started), his crew-cut 'Nazi' hairstyle which contrasted with the long hair worn by most boys in Gregory's school class, and his stiff and 'regimental' demeanour which they jokingly and naïvely said reminded them of a Nazi death camp warden.

Hans' story was also directly related to the second world war, although Gregory had only started thinking about this long after they had left school. As his surname betrayed, Hans Schlesier's parents had been escapees from *Schlesien* (Silesia) which had been part of Germany before the Second World War, but which had become part of Poland after the war. Although Gregory did not know the details of exactly how and why Hans' family had ended up in Heidenhausen, he knew from historical books and novels written by escapees from this part of the world how harrowing their escape from the advancing Russian army must have been. Gregory knew that Hans' parents had settled in Heidenhausen sometime in early 1945, just before the end of the war but after Silesia had already been overrun by the Russians, probably because one of their relatives had already established a plumbing business in Heidenhausen in the 1920s. Gregory did not know whether Hans' ancestors in Silesia had been plumbers or what other work they may have done but, in hindsight, he suspected that they were at most two generations away from being farmers. Hans' dad, Bernhard, had eventually taken over the family's Heidenhausen plumbing business sometime in the 1950s, and, in Gregory's mind at the time, their three-bedroom terraced house suggested modest wealth that showed that the business was going well. But Hans' family, nonetheless, appeared to be in need of additional income. As a result, they had taken in a lodger to help make ends meet – a person that would later prove to have played a key role in Hans' bumpy life pathway.

4

25th March 1974. Hans was walking back from school. His house was not far, only about 1.5 km from the school gate and it was an easy walk for a kid on his own. First it took him past the local *Gasthaus* (pub-restaurant), with its pub sign of three wrestling brown bears, located at the intersection of the road that led to the school. Then he walked over the large intersection, with traffic lights that made it easy for him to cross what was usually a busy road that led down the hill towards the centre of Heidenhausen located in the valley below. And, finally, his walk back took him along the road that cut through the last undeveloped patch of *Heide* in the area – a juniper heathland that was characteristic for the eastern *Schwäbische Alb* – surrounded by housing developments built in the 1950s and 1960s. Hans' house was located in one such development, towards the end of a cul-de-sac and bordering directly onto the heathland.

But Hans was not in the mood to admire the beauty of the *Heide*. It had been a bad day at school. A very bad day. He had received the result of their last Maths test, and, as he had feared all along, he had done abysmally in the test, with a grade of only '5' (equivalent to a 'fail' in the British and US school systems; German school grades are based on a gradient from 1 to 6, with 1 the best grade; pupils need an average of a '4' to pass a subject, and failure to reach at least a '4' in two subjects leads, rather harshly, to a pupil having to repeat the entire school year [called *Sitzenbleiben* in German, i.e. 'staying seated at one's school desk']). For Hans this had been the second Math test this term out of four overall, and the second time he had only achieved a '5', putting him in danger of having to repeat the whole year. This would be unthinkable and completely unacceptable to both himself and his parents.

"Stupid! Stupid! Stupid!", Hans shouted out while tears welled up in his eyes, "I am so bloody stupid!". In anger, he kicked a small stone from the pavement onto the road, but luckily there was no vehicle in sight. "And these bloody *Schweisser*s with parents who can help them with Maths! They always do well!", Hans mumbled, not realising that some *Schweiss*-Kinder, like Gregory, were doing just as badly in Maths as him.

Hans had reached the door to their terraced house and fumbled in his pocket to find the key. He was afraid. He was very afraid. At age 13, nearly 14, he was aware of the pressure his parents put on him as their only child to do well at school. As refugees from Silesia, his parents had always instilled in Hans the goal to 'do better than them', to get a 'proper education', and to eventually go to university with a degree that would lead to a secure and well-paid job. Although his father, Bernhard Schlesier, had always shown some pride in having successfully taken over the plumbing business from his uncle a few years after they had settled in Heidenhausen, Hans could not escape the feeling that his father felt like a failure, that he 'could have done better in life'. Indeed, ever since Hans could remember, there was always a feeling of unhappiness, maybe even depression, around his father, who always seemed rather withdrawn, taciturn, moody and was, at times, violent towards both Hans and his mum Sigrid. His father's mood swings were certainly also influenced by the fact that Bernhard had suffered since childhood from acute psoriasis, a severe and difficult-to-cure illness characterised by very painful raw bleeding skin and unsightly flaking scales. As a result, Bernhard always had ugly-looking bleeding flakes of skin around his neck and on parts of his face, and Hans was not sure whether other parts of his father's body were similarly affected (as he had never seen his father naked). Undoubtedly, Hans knew, this also increased Bernhard's irascibility and moodiness.

Standing in front of the entrance door, Hans was so afraid that his hands were sweaty, and shaking so much that his house keys fell to the ground and only narrowly missed the water drain. "You fucking useless cunt!", Hans chastised himself again while opening the door. He tried to make as little noise as possible, for fear that Bernhard was at home and would hear him come in. *What can I do?*, Hans fretted while standing undecided in the narrow porch. *But I have to tell them sometime that I have failed the Maths test again! I can't hide this for long!* He almost wet himself with fear about what his father had done to him after his most recent Maths test failure and realised that he needed the loo urgently. What a spanking he had received then! The thought made him shake even more with fear.

He slowly and quietly made his way through the immaculately clean porch where every shoe and umbrella stood in exactly the correct place in very Germanic fashion, and up the stairs, cleaned so spotlessly daily by his mum that it would have put a sterile hospital ward to shame. A few meticulously tended flower pots stood guard on the staircase. Again, there was no dead leaf in sight and even the soil in the pots had been cleaned from any unfitting speck of dirt and dust. But Hans was oblivious to all this German cleanliness, as he was hoping to get past his parent's living room door on the first floor unscathed, and then to escape into his own room under the roof on the 3rd floor. As a single child he knew that he was lucky to have a whole room to himself, next to his parents' bar and disco room where they had friends around regularly for a bit of dancing and drinking. Indeed, many of the schoolboys he knew, especially the ones from the rural villages near Heidenhausen, had to share rooms with their siblings, sometimes even with their sisters.

Hans had almost made it past the living room door with its frosted glass pane when he saw his father's shadow come up behind it. Hans had hoped that his father had gone back to work after his lunch break, but as it was only about 1pm (at the time, German school days started as early as 7.45am and often finished around lunchtime), Hans realised that this had been wishful thinking. An indescribable fear paralysed Hans on the spot. Bernard burst out of the door and blocked Hans' path on the landing. Although Hans had grown a lot in the last year, Bernhard still towered over him. His father was a stocky and burly man with a receding hairline, dark brown eyes, a square clean-shaven face, and a massive body that showed that he was strong as an ox. Bernhard had often talked about his youth in Silesia where he had trained to become a boxer and where he, apparently, had had several successful boxing bouts, knocking out opponents who had been taller and stronger than him.

Without saying hello to his son, Bernhard planted himself in front of Hans and bellowed out "Well? What's the verdict?", knowing full well that it was the day when Hans had received his Maths result. Although not entirely unexpected, Hans was taken aback by his father's directness, and was momentarily too stunned to answer. Bernhard grabbed Hans' shoulders and shook his son. "What grade did you get!?", Bernhard shouted out more loudly. Hans opened his mouth, but no words came out. Tears welled up in his eyes again and started running down his cheeks. Hans could feel a warm feeling in his crotch and around his thighs. He had wet himself!

"What the hell …!", Bernhard shouted, looking down at the wet patch forming at the front of his son's trousers. "What is going on, you little pussy!", Bernhard screamed, violently tearing Hans' backpack from his shoulders. "What are you hiding from me, you little shit!", Bernhard bellowed as he tore through Hans' pack, rifling through school books and notebooks and throwing them out onto the landing. After a short while he held Hans' Maths results in his hands. Hans had started to tremble almost uncontrollably, a wet patch of urine had now formed around his shoes, drenching some of the discarded school books and papers. "A '5' again! My son has again only achieved a '5'! And you did not dare tell me, you little useless shit!", Bernhard shouted straight into Hans' face. "After all the sacrifices I and your mum have made, all our savings going to your expensive and useless Maths tutor ... three times a week you see this idiot ... and still no improvement in your results! What is wrong with you ...?", Bernhard shouted angrily while shaking his son.

Hans just stood there trembling, flabbergasted and dumbfounded. He did not know what to say or do, as he felt the heavy and large bodily mass of his father hunkering over him. Tears continued streaming down his face, but he was speechless. "I will teach you what happens when you come back with such crap results!", Bernhard shouted while tearing at Hans' trousers, opening his belt and zipper, and eventually pulling down Hans' pants and drenched underpants to his ankles. Hans knew what was going to happen, but it was almost as if his mind had left his body and that he was no longer inside himself. He looked down at his naked self, he saw his penis wobbling from left to right as his father kept shaking him, the faint trace of emergent pubic hair at what he had always thought were the most private parts of his body, not even to be seen by his parents, the wet stains of urine still visible on his legs, and the yellow puddle by his feet. He felt his father bend him over, with Hans half hanging over his father's knee, but Hans was in no state to offer resistance. He heard Bernhard fumbling and retrieving his own belt from his trousers, and even when he felt the first lashes of the hard leather on his bare buttocks he did not flinch, move, or utter a sound. "That will teach you to do better next time", Bernhard shouted as he spanked Hans hard, five times, ten times, leaving red streaks on Hans' white buttocks. Hans felt intense pain, as if the skin of his bum was being torn apart, but still he did not move or utter a sound. His father stopped, evidently irritated by the lack of reaction from his son. For a while, Bernhard just kneeled motionless, breathing heavily with his naked son strung over his left knee. Eventually Bernhard threw the belt on the floor and pushed his son up. He slowly pulled up Hans' underpants and trousers. While doing this he desperately tried to avoid staring at Hans' penis and sprouting pubic hair, but he could not stop himself from keeping his eyes fixated for a few seconds on his son's pubescent private parts.

Hans slowly turned his head around and stared into his father's eyes. Hans had never felt so utterly humiliated, although he had been spanked even harder several times before. But he was older now, he was no longer a child. How could his father dare still spanking him like this? Hans' stare was one of abject hatred, a stare that suggested that Hans would know that, eventually, his time of revenge would come, that whatever Bernhard did to him, or indeed to his mother, would eventually come back to haunt Bernard. Holding back further tears, Hans held his father's gaze for a long time. And for what seemed an eternity father and son just stood there, dead quiet, with only Bernhard's breathing audible in the cavernous and sterile staircase.

After a while, Hans lowered his gaze, picked up his belt and his partly drenched books and papers, and made his way up the stairs, leaving Bernhard standing dumbfounded on the landing near the puddle of piss that remained as the last evidence of Hans' humiliation. Although Bernhard wanted to shout after his son in the hope that this 'lesson' would compel Hans to work even harder, Hans' stoic behaviour during and after the spanking had clearly thrown Bernhard off guard. He saw his son's stooped frame disappear up the stairs, leaving stains of urine on every step, but he did not dare follow Hans. With a shudder, he remembered how Hans had looked at him after the spanking with a hatred and determination he had not seen before, and this made him pause and avoid further confrontation. Bernhard looked at the puddle of piss by his feet, shook his head, picked up his belt, adjusted his trousers and shirt that had become dishevelled during the spanking, and stomped back into the living room.

5

26th **July 2019.** Racking his brain, Gregory could not remember much interaction with Hans before they were about 13 or 14. Theirs was, evidently, not a close friendship that had started like most people's school friendships early on in primary school. But Gregory certainly remembered Hans always being 'in the background', both at primary school and then in their early years of secondary school. But looking back through the abyss of time spanning several decades, Gregory found it hard to recollect exactly which friends had come in and out of favour and when. As for most children below the age of 12 or 13, friendships had formed quickly and also vanished rapidly, and often friends were rather 'pragmatic acquaintances', because one walked together to school with a neighbouring kid, for example, rather than because of specific traits that may have attracted one to a specific person. This changed somewhat after the age of about 13 or 14, when friends began to be chosen more on what they represented as persons rather than just being 'there' and 'available' as neighbour's children with whom one could play in the street. In Gregory's cluster of friends, Hans was evidently in the latter group and was a person 'chosen' by Gregory to become his friend. Or was it the other way round, that Gregory had been chosen by Hans?

Gregory was well aware that his choice of friends around the age of 11 and 12 had been negatively affected by the fact that his family had briefly moved from Germany to France. Gregory's father Ron, an ambitious and rather selfish man, had left *Schweiss* and taken up an even better paid job at a research institute near Geneva, but he had done so without consulting his wife or his children as to how this would affect them. The decision turned out to be a disaster for the family. The newly built house they were meant to move into near

Geneva was not ready, which meant that Ron had gone ahead, while Gregory, his mum Alice and his brother Max stayed behind in Heidenhausen, in limbo until things got sorted out in France. In the meantime, horny Ron had met another, much younger, woman, but had not dared tell his wife who, naïvely, moved to France with her two sons to join her husband. Things came to a head soon afterwards and led to an acrimonious separation, eventual divorce, and the return of Alice, Gregory and Max to Heidenhausen, where, luckily, Alice was given the opportunity to return to her old job as a school teacher.

For Gregory, this disruption, although brief, had severely disrupted his life at the age of 11 and 12, when peer groups and peer bonding were becoming particularly important. Although he had missed about eight months of school in Germany (not helped by attending a rather inferior school while in France), Gregory insisted on returning to his old year group, in the hope that he would easily slot back into his old circle of friends. However, Gregory had underestimated that eight months was a long time for children aged 11 or 12, resulting in the fact that his old friends had consolidated their friendships with others, which made it difficult for Gregory to re-enter his former peer group. But he had also underestimated the narrow-mindedness of his fellow pupils when it came to children from 'broken' households. Gregory was very disappointed in many of his former friends, who suddenly regarded him as an outcast and pariah just because his parents had separated, although he felt himself that he had not changed at all. Maybe then it dawned on Gregory, how parochial and narrow-minded some of his classmates were, possibly influenced by the rural, religious and rather conservative faction of pupils in his school class?

This situation had left Gregory in limbo at the time and in search for new friends. It was at this point that Gregory recognised the importance of having been part of the *Schweiss*-Kinder in-group. Although his parents were separated and he was technically no longer with a father who worked at *Schweiss*, his label of '*Schweisser*' still stuck and two of his new friends, Bill and Rufus, were also both *Schweiss*-Kinder. However, from the vantage point of decades in the future, it was impossible for adult Gregory to tell whether it was his coincidental label of being a '*Schweiss*-Kind', or the fact that children of *Schweiss* workers were socio-culturally more similar to him – more international, with better educated parents, and with possibly more 'sophisticated' outlooks on life – that bound him together with these new friends. Bill, in particular, had just arrived from America and his father had been offered a senior position at *Schweiss*. Bill was, like Gregory, from an international family and bi-lingual (mum American, father German, Bill spoke English and German fluently; Gregory spoke French and German fluently but only learned English at school and became trilingual later on after living in the UK). Bill, as a new kid in class, was 'ready' for a new friendship and the two of them quickly found each other and became the best of friends. Rufus, the other '*Schweisser*' who became Gregory's friend after his disastrous spell in France, on the other hand, had German parents, but was interesting to Gregory for his slightly rough demeanour and his wide circle of friends from other Heidenhausen schools, boys Gregory rather liked and admired as they were a bit different from the kids from *Franz-Bosch-Gymnasium*. Bill, thus provided a safe and sophisticated environment, while Rufus was attractive as a friend for his rough edges and a wide-spanning network of likeminded kids from other schools, which helped Gregory open up new horizons.

So, my lack of recollection of Hans before I was 13 is probably also affected by the fact that my family and I had lived in France when I was 11, and that it took me a while to re-establish a new circle of friends after coming back from France, adult Gregory admitted to himself while scratching his itchy chin. *This must certainly also have provided an opening for Hans to enter my peer group at what was undoubtedly a psychologically vulnerable time for me?*, he mused. *But was it me who suddenly discovered Hans' qualities as a friend, or was it the other way around, i.e. that I became interesting to Hans precisely because of my recent family history and the fact that my parents were now divorced? In other words, was it that in the past I had been almost 'too perfect' for someone like Hans, who came from a more modest non-Schweisser background? That I had been a Schweiss-kid with a perfect and sophisticated family background before, while now I was suddenly somebody who, with a broken home and associated problems, had become more accessible and, indeed, more acceptable as a potential friend? Had I left the aloof realm of the privileged Schweiss-Kinder and 'come down' to a level that was more acceptable to somebody with a less international background like Hans? In many ways, through my simultaneous friendship with both Bill and Rufus and with*

Hans, I myself maybe tried to juggle the complex interface between the two complex classroom worlds of the Schweiss-Kinder and the Heidenhausen kids – a world that had only opened itself after I had become more 'normal' and 'acceptable' after the chaotic breakup of my parents?

But what had attracted Gregory to Hans at that specific time and what had changed, irrespective of Gregory's chaotic family breakup, compared with the time when they were together in primary school or the first years of secondary school? The simple answer was: girls! At 13 and 14, for reasons then completely unknown to Gregory, Hans had suddenly emerged as a kid whom the girls rather liked. Although Gregory vaguely remembered Hans as a slightly chubby almost bland looking kid during primary school – a view reinforced by the classroom picture in the newspaper cutting in Gregory's mum's photo album – by the age of 13 and 14 Hans had lost his early childhood baby fat to grow into a slim, brown-haired and brown-eyed good-looking boy whose voice had broken relatively early, partly aided by the fact that Hans was almost a year older than most other kids in their school class. As part of the stern development programme for their son, Hans' parents had also enrolled him into the local, rather expensive, tennis centre (*how could they afford this?*, Gregory had always wondered), which meant that Hans also developed the swagger, flamboyancy and demeanour of a permanently tanned 'sporty' kid.

What attracted the girls to Hans most, however, was not just his good sporty looks, but the fact that he could put on the most heart-warming smile amplified by a lost-puppy-dog-look, and, most importantly, that he oozed mature self-confidence when it came to approaching and talking to girls. In contrast, younger kids like Gregory, Bill and Rufus seemed to be stuck in eternal pre-pubescent purgatory, still childishly lanky, all knees and elbows, and with wimpy voices that had not broken yet at the age of 13. Rumours quickly spread that Hans had several girlfriends on the go, both from within their school class and from other schools, and that he had already 'done it', i.e. that he was indeed already making love to one or several of his girlfriends. As a result, out of early childhood obscurity, and just at the time when Gregory had come back into his old school class after his family's disastrous foray into France, Hans had emerged as this new classroom superstar, a flamboyant 'hunk' and idol of most boys to aspire towards when it came to meeting girls, going out, and 'doing it' with girlfriends. To kids like Gregory, who were beginning to show an innocent and naïve interest in girls, it became, therefore, a privilege and honour to know Hans and to be seen as one of his friends. Indeed, being seen to be with Hans at the time elevated one to an inner circle of 'cool' kids who felt superior vis-à-vis their schoolmates. Gregory remembered very well that he, therefore, felt very proud of having been accepted by Hans as one of his best friends.

6

26th July 2019/October 1974. Looking out of the living room window, adult Gregory paused to think about the first time Hans had taken him home. *I guess it was sometime in October 1974 at the start of Year 7, when I would have been 13 and Hans, who was 11 months older than me, would have been 14 at the time*, Gregory tried to remember with a pensive look on his face. They had walked together after school to Hans' house and, Gregory remembered, they had chatted mainly about their school teachers. As they entered the porch to Hans' terraced house, Gregory particularly recalled being asked to take off his shoes (which Gregory found pretty weird) and vividly remembered the antiseptic smell inside the freshly cleaned stairs. To Gregory's eyes – who lived with his mum, brother and grandmother (his mum's mother) in a relatively chaotic apartment full of stuff and, although regularly cleaned, rather messy and chaotic in places – the porch and staircase in Hans' house looked and smelt completely sterile, more like a hospital ward than a living space.

Gregory's initial impressions were confirmed as they walked up to the first floor where they met Hans' mum Sigrid cleaning the first-floor landing. She looked up briefly, and Gregory could not escape the feeling that she felt irritated by his presence. She had a large gash above her right eye and her right cheek looked also red and swollen. Had she had a fall recently or had somebody beaten her up? Although she did not say it, Gregory could see in the way she looked at her son that she reproached him for not having warned her that Hans would bring home a friend. Again, this situation was unfamiliar to Gregory, as in Bill's and Rufus' houses kids went in and out as they wanted (not having to take their shoes off), and the parents never quite knew what their kids were up to, where they were during the day, and with whom they were playing.

When she saw Gregory, Sigrid awkwardly and almost apologetically tried to hide her scabby facial wounds behind one of her hands and adjusted her apron and dishevelled hair with her other hand. Rather frostily she greeted Gregory, and told Hans to be quiet upstairs as she was not sure whether Hans' father would come home for lunch and then take a nap. At the mention of Hans' father, Gregory thought that he detected a change in Hans' demeanour, a slight tightening of his spine, a change in his normally relaxed facial expression, maybe even a flicker of fear? *Was it the dad who had beaten up Sigrid?*, Gregory already suspected then while they walked past Sigrid and carried on up the stairs. Hans had mentioned his dad a few times at school, but only in the context of his father having great expectations for his only child, possibly with a hint that both his parents, because of their modest backgrounds, were putting a lot of pressure on Hans to perform well at school.

At the time Gregory did not know anything about the heavy spanking Hans was suffering from his father, although he would soon enough find out more about Hans' problematic relationship with Bernhard. But most of this, and other things that were happening at Hans' home, such as the father regularly beating up his wife, only came out much later, long after their school years. Had Gregory known there and then what was happening to Hans, maybe the whole sad story about Hans and his psychological meltdown would have taken a different turn?

The two boys made their way past the second floor, where Hans explained that a 'lodger' was living without saying much more, although Gregory had the impression that Hans had gazed at the entrance door to the lodger's room longer than necessary. Little did Gregory know at the time, that only a few months earlier this lodger had become one of the many key elements in Hans' quickly evolving life pathway that may have been the cause for the many problems he developed later.

Another flight of steps up, Hans opened the door to the rooms on 'his' floor. For a brief moment Gregory stood there flabbergasted and with an open mouth. The door opened to a large party room (or 'disco room' reflecting the pretty awful 70s dance music tastes of the time), a large room of over 30 square metres with a well-stocked bar and a counter with four bar stools. Everything was kitted out in typical 70s fashion, with a large mirrored 'disco' ball hanging from the ceiling that, when lit from the sides, would send sparkling lights around the dancers; garish Formica and mock-wood panelling adorning both the walls and the side of the bar; and yellow plastic reclining chairs, which looked incredibly uncomfortable, placed strategically in three corners of the room. A large window provided stunning views of the *Heide* juniper landscape and the new housing developments in the distance.

Gregory did not know what to say, as he was both appalled by the obvious garishness of the decorations, but also impressed by the fact that Hans' parents could afford to keep such a large room just for fun and entertainment in what did not appear to be a very spacious house overall. Again, this all seemed so different from Gregory's flat which was full of bookshelves and with copies of famous paintings and photos on the walls. But Gregory was also waiting to gauge Hans' reaction while being shown the room. Did Hans show pride at what this room was representing, or was there also a hint of a cynical smile on Hans' face that betrayed that he was not so impressed with what his parents had attempted to present here? Gregory was not sure, so he just uttered some words of appreciation as they walked quickly towards the bar. Gregory was certainly impressed by the various bottles on display in the bar, the meticulously placed cocktail glasses aligned in perfect symmetry, a symmetry further amplified by their reflection in the mirrored wall at the back of the bar.

"Let's have a drink!", Hans said, out of the blue and completely surprising Gregory while they sat down on the bar stools. Hans picked up one of the most garishly coloured bottles – Gregory remembered that it may have been *Bolts Blue* – and poured the liquid into two cocktail glasses. While pouring, Hans looked surreptitiously towards the entrance door. He was obviously listening out for his father, but he had a self-determined, almost stubborn, look on his face which suggested that Gregory should not decline the offer of a drink. Aged 13, Gregory had never tasted alcohol before in his life, not even beer or wine, let alone a 'stronger' drink like the one Hans was pushing towards him on the counter. Hans looked at Gregory with his self-determined look and gulped down the content of the cocktail glass in one go, wiping his mouth with the back of his hand afterwards and, seemingly, showing no ill effect or even tears in his eyes from the stinging alcohol.

He has clearly done this before!, Gregory thought impressed, even more in awe of his new friend than before. Gregory put the cocktail glass to his lips, but even the smell of the strong alcohol wafting towards his nose made him cough so that he had to put the glass down again. Hans smiled back at him, but said nothing. Gregory raised the glass again. He had intended to gulp the content down like Hans in one go, but, pouring just a little bit of the blue liquid into his mouth and swallowing it felt like an explosion in his mouth: Gregory felt the strong alcohol burning his oesophagus, the alcoholic fumes assaulting his nose, and the liquor burning the roof of his mouth. Gregory coughed uncontrollably, his eyes watered as he fought for breath, barely able to put down the still over half-full glass on the counter without spilling its content. For what seemed like an eternity he coughed, wheezed and fought for breath, while Hans looked at him laughing.

"Your first one, ey?", Hans said, patting Gregory gently on the back. Gregory could not speak and simply nodded in acknowledgement, embarrassed at his obvious lack of drinking experience. "Never mind, I'll finish it for you", Hans said and again downed the remains of Gregory's glass in one go with seemingly no side-effects. Hans quickly cleaned the glassed in the sink, dried them with one of the towels, and placed the glasses back exactly in the same spot where he had found them. "Don't worry", Hans said as he saw Gregory's worried look, "I do this quite often with my girlfriends but always with a different bottle, so my parents never realise that a bit is missing. We never start a new bottle and never finish one either, otherwise it would be too obvious. My parents get so pissed in here anyway with their friends that it would be a miracle if they found out if a drop is missing!" On hearing this, Gregory tried to imagine Hans' rather demure-looking mother Sigrid whizzing around the dancefloor drunk and out of control – a picture he found difficult to visualise.

Hans took Gregory to his room which directly adjoined the disco room. Indeed, one had to walk through the disco room to get to Hans' room, so Gregory wondered what Hans did when his parents were partying next door, but he did not dare ask yet. Maybe Hans took part in his parents' wild parties and maybe that was why he was used to drinking strong alcohol and chatting up girls?

Gregory was not sure whether Hans' room was what he had expected. And had he expected anything anyway, as it seemed that he still knew so little about his new friend? The room was middle sized, with two windows, one on the side overlooking the *Heide* with Hans' desk just below it, and another large Velux-type window in the roof looking straight at the sky with Hans' bed right below it. Gregory had never seen a roof window like this in someone's room before, and he immediately imagined how great it would be lying on the bed below and looking out at the stars at night. Maybe with a girl in your arms? Like the rest of the house he had seen, Hans' room was immaculately clean and orderly, very different from Gregory's own room where he could barely make it to his bed with all the stuff and clothes strewn all over the floor and blocking the way. Gregory's mum had long given up admonishing her son for his messy room. Hans' desk was covered in papers, books, pens, a calculator, and a few other things, but again everything was tidily arranged and seemingly in perfect place. A quick glance at the books and paper showed Gregory that Hans was working on preparing for their next Maths test. Gregory was aware of Hans' problems with Maths, and they had even talked about swatting for the next test together, although Gregory was well aware that this may be akin to the 'blind leading the blind' as he knew that Hans struggled as much as himself with Maths. Hans' bed was immaculately made up, with the sheets nicely tucked in and the duvet folded in a very orderly manner on top of the sheets. The floor was empty and no clothes were lying around, all evidently neatly tucked away in the wardrobe at the back of the room.

"Nice room!", Gregory said, not really knowing what else to say. It almost felt that Hans was 'presenting' his room to Gregory, maybe to show him how neat and tidy everything was arranged, while at other friends' houses Gregory had never really given a thought about their rooms and whether they were neat and tidy. Everything seemed a bit staged for Gregory, a bit different, a bit out of his comfort zone. Indeed, the room was more like an adult's room than that of a child of 14, and again confirmed to Gregory that Hans seemed to be well ahead in terms of maturity and way-of-life. At the same time, he also felt sorry for Hans, as the room did not seem to be lived in, a room where someone could have fun in. But then the room was probably also the place where Hans had made love to all these girls, if the stories about him were true, Gregory thought while biting his lip slightly embarrassed and looking surreptitiously at the bed. In his mind and aged 13 he could not yet envision what two people making love looked like, but he imagined mingling and sweating bodies, heaving and panting, and dishevelling all these beautiful neat and tidy bedsheets! How did Hans manage to clean up afterwards?

"I bought a new music record yesterday, would you like to hear it?", Hans said, taking Gregory out of his reverie.

"Yes, sure!", Gregory tried to reply self-assuredly. Again, he did not want to admit that he did not know much about modern music. For some reason his brother Max, who was only 10, seemed to know much more about music than Gregory. Music had not yet much interested Gregory, for whatever reason. Hans placed the brand-new vinyl onto his record player. Gregory noted that it was an expensive high-quality and newish German-made *Dual* record player where, at the push of a button, the arm with the needle would automatically find the start of the record. Again, it seemed that no expense had been spared by his parents to provide Hans, their only child, with the newest kit. While the first sounds of a complex rock song wafted out of Hans' 80-Watt *Brown* speakers, Gregory grabbed the sleeve of the album which said *Machine Head* by a band called *Deep Purple* Gregory had never heard of before. Gregory's mum, busy as a school teacher and now as a single mum, never seemed to have much time to listen to music, and although they had a record player, a few nondescript and dull-sounding records from the past when his parents were still married, and a radio, Gregory had, so far, never felt much of an urge to listen to music.

After a few seconds of the first song, 'Highway Star', Gregory was completely enthralled by the music. He had never heard anything as beautiful and exciting as this song, with Richie Blackmore's fantastic guitar soli, John Lord's masterful organ play, Roger Glover's enticing bass rhythm, Ian Paice's unbelievably virtuosic drumming, and Ian Gillan's fantastic singing. Hans saw Gregory's reaction and turned up the music really loud, obviously forgetting Sigrid's earlier warning. The 80-Watt speakers made Hans' room shake with the bass and drum rhythms, and for a few minutes both Gregory and Hans just sat there, eyes closed, and letting themselves be surrounded by the rock music. Gregory had never felt anything like this before, surrounded and completely overwhelmed by a musical universe, carried away into another dimension by rhythm, sound and soaring soli. It was the most beautiful thing he had ever heard, he was utterly hooked.

Suddenly the door burst open. Hans' father Bernhard stood there, hands on hips, glaring menacingly at his son. "What do you think you are doing, making such a racket!", Bernhard said, stomping forward, opening the lid of the record player and violently shoving the record player's arm aside, causing it to scratch the vinyl record.

Hans looked at his dad, evidently unsure how to react. He had enjoyed the brief moment of bliss evident in his friend Gregory's face as they listened to the crescendo of Richie Blackmore's 'Highway Star' guitar solo, and now the moment was gone. In his eagerness to impress Gregory, Hans had to admit that he had forgotten that his father may be back for lunch and a nap. He stared at his father and started trembling, oblivious to Gregory's worried look with eyes darting nervously back and forth between Hans and his father.

Bernhard had clenched his fists and had moved towards Hans who was cowering on his bed, instinctively shielding his face from the expected attack. Gregory could hot believe what he saw. He had never seen such anger before in an adult, and, when Bernhard had smashed the record player, Gregory had automatically crouched into a protective foetal position, hugging his knees, and not daring to look Bernhard in the eyes. Bernhard stood over his son, breathing heavily and ready to strike his son, but a quick glance sideways reminded him that for once there would be a witness to him beating up his son. With the utmost difficulty he controlled his anger, unclenched his fists and turned around. At the door he shouted: "I don't want to hear a peep from you two again while I have my nap!" Turning around and pointing at the record player he bellowed: "… and the biggest mistake was giving you this wretched record player as a birthday present!" Bernhard slammed the door behind him and left the two boys sitting there, stunned and scared.

Gregory looked at Hans, who, in the blink of an eye, had been transformed from a self-confident boy idolised by all his classmates to this hunkering, shaking, whimpering and scared wreck of a human being. Hans' body was still stiff with fear and only slowly did he sit up while letting his arms, raised earlier to protect himself from the expected vicious blows, slide to the side to prop himself up on the bed. Gregory could see that Hans was fighting hard to keep back the tears, not to lose the last shred of dignity in front of his new friend.

"You better go now, Greg", Hans said with a slightly trembling voice. He looked Gregory deeply in the eyes with his intense brown-eyed stare: "And please don't mention this to anyone, promise? I don't want the other kids to know about my father."

Although Gregory was still deeply shaken by what he had witnessed, these last words of Hans instilled in him a deep sense of pride. Not only had Hans used Gregory's shortened name 'Greg', which reinforced their new-found intimacy and had only been in use for the last few days, but he had also asked Gregory to keep what had happened a secret, thereby confirming to Gregory that he had been accepted into Hans' inner circle, that he had become one of Hans' 'best friends', based on the secret insider knowledge he now had about the complex and fraught Bernhard-Hans relationship. In the following years to come, at least until Gregory was about 17, this intimate insider knowledge – gleaned on this fateful day early on in their growing friendship – would prove to be reinforced over and over again, as Gregory emerged increasingly as Hans' best friend and one of the few who knew about some of the problems – and not only with his father – Hans was facing.

In hindsight, Gregory also wished that he had known much earlier about what had happened at home during Hans' 14th birthday, a few months before this first visit to Hans' house, as this would have undoubtedly helped explain some of Hans' very early seemingly 'mature', but also at times odd, behaviour with and around girls. It would have also helped place Hans' future behaviour into a wider, and arguably more critical, context. But in the end, Gregory realised from his adult vantage point, that even best friends could only tell each other so much about their inner secrets and fears. He, therefore, thought back to his younger self with no indulgence, but with no blame either. What had happened to Hans on his 14th birthday was so unspeakably weird that even an adult would have found it hard to talk about it, let alone a 14-year-old kid at the time it happened.

7

7th July 1974, Hans' 14th birthday. Like every year, Hans had looked forward to his birthday. Usually, his grandparents who lived nearby would visit and bring presents and cake, but this year, for some reason, they could not make it, and Hans would be celebrating alone with his parents. But he did not mind that, as this day was special and one of the few where he was relatively sure not to expect one his father's unpredictable tantrums. Indeed, on the whole, he knew that he could always expect plenty of presents, some of which were quite expensive. For his 13th birthday a year ago, for example, his parents had not only given him a new bike but also paid for his membership at the local tennis club for the first time – a membership, Hans knew, that was usually reserved to the posher middle-class families of Heidenhausen, and not normally for refugee families 'from the East' like his own. As a result, and partly also to please his parents and to show that he appreciated what they did for him, he had put a lot of effort into his tennis and, after 12 months of intensive twice-a-week training and practice, he had become quite good at it. He had good hand-eye coordination, a knack for strategy about how to outplay his opponents, and he was quick and nimble when running towards the ball and hitting his vicious passing shots from the baseline and winning volleys at the net. Of course, he also knew that the girls quite liked tennis players and that the exercise and outdoors activity also helped him get tanned and fitter.

One of last year's birthday presents had also been payment for three sessions a week with his new Maths tutor, a present Hans appreciated but which put even more pressure on him to perform well in Maths. Hans still vividly remembered the recent humiliating spanking by his father resulting from his continuous poor performance in Maths, and Hans felt that the relationship with his father could never be the same after this incident, especially after the humiliation of his father seeing him butt-naked in front of him after violently pulling down his trousers and underpants.

Hans realised that something must have also changed in himself recently, as during spankings in the past, when his father had equally pulled down his trousers to hit him on his bare bottom, he had never been worried about being naked in front of his dad.

But despite the tutoring lessons as a rather awkward recent birthday present, Hans looked forward to his 14th birthday. Although he was not meant to know, he had gleaned from his parents' discussions that he would be given a new expensive *Dual* record player, something he had wanted for a long time. He was sure there would also be the ubiquitous book from his grandparents – usually they chose something like Enid Blyton that was now much too childish for Hans – but he did not know what other presents to expect this time. Maybe the *Minolta* camera he was craving? Or a new superfast calculator as a 'school-related' present so fashionable with his ambitious parents?

Hans peeled himself out of bed, put on his clothes and made his bed as usual. He quickly made his way downstairs to the first floor where his parents were already waiting for him at the breakfast table. His birthday happened to fall on a Sunday, which gave the whole family an opportunity to celebrate together in a relaxed manner and with no rush to go to work or school or to clean the stairs (as good Catholics, Hans' mum refrained from cleaning the house on 'holy' Sunday). But as he entered the living room where his parents already sat at the breakfast table, Hans quickly realised that something was wrong. Instead of greeting him warmly as they would usually do on his birthday, his mum looked away while his dad looked sternly ahead. Evidently they had just had an argument.

"Good morning son, and happy birthday", his dad eventually said, pointing at the chair next to him and inviting Hans to sit down. Sigrid turned her head and looked at Hans and then at her husband. She placed her hand on Hans' hand and smiled gently at him, then looked back at her husband. "Are you sure you don't want to reconsider …?", she asked Bernhard pleadingly. Bernhard looked back at her with the stubborn and angry face Hans knew all too well.

"One more word from you and you'll get again what you deserve!", Bernhard bellowed back at Sigrid, clenching his thick boxer's fists.

Sigrid looked demurely down. She knew when it was time to yield to Bernhard, especially on her son's birthday. She had long given up trying to stand up to her bully of a husband, and had resigned herself to her dull life as a housewife who was expected to keep the house clean, cook, and help look after their son. She looked again at Hans, almost pleading for him to understand, but Hans did not have a clue about what was going to happen. When entering the room, he had seen the small heap of presents on the side table. The larger rapped package suggested that this was indeed the record player and loudspeakers he had wished for, and a few other smaller items suggested books and other small presents. Nothing seemed out of the ordinary.

Bernhard cleared his throat and looked first at Sigrid, then at Hans. "You can open your presents later", Bernhard said with a forced conciliatory voice and pointing at the heap of wrapped packages. "Your mother and I…", at which point he sent a sharp look back to Sigrid which unequivocally told her to keep quiet, "will give you a very special birthday present this year."

Hans looked again at both his parents, trying to guess what was in store. This 'special' present was obviously not in this room. Hans looked questioningly at his dad.

"You are 14 now and growing into a man…", Bernhard said awkwardly. At this point Hans remembered again with anger how his dad had looked at his sprouting pubic hair a few months ago while he hung in a humiliating posture over his father's knee, trousers and underpants at his ankles, receiving a spanking on his bare buttocks and standing in a puddle of piss.

"It is time for you to know about women and to …", Bernhard paused again, trying to find the right words, "… and to know how to please them".

At this point, Sigrid looked away again. Evidently, she was not happy about this. Was she fighting back tears? *Had this been the reason they had argued?*, Hans wondered. *Where is this leading to? Does Dad think I have not had a girlfriend yet, or what is this all about?,* Hans continued his thoughts, suddenly regretting that he had not yet introduced some of his fleeting girlfriends to his parents.

For the past 12 months or so Hans had begun to approach girls. While his schoolmates were still shily joking and giggling about girls but not daring to approach them, Hans found it easy to talk to girls, and he also thought that they were attracted to him. He knew that his looks had changed over the past two years or so; that he had entered puberty earlier than others, with his voice breaking just when he had turned 13 and with pubic hair and hair under his arms beginning to sprout, while most of his classmates were still hairless pre-pubescent kids; that he had grown taller than others, at least for the moment; and that his tanned sporty looks attracted the girls. He also knew that his schoolmates had started the rumour that he had already had a few girlfriends and that he had 'done it' with some of the girls. Although there was no substance to the rumours about having 'done it', Hans had felt that his position with his schoolmates had suddenly positively changed because of this. As a result, he had not put any effort into dispelling the rumours about his sexual prowess and had, instead, revelled in the new-found attention he was receiving from his schoolmates who, until recently, had been rather indifferent towards him. Sure, he had kissed Bettina, he had flirted avidly with Sonia, he had briefly fondled Martina's budding breasts through her sweater, but without any of this leading to anything further. Although just last week, in a hidden corner of the school playground, he had thought that he could go further by slipping one of his hands into Martina's panties, she had slapped him hard, putting an abrupt stop to what had been his most daring foray into a girl's body so far. Hans also remembered a recent kiss with Martina at the same spot in the playground when she had allowed him to put his tongue into her mouth. But although this had caused him to get an erection, he had felt embarrassed and had moved away from Martina so that she could not feel the rising bulge in his pants against her hips.

So, despite of all his bluster and his schoolmates' misconceptions about his sexual prowess and exploits, Hans had to reluctantly admit that he had never seen a girl naked, not even in pictures, and neither had any girl ever touched him 'down below' yet. He certainly could not remember ever having seen his prudish and demure mother naked, let alone his father. Indeed, it was hard to imagine them without clothes on or that they did 'it' together. No, he could not imagine his parents 'making love', and he briefly shuddered at the thought while placing a piece of ham on the *Brötchen* (small bread bun) on the plate in front of him, whose crust was covered with a delicious assortment of seeds (his mum had especially bought his favourite poppy-seed covered *Brötchen* for his birthday).

Of course, he knew all about erect penises and sperm and that you could make yourself 'come' by stroking and caressing your penis. Hans had started masturbating just before his 13th birthday and he vividly remembered his first orgasm. Although his mum had tried to tell him awkwardly and with visible Catholic embarrassment a few months before that it was 'bad for boys' to touch their penises, curiosity had, of course, gained the upper hand. He did not believe some of the stories going around the playground at school, where his schoolmates had started increasingly to talk about sex, that masturbating made your brain go mushy, or that any man only had a certain number of 'shots' over a lifetime which should not be wasted by jerking off. Hans was bright enough to understand that these stories were made up by religious bigots and conservative parents who had been told the same mumbo-jumbo stories by their parents.

A few weeks before his 13th birthday, as a new bedtime routine just after his mum had closed his bedroom door and wished him good night, Hans had started rubbing his penis almost every evening before going to sleep, and he increasingly liked the feeling of being aroused. At first he was not sure how best to do it, but he quickly learned that a specific cadence and movement of his fingers around his foreskin and top of his penis increased the pleasure. It must have been just before his 13th birthday when he had rubbed his erect penis a bit faster and more forcefully than usual, when an indescribable feeling began welling up in him, growing stronger and stronger, a feeling of having reached a point of no return, that something was about to happen that could no longer be stopped, something huge and awesome coming from deep inside him that he could no longer control or hold back. He had felt his penis grow harder and harder, bigger and bigger, and suddenly his whole body had become one giant penis, an exquisite and beautiful feeling he had never experienced before. It felt as if all the synapses in his brain were firing simultaneously and that all his pleasure centres were being stimulated at once. He could not stop pulling and pushing his foreskin up and down faster and faster until his penis seemed to explode, his whole body heaving, convulsing and tightening, his back arching, his eyes closing, and an almost inhuman groan coming out of his throat. With rhythmic jerks his penis squirted out a few drops of a whitish liquid that shot out onto the pillow. After a few seconds, the explosion abated, his body relaxed, and his breathing slowed down.

Hans remembered opening his eyes and looking guiltily at the stain on the pillow, and quickly turning around to see whether his bedroom door was opening with his father barging in, surprised at all this panting and moaning. But all was quiet, his parents had obviously not heard his animalistic groans of pleasure. Hans knew immediately that he had had an orgasm, after all that was what all the boys at school kept harping on about – although he doubted that many of them had so far experienced an orgasm themselves, with most of them being younger than him and still not in puberty – but he certainly was also a bit overwhelmed by what had just happened. Never before had he felt so aroused, had he felt so exquisitely led by his own urges and out of control. Out of curiosity he touched the sperm stain with his finger. It was moist and sticky and although initially white it had become almost transparent, like a wet watery stain. He quickly grabbed a tissue from the pack near his bed (in those days tissues – *Tempo Taschentücher* – came in little plastic packs of 10 folded tissues) and tried to wipe the stain off as best he could. There was not a lot of sperm, but Hans was nonetheless worried that his mum would see the stain when she next took the pillow covers for washing. From now on, Hans knew that he had to be careful and use a tissue from the start when jerking off.

Hans also remembered that the next evening after his first orgasm he had tried jerking off again, but that this time nothing happened. Instead, his penis had become a bit sore from all the vigorous rubbing, and he had to wait a few days before being able to touch his foreskin again. He was very disappointed at the time and thought that maybe his orgasm would be just a 'one-off', but he quickly learned to pace himself and that, as he grew older, his orgasms would come with greater and greater frequency. Now, at 14, he could pride himself at being an expert masturbator, also very adept at hiding his regular jerking-off sessions and the resulting accumulation of discarded tissues from his parents.

Hans looked up guiltily at his parents. *If only they knew what I just thought about?*, he chuckled inwardly, while briefly glancing at his mum sitting next to him at the breakfast table. Despite all these thoughts about his own body, he could not think of his own mum as having a body at all under her rather traditional dress. Even with a somewhat 'experienced' boy like Hans when it came to girls, there was still a gulf, an abyss, between him and girls' bodies. So, what was his Dad talking about when he mentioned 'how to please women'. Although Hans felt uncomfortable, especially from gauging his mother's reaction to all this, he nonetheless had to admit that his curiosity had been aroused. Had his dad managed to get one of his girlfriends – Bettina, Sonia, Martina – to come here today?

"Back in Silesia, my parents had done the same for me when I was about your age", Bernhard continued, having regained his poise, "and it certainly did me a lot of good knowing how … how things worked and … and especially what women like".

Hans was flattered that his dad, who had lately seemed to be increasingly angry with Hans over his school performance, was admitting such intimate secrets about his youth. But Sigrid was still looking away, not daring to look Hans in the eye.

"So, we asked our lodger, Miss Schmidt, to help out a bit", Bernhard said almost with pride in his voice. "She has agreed to … to help you in that respect, and we will not charge her rent for this month in return. This will be your main birthday present … from us … to help you become a proper man." Bernhard had stumbled a bit again towards the end, and even seemed a bit embarrassed by all this.

Hans did not know what to say and looked at both his parents with open mouth and a questioning stare. He knew Miss Schmidt from passing her on the stairs, he knew she was about 24 and unmarried, and he seemed to remember that she worked in one of the newly-opened retail stores in town. But Hans had to admit that he had never looked at her as a 'woman', as all the girls he had met so far were his age or younger. Bettina was still only 12, while Martina was a few months younger than himself. What was he going to do as a barely 14-year-old with an old woman of 24? To be sure, based on his own experience with regard to knowing how his penis 'worked' and knowing all about orgasms, Hans had no concerns about his father's plan in that respect. But jerking off successfully was one thing, making love to an adult woman – if that was what his parents and Miss Schmidt were planning – was quite another!

Nonetheless, he had to admit that, although shocked, he was not dismissing his father's suggestion outright, and he felt increasingly curious about how it would feel if a girl – or indeed a fully-grown woman – touched his boner. After all, had his father not just admitted that his parents had done the same with him at about his age, and had Bernhard not said that it had greatly helped him to better 'understand' women? As the girls Hans had known so far seemed so reluctant to let him go further than just a kiss and an innocent fondle, maybe there was something to be learned from an older, more mature, women? How would an orgasm feel inside a woman?

Bernhard saw that his son was thinking hard about what he had just suggested. "Don't worry, son", he interjected, taking Hans out of his thoughts, "Miss Schmidt, Elke Schmidt, has been fully informed, and she looks forward to seeing you. Don't worry, she is not a hooker or anything like that, she is a good clean girl from a good family, and she just wants to help you and make a bit of money on the side. Nothing wrong with that. She said that she is looking forward to it and waiting for you to see her."

Hans knew that hookers were women who had sex with men for money, but again he had to admit to himself that he did not know much else about what these women actually did with men. Of course, he knew that Elke Schmidt was not a hooker. The few times he had seen her on the stairs, she looked like an upright and hard-working woman just trying to make a living. Before he could reply, or ask his mum again for her view on this, Bernhard stood up, grabbed Hans' elbow quite hard, and pulled him towards the stairs.

"C'mon then, she is waiting", Bernhard said, feeling resistance while pulling Hans up the stairs. Hans was still waiting for his mum to give her approval, be it through a cursive nod or a faint smile towards Hans, but Sigrid demonstratively looked away. As a result, Hans hesitated. *Is this the right thing to do if mum does not approve?*, he wondered.

"Don't be a pufta, son!", Bernhard shouted. "This has to be done. You'll see, at the end of it you'll thank me … us … for what we are doing here, you'll see."

Seeing his mum look away, Hans was indeed offering some resistance, and, although he was curious, he was not at all sure about this. What was he expected to do? How would he know what to do and how to do it right? Yes, he wanted to 'do it', but why with someone like Elke whom he did not know and who did not know him? What if she was really ugly, with warts all over, sagging breasts and a tummy bulging over awful granny panties? What if her breath smelled of alcohol and cigarettes? But then, this was also a 'big' birthday present which it would be impolite to turn down, and, although his mum was obviously not very happy about the idea, his parents only wanted the best for him. *One month's rent!*, Hans thought flattered, *that must be at least 200 Marks or more. A fortune! And all that for me, to show me how proper sex works!*

While all these thoughts were going through Hans' head, Bernhard had dragged him towards Elke Schmidt's door on the second floor. Hans realised that it was now too late to withdraw, to tell his dad that he did not want to do it, that he was scared. Hans certainly did not want his father to think he was a 'pufta', somebody who shied away at the first opportunity to make love to a real woman. *Maybe if I do it, it will improve my relationship with dad?*, Hans thought hopefully, giving him a further reason to go ahead with it. *If I say 'no' now, this will probably be the end of my attempts to patch up things with him!*, Hans realised. *He would never respect me again if I reject this!*

The door opened and Elke Schmidt stood in front of them. It was the first time Hans had really looked at her. Elke was tall, taller than Hans remembered, indeed she seemed to tower over him who, at 14, was just entering one of his main growth spurts. Hans thought that her face, framed by wavy brown shoulder-long hair, looked quite attractive, with slim cheekbones, a little tanned, with dark green eyes and a sharp nose. As it was mid-summer, Elke wore a loosely fitting summer dress with a pattern of pink roses on a beige background. She was barefoot, which Hans rather liked as it made Elke look more informal. Hans could not make out whether Elke wore a bra.

"Well, hello there …!", Elke said to Hans with rather exaggerated jocularity. She held out a hand towards him, which Hans shook. Her hand felt limp and a bit moist.

"Right, I'll leave you two to it!", Bernhard said while looking at Elke. Was he telling her with his eyes to be gentle with Hans? It was hard to tell.

After closing the front door, Elke led Hans through the small hall straight into her bedroom. Hans still felt very unsure about the whole project, but he followed Elke towards the bed. The room was small but ideal for a single person, with a single bed along the left side wall, a small desk under a large window looking over the juniper heath, and a half-open wardrobe on the right wall that showed an assortment of dresses in colours and shapes fashionable in the mid-70s. The room was tidy and clean, but not quite as sterile and immaculate as Hans' own room or the rest of the house.

"I know this is awkward for you", Elke said while patting the place next to her on the bed and inviting Hans to sit next to her. "Believe, me I've never done anything like this before!", she said with what seemed to be a genuine smile, "but when your father asked me and said that this would be your birthday present I could hardly refuse ... especially as they will also refund me one month's rent, which I can certainly do with!", at which point she could not refrain from chuckling out loud, putting her hand in front of her mouth in embarrassment.

Hans sat next to her, not knowing what to say or do. This was so different from his previous encounter with girls, indeed he had never been in another girl's room on his own before.

"Oh, don't worry", Elke said, possibly misinterpreting Hans' inquisitive look. "I have had a few boyfriends before, you know, nothing serious, just a bit of sex, so I know what it's all about and what men like". She hid her mouth again behind her hand while smiling naughtily. "I have not yet met 'Mr Right', which is why I am not married yet," she continued while scrutinising Hans' face as if searching for something appropriate to say, "but you also know that in this day and age girls no longer just jump at any opportunity to get married. So, plenty of time for someone like me still, after all it's the Hippie-70s and we are meant to be able to do what we want!" There was that smile again which, Hans had to admit, made Elke even more attractive, amplifying the little crow's-feet-wrinkles around her eyes.

After a little pause she asked Hans whether her parents had told him what they were expected to do, at which point Hans just nodded. He still had not said a word. Elke then asked him to say a bit about himself, whether he had a girlfriend, which Hans thought was rather nice and polite of her. He briefly told her about Bettina, Sonia and Martina, but without giving any detail about his lack of sexual experience with them. Although Elke pretended to be impressed by Hans having not one but three girlfriends at the same time, Hans nonetheless guessed that Bernhard had told Elke that he was still a virgin, which made Hans feel a little uncomfortable.

"So, your parents want me to show you how to have sex, how to make love", Elke said frankly, suggesting to Hans that they were now moving towards the 'business end' of their meeting. "I'll be as gently as I can, and you just have to tell me if you want me stop at any time. I know from my own experience that the first time with somebody can be quite overwhelming."

At this point, Elke placed a hand on Hans' knee. Despite the summer heat, Hans was wearing jeans and a cotton t-shirt. He felt his heart beginning to race, and he suddenly felt very hot. Elke moved her hand up Hans' thigh and then further up towards his crotch. She felt his penis through his trousers and started gently rubbing it through the tough denim. Nobody but himself had ever touched him there, and he had to admit that it felt nice. He felt his penis immediately harden and closed his eyes with pleasure.

"You like this, don't you", Elke said gently, placing a kiss on his hairless cheek. "Your skin is so soft", she whispered while pulling Hans gently towards her, turning his face towards her and kissing him intensely, slipping her tongue into his mouth. Hans did not quite know what to do, but quickly realised that she wanted him to respond by touching her tongue with his. This wet kiss aroused him further.

While she was kissing him, Elke had begun opening the zipper of Hans' jeans. She opened the trousers and pulled down Hans' underpants, touching his erect penis with her hand. It felt very different from touching himself, much more intense and arousing. Elke started rubbing Hans' penis back and forth. Hans lay back on the bed, closing his eyes and enjoying every moment of it.

"You are such a beautiful boy!", Elke said while looking at Hans' penis and sparse pubic hair, stroking him more vehemently. "Your girlfriends are very lucky!"

Hans did not want her to stop, so he said nothing, and still lay back with his eyes closed in complete bliss. Elke stopped stroking him, got up, and took off his jeans and underpants. She pushed Hans into an upright position and asked him to raise his arms and took his t-shirt off. He felt just like a doll in her arms, ready for anything. He now was stark naked in front of her, with a huge erection, but it did not embarrass Hans one bit. He desperately wanted her to continue stroking his penis.

Elke now stood in front of him and slowly unzipped her dress, which floated to the floor with one quick twist of her hips. She wore no bra and Hans looked amazed at her breasts. This was the first time he had seen women's breasts. He thought her breasts were beautiful, as was her skin. No warts anywhere to be seen, instead Elke's skin was tanned along the face and neck, with white lines showing where she must have been sunbathing recently in a bikini. Her breasts were relatively small and firm, not hanging at all, and her small dark red nipples were slightly erect. Elke was much slimmer than Hans had imagined, her hips slender and her legs long and rather thin and nicely tanned under the bikini line. Her body looked almost boyish, although Hans could not draw any comparisons with anyone else. He thought Elke looked beautiful, the most beautiful person he had ever seen.

"Do you want to take off my panties?", Elke asked rather shyly.

Hans could not take his eyes off Elke's breasts, but he sat up on the edge of the bed and started slowly pulling down Elke's panties. Her panties were rather small and bikini-shaped, as was the fashion at the time, but they fitted so tightly that Hans had to place one hand on Elke's bottom to help wiggle them down her slender hips. At first, Hans did not dare look at the bush of brown pubic hair appearing, but his curiosity got the better of him. He had pulled down Elke's panties to her knees and stared at her pubis. It was different from what he had imagined, all this hair everywhere! Like most German women at the time, Elke did not shave her pubic hair, and being brown-haired she was rather hirsute. Hans carefully touched Elke's pubic hair, it was soft to the touch, almost like cat's fur. Elke had pulled down her panties to her feet and had flung them with one foot towards the corner of the room. Still standing in front of him, she gently guided Hans' hand between her legs. Hans could feel something moist among all this pubic hair, as Elke carefully placed his hand between her vaginal lips. With his hand in hers, she slowly started gently caressing her clitoris with one of his fingers.

"This is where you find the clitoris", Elke explained in a schoolmistressy tone. Hans had never heard the word and did not understand what Elke was doing. "Women like it if you rub the clitoris gently", Elke said. Hans, still guided by Elke's hand, slid his finger gently back and forth where Elke had indicated. He could feel a pea-sized hard and knobbly protrusion with his finger and Elke let out a deep sigh of pleasure as he caressed her clitoris gently. "Yes, that's it, that turns me on!", Elke said with her eyes closed.

Hans felt his penis stiffen further, and he was so turned on by what Elke was asking him to do that he felt the early onset of an orgasm, and all that even without touching his penis! As Hans closed his eyes and started breathing heavily, Elke must have realised what was going on and she immediately gently pushed Hans' hand away. "Ah careful, we can't have you come yet. We want this to last a bit longer, don't we?"

Hans opened his eyes and could feel the rising feeling of orgasm slowly abate. But he was still very aroused, much more than ever before. He felt a strong urge to come inside Elke, to make love to her.

Elke kneeled in front of Hans and gently took his penis into her hand. "And now for something your girlfriends need to learn pretty soon!", she said smiling naughtily at him while taking his penis in her mouth. Hans could not believe how beautiful it felt! Elke had gently pulled back Hans' foreskin with one hand and her wet mouth was gently moving up and down his shiny and rock-hard glans, stimulating him almost to the point of no return. When she felt his oncoming orgasm, she stopped and briefly squeezed his penis with her hand, which made the feeling of coming abate a little. Then she would take him into her mouth again, right up to the point of orgasm, then stopped again.

"I bet you want to come inside me now?", Elke said after a while, lying down next to Hans on the bed. "We will try to make it last as long as possible, so don't move too quickly to start with. Just come inside me …". She was lying on her back and spread her thin legs so that Hans could look straight at Elke's vagina. He did not know exactly what to do, but he knew that making love had to do with women's vaginas, and that you would come with your penis inside them. He could not stop staring at the wet and red opening, half hidden by tufts of brown pubic hair. Elke took Hans' penis in her hand and guided him gently inside her. Hans felt so stiff, and he was keen to thrust as quickly as possible, to come inside Elke, but she held him back a bit by placing her legs on his hips and gently dictating the pace. Hans could not believe how wonderful Elke's vagina felt. It was even wetter and slippery than her mouth, it seemed to completely and perfectly envelop his penis.

After a short while, Elke opened her legs further and let Hans slide into her as deeply as possible. She now let him dictate the rhythm of thrusts. Hans' body seemed to take over, somehow knowing what to do, how deep to push in and what cadence to use. Elke started moaning gently with her eyes closed. Hans looked at her and supposed that Elke was enjoying what he was doing. He saw Elke's small breasts bobbing up and down with the rhythm of his thrusts, her face suggesting rising pleasure. But after a while, he could no longer keep his eyes open, his penis took over more and more. He could feel a massive orgasm rising slowly and inexorably from deep inside him, beginning to completely overwhelm him. Enveloped by Elke's wet vagina, the onset of orgasm was longer than he had ever experienced in his bouts of masturbation. It seemed to go on for ever, until he exploded inside Elke, his whole body convulsing uncontrollably, his back arching backwards, and letting out a loud groan of pleasure. He seemed to come for an eternity, his cadence slowly reducing, Elke's loud breathing slowly getting back to normal. Hans opened his eyes and smiled at Elke, who looked back at him with an almost loving expression on her face. This had been the most beautiful thing Hans had ever done. He had made love to a woman! He very slowly slipped out of Elke, his penis still erect and his glans still glistening wet, lying next to her, still panting from the exertion.

"Wow, that felt like a big orgasm!", Elke said, caressing Hans' face and kissing him gently on the neck. "I could really feel you coming inside me!", she whispered, tugging at his ear with her tongue. "But now it's my turn!", she said, "if you are not too exhausted". She gently took his head and guided him down between her legs. Hans did not know what she wanted him to do. "And now lick my clitoris ... you know, that hard knobbly thing you felt with your hand earlier ... I would like that very much, and maybe I will also come." Hans thought that Elke had automatically had an orgasm when he came inside her, but he realised now that that may not have been the case. *Maybe that's what dad had referred to as understanding 'what women like'*, he thought. *Maybe it's not just about me coming inside her, but also about making the woman you are with enjoying herself and having an orgasm.*

Hans stuck out his tongue and tried to find the knobbly protrusion of Elke's clitoris. Her wet pubic hair was caressing his face and a strong fish-like smell emanated from Elke's crotch, not unpleasant but something Hans had never smelled before. As Hans' tongue was trying to find the right spot, Elke guided him patiently towards her clitoris by nudging his head back and forth, and instructed him about the right pressure and cadence needed to maximise her pleasure. Breathing in the musky smell of her crotch, Hans gently caressed Elke's clitoris with his tongue. He could sense through her hand still guiding his head and through the increasing cadence of her breathing that she enjoyed what he was doing. He increased the pace of his tongue a little and Elke's breathing increased simultaneously. After a while she let go of guiding his head, leaving Hans on his own to find the best position. Just when his tongue was beginning to tire and ache form the effort, Elke's breathing suddenly became louder, she started to moan and wiggle her pelvis. "That's it, just a little bit more … just a tiny bit to your left … yes … yes!", she moaned. Suddenly her whole body went into spasm, her back arched, her hand pressed Hans' head and mouth right into her crotch and she let out loud cries of pleasure. Her orgasm seemed to last an eternity and Hans, encouraged by the hard pressure of Elke on the back of his head, continued licking her until the final spasms had abated. Hans stopped, his tongue rather exhausted, and looked up at Elke from between her legs.

"Wow! Well done, Hans. I wasn't sure whether you could make me come, but that was a very nice orgasm." She pulled Hans towards her and they both kissed intensively. Hans thought that his breath must surely smell of her vaginal fluids, but Elke did not seem to mind.

For several minutes they lay there, eyes closed, and feeling each other's bodies. Hans was very happy. Although he had not known what to expect, he now thought that he had learned a lot, how to make love to a woman and, maybe most importantly, how to make a woman come. He was very proud that he had not been nervous at all, that his body had taken over by itself at the right moment and that it had all seemed very natural. Maybe he could take this knowledge back to his girlfriends, to Martina, who was maybe most ready to explore sex a bit more, maybe to Sonia or even to 12-year-old Bettina? Not once did he think that what he and Elke had just done was very unusual, outrageous, unheard of, barbaric, indeed rather abnormal, for a barely 14-year-old boy.

8

26th July 2019. Gregory did not know what to make of the story of Hans' 14th birthday 'present' when he finally found out about it. Hans only told him this story a few years later, and, back in 1974, neither Gregory nor any of his friends knew anything about what Hans' father had made him do with Elke Schmidt. Gregory was sure that, had they known, him and his friends would have been outraged, maybe they would have never wanted to see Hans again? Nobody would have ever heard of a thing like this, not in their circles, certainly not among the *Schweiss*- Kinder. Hans' 'act' with Elke Schmidt smacked of something dirty, something that was simply not done among civilised people. Maybe it was something that 'uneducated working-class people' would do, but, as this thought surfaced, adult Gregory knew he was on shaky ethical ground. Better not go there with his thoughts …

But Gregory was nonetheless certain that what Elke did with Hans on his 14th birthday was yet another building block in Hans' eventual psychological demise. 'Doing it' with Elke Schmidt was so different an act for a merely 14-year-old, so out of the ordinary, so … weird, that it had to leave a mark on a young person like Hans. Hans, when recounting the story years later, had claimed that he had greatly enjoyed making love to Elke, and that he had indeed learned a lot about 'what women like' in the act. But, after Hans had told him about it, Gregory never believed that Hans could so nonchalantly brush away what had happened. Had Hans just fooled himself after making love to Elke Schmidt that this was what 14-year-old boys were meant to do? Had he not realised that for all his schoolmates this would have been something totally unacceptable, barbaric, vicious and completely abnormal? Was the story even true, or had Hans made it up to boast in front of Gregory? But Gregory never doubted that Hans had made love to Elke Schmidt on his 14th birthday. It was difficult to explain why, but Hans was not the type to make up a story like this. But Gregory also fully understood why Hans had waited a few years before telling him and Bill about his experience with Elke. And yet it was the very fact that it almost seemed 'natural' to Hans that his dad had 'given him' Elke as a birthday present, that made Gregory wonder whether Hans at the time was already beginning to live in cloud-cuckoo land, in an abominable and abnormal sexual world of his own, with its own strange rules and boundaries? Hans' subsequent behaviour with girlfriends – especially when he was older – possibly lent support to this hypothesis.

While he let his mind re-absorb the sad story about Hans and Elke Schmidt, adult Gregory wondered how such a story would have played out in today's day and age. First of all, what Hans' father had facilitated, and Elke Schmidt did, would be highly illegal, as it obviously involved sexual intercourse with a minor, which should be punishable for both the father for soliciting the act, and the lodger for perpetuating it. As far as Gregory knew, the legal side of things would not have been much different in 1970s West Germany from what it was today. And yet, was there maybe something particularly 'West German' about this story in that West Germany – with all its 1970s burgeoning post-war idiosyncrasies, peculiarities and tastes – provided both the backdrop and ecology for Hans' life story and pathway? West Germany had certainly been heavily influenced by the post-1968 youth revolution – especially by the radical activist philosophies of Daniel Cohn-Bendit and others, and by the murder in West Berlin by the police of West German student activist Benno Ohnesorg, which was one of the sparks for West Germany's very active and politically vocal post-68 movement – much more so, Gregory thought, than in the UK or the US, for example.

Although Gregory was too young to judge this at the time, what he had read since suggested that West German culture was, at least in parts, heavily influenced by the post-1968 spirit – the Hippie culture, free love, criticism of established societal mores, etc. – and maybe such a culture would have seen sex with minors, even if instigated by adults, as something more acceptable than today? Gregory knew that a decade later the German Green Party, established in 1983, had, at one point in time, misguidedly advocated bringing the age of sexual consent down much below 18, and Gregory seemed to remember that the age of 14 had been mooted by some Green politicians. And yet, Gregory was not willing to accept that Hans being enticed to make love to Elke was a particularly 'German thing'. Surely, this may have happened in any family outside Germany, albeit in families that had very strange views about their children's sexual education. And on top of this, Hans' parents were certainly not at all involved in, or indeed influenced by, the post-1968 revolution. On the contrary, with their narrow-mindedness, shallow petty bourgeois values, and obsession for sterile order and cleanliness, they epitomised German conservativeness with a small 'c', the much-derided German *Spiesser* (bigot), which made Hans' act with Elke Schmidt even more preposterous and incomprehensible.

A possibly more important distinction between what happened to Hans on his 14th birthday in the early 1970s and the present day was the fact that teenagers like Gregory, Hans, Bill and Rufus had no access to information sources such as the internet at the time. How easy was it for today's kids to see millions of naked women from all walks of life and from all over the world, to glean from thousands of porn sites what love making was all about (albeit rarely in a realistic setting), to see more positions than the Indian *Kamasutra* could have ever dreamed of, and to see all kinds of sexual acts by people of various ages, genders and colour. But in early 1970s West Germany, the only access to sexual material was either through 'men's magazines' which could be purchased in shabby kiosks and which showed blurry nude pictures of women, or through hard-core porn magazines obtainable only in 'sex shops', both inaccessible and unobtainable for young teenagers. Gregory remembered how the only sex shop in Heidenhausen, located near the railway station, was always talked about in hushed tones by his schoolmates as a site of crime, vice, grubbiness, and full of dirty and desperate old men. Only much later, when they were nearly 19, did Gregory and some of his friends venture into that sex shop for the first time to flick through the grubby and uninspiring magazines. It should also not be forgotten that the early 1970s were also a time when even sex videotapes and films had not yet been widely available. It was, therefore, almost impossible for young kids to find visual information about sex. This was in no way an excuse for what Hans' dad and Elke had done to Hans, but it highlighted how different the conditions were then when compared to the present day. For most of today's kids, it would have been unfathomable how difficult it was for young kids in the 1970s to even see the naked body of a woman.

Recalling the story of Hans' 14th birthday present with Elke Schmidt left a decidedly sour taste in Gregory's mouth. Something was clearly wrong about this behaviour, about Hans' family, about the whole idea of introducing a child to sex in such a way. Gregory preferred to see Elke Schmidt as a poor gullible pawn in Hans' father's plan, swayed by the forgiveness of one month's rent, and possibly lured to perform the act by a hint of curiosity about what it would feel like to make love to a young boy, rather than seeing her as fully complicit in the whole sad affair. But whatever the motives and reasons for this distasteful and abominable act had been, once it had happened it could not be taken back, the clock could not be turned back, the die had been cast. Hans had, for better or worse, been put on another misdirected and misguided rung of his life pathway's ladder.

9

17th June 2019. Hans woke up with a jerk. Where was he? It took him a while to realise that he was still behind his sofa, crammed in between the back of the sofa and the wall of his living room, soiled sheets around him as well as an increasing pile of food wrappers and remains of old food. He kept as quite as possible, trying not to move so that he could listen out for any noise made by the intruders. He was sure they were still in his flat, even after eight days of rummaging through his clothes, of rattling pots and pans in his kitchen, of shuffling along the corridor, of touching his things with their dirty, calloused and sweaty hands.

Why do they never show themselves?, Hans kept wondering. *What are they looking for that they could not find after eight days of searching? Of course, they are looking for me!*, he suddenly realised with his pulse racing and breathing more heavily. *What will happen if they find me?*, he fretted, chewing his fingernails.

For a long while he did not dare move, listening out for the slightest of sounds. There, something was banging against something; or there, a clicking sound; or there, again this sound of something rustling against the wall. It had to be them! But Hans desperately had to go for a pee. This was probably what had woken him up. Very carefully he moved his heavy and morbidly obese body towards the corner of his den, where several turds were floating in a puddle of piss. He was oblivious to the acrid and pungent smell. After relieving himself the last time, he had left the zipper to his filthy trousers open, so that the noise of zipping his trousers up would not alert the intruders. Hans very cautiously took out his penis and emptied his bladder into the festering puddle of piss. Although he crouched down as low as he could to the floor, he could not prevent the noise made by the gushing urine. To him it sounded not like a mere trickle, but like the Niagara Falls! He was very worried that the intruders would hear the gushing piss. He stopped as quickly as possible, tucked his dripping penis back into his underpants again without zipping up his trousers, listened out for approaching footsteps, and crawled back towards the other end of his den. As far as he could make out, the intruders were still in his hallway, touching his coats, shuffling along the wooden floors, and even playing with his door keys dangling from their brass hook.

Tears welled up again in Hans' eyes. How long did he have to endure this ordeal? How long would these bloody intruders force him to hide in his den? Had they been sent by the social services to check on him, to see whether he was still able to live on his own? After all, it was Heidenhausen's social services who had allocated him this flat, who were paying his rent, who sent around a care worker once a month to check on him, especially whether he was taking his medication. His medication! Suddenly, and for the first time in eight days of hiding, Hans realised in a brief moment of lucidity that he had forgotten to bring his medication to his den, these small blue pills he hated so much that fogged his brain, that left him in a zombie-like existence, that destroyed the last shreds of his remnant free will. How he hated having to take these pills! They changed him, they made him another person he no longer recognised, and, worst of all, they made him feel as if he had retreated from life, as if he was giving up trying to live a 'normal' life with laughter, joy and meeting other people. In that sense, it was good not to take his pills, he thought while clenching his fists hard. Maybe this was his last act of rebellion? But then, had his doctor not clearly said at their last meeting that if he did not take his pills regularly his paranoid delusions would take the upper hand again? Hans had to smile at this thought. Did the doctor and his care worker really think that the intruders did not exist, that they were a figment of his imagination? Ha! How wrong they were, as he could clearly hear somebody just at this moment again going through his clothes drawer. They were clearly there, rummaging through his stuff again, pulling out his shirts, tearing at his underpants, ripping his socks. But he did not dare look over the rim of his sofa and shout at the intruders to go away. What if all they were looking for was himself? What if they would kill him if they found him in his den behind the sofa?

But suddenly another thought occurred to Hans. What if these intruders had not been sent by the social services but by his father Bernhard? Indescribable fear suddenly overwhelmed Hans. Maybe it was his father himself who was at this moment going through his clothes in his bedroom, who was stomping around in his kitchen, whose footsteps were approaching, betrayed by the creaking of floorboards in the living room, right next to his sofa? Hans started sweating profusely with fear, he began hyper-ventilating with angst, and trembling uncontrollably. *That's it! It's been dad all along! He is trying to find me, he is trying to kill me for what I did to him all that time ago!* His uncontrollable fear made him empty his bowels into his trousers. Hans could feel the diarrhoea seeping through the already soiled back of his trousers, running down his thighs and oozing out onto the bedsheet underneath him. His sobbing increased, he simply no longer knew what to do. Overwhelmed by fear, his heavy obese body slumped back onto the bedsheet, Hans closed his eyes, wishing all his abject fears, all these fearful noises, all

81

these dreadful smells, to go away. *Leave me alone! Just leave me alone!*, he thought in desperation as he closed his eyes.

Part 2

Rupture

10

1st August 2019/late 1975 and early 1976. A few days had passed. Adult Gregory busied himself around the house while his wife Amelia was at work. Retirement suited him well, with several projects in and around the house and the garden on the go, and boredom, that many workaholic colleagues or friends had warned him about, had never been a problem so far. And yet, despite all these distractions, and ever since coming across the photos of Hans on the school trip to London in 1978, Gregory could not stop thinking about his former schoolfriend. It was as if a long-closed box had been opened, as if an old wound had reappeared, as if a ghost from the past had come back to haunt him until the whole story of Hans' life was retold in his mind again in full. It was an exorcism of sorts that detracted him from his retirement projects, and that took up large chunks of his day, as he could not stop thinking about Hans and their childhood and youth. But Gregory knew that recounting Hans' story was also brought about by feelings of guilt on Gregory's part, guilt for having 'abandoned' his former friend after their last fateful meeting ten years ago in 2010.

Gregory was back in front of his large living room windows, in one of these time-consuming and all-enveloping 'thinking-about-Hans-moments', and looked out across the village towards the estuary along which wealthy mansions were huddled – some architect-designed and ultra-modern, some more old or traditional in style. He closed his eyes, waited for pictures of him and Hans to appear, but, as had often happened these past few days, there were only a few. Gregory realised that his memories of Hans and him continued to be just snapshots – snapshots over a long abyss of time, possibly distorted, certainly incomplete. Maybe he did not really know Hans well after all, especially since they had stopped being best friends so long ago?

Gregory wished he had more photos of Hans, photos of this crucial time when they were aged between 13 and 16, as these would help further jog his memory. But there were none. A side-effect of Gregory's parents' separation had been that very few pictures were taken by his mother of him and his friends after the age of 11, as his father had kept all their cameras (a nice and expensive *Rollei* single-lens reflex camera and a *Fuji Single 8* film camera). At the time, his mum had shown no interest or inclination to purchase another camera and to take photos. Indeed, as a single working mum, Gregory's mother was so occupied with other things that he could hardly blame her for not having had the time to think about taking photos. And yet, this camera- and photo-less time had left a yawning void in Gregory's childhood that was difficult to compensate with the odd snippets of distorted memory that occasionally came to the surface.

In addition, when they were best friends Hans had very rarely come to Gregory's flat, so there would have been only few opportunities when Gregory's mum, if she had had a camera, could have taken photos of them. It had been

Gregory who had gone to Hans' house instead, partly because Hans lived closer to school, but maybe also, Gregory had to admit, because he was a bit embarrassed to take Hans, a non-*Schweisser*, home. It was not that Gregory's mother was a snob or anything like that, but maybe that rift between *Schweiss* and non-*Schweiss* Kinder still played an important role in social stratification at home? From his present vantage point, Gregory was not sure. He simply could not remember whether such a snobbish attitude could have played a role in the fact that Hans almost never came to Gregory's flat, at least at the beginning of their friendship.

Partly as a result of this and the fact that Gregory's mum had no camera anyway (apart from the lonely picture from the newspaper cutting he had discovered recently that coincidentally showed Hans and Gregory sitting in the same primary school class), Gregory had no pictures of Hans, or of any of his other friends, until he was given his own camera at the age of 16. And even then, Gregory did not initially take pictures of his friends, but instead rather boring and innocuous pictures of their flat and his family, mainly on holidays, and many pictures of things such as cars, their cats, or buildings which must have been interesting to Gregory at the time but which were of little use when it came to recreating memories of his teenage years. Indeed, the first pictures taken by him of his friends must have been those that had jogged his memories of Hans in the first place, pictures taken during their school trip to London in 1978 when Gregory would have been 17 and Hans 18. Gregory grabbed his laptop and searched for the picture folder labelled '1978' where he immediately found the scanned photos in question: the picture where Hans looked at the camera with a lost-puppy-look in his brown eyes and a sheepish grin that suggested that he had been caught unawares when the picture was taken, and the other rather interesting photo in which a hint of jealousy was perceptible in Hans' facial expression as he stared jealously at Bill who was standing a bit further away in front of some statue – possibly Churchill – smiling at the camera with a confident, almost arrogant, look on his face.

And yet, although Hans had faded into the background a long time ago, at least since their last difficult meeting in 2010, there were nonetheless snippets of memories, fragments that came to the surface, jogged not necessarily by thoughts about the catastrophes that befell Hans, but by simple day-to-day activities that had been typical of the time when they were young teenagers. These emergent memories of Hans and Gregory were like skipping stones across water, only occasionally touching the surface, but nevertheless creating ripples that, eventually, intersected to connect together other bits of memories and stories. Two of these memories, for example, that could not have been sparked by photos, but that nonetheless had left a deep impression on Gregory, involved Hans and him riding their mopeds through the streets of Heidenhausen at night in 1976 when Gregory would have been almost 15, and the other memory involving an earlier scene, in late autumn 1975, with Hans and two of his girl-friends lying in the grass just outside their school a few months earlier.

Gregory vividly remembered receiving a small *Peugeot* moped with a one-stroke 50cc engine. Although this was meant to be for his 15th birthday, he was still only about 14 and a half when he got it. This was yet another present by his father who felt forever guilty of having 'abandoned' the family for a younger woman – one way to placate his guilt of virtually never seeing his two sons with almost endless showers of monetary and other gifts. Although in West Germany you were only allowed to ride a moped (with a maximum engine size of 50cc) from the age of 15, Gregory and his friends knew that the police rarely checked teenagers' IDs when they stopped them, unless the kids riding the mopeds looked really young. As a result, Gregory rode his moped from the moment he received it without his worried mum being able to stop him. After all, why did they get him this moped so early if they did not want him to use it?

Like many of his friends, Gregory was changing fast at the time, his voice had broken, and he was beginning to show an interest in girls, not the giggling innocent pretence-interest of pre-pubescent times, but a 'real' interest in going steady with a girl, in maybe having sex with her, although what this exactly meant was still a rather abstract notion to Gregory who had not even kissed a girl yet. He had also begun to let his hair grow long, as was the style of many teenage boys in the mid-70s, based on the growing number of long-haired rock musicians they idolised. Gregory saw both the moped and his friendship with Hans as a key to possibly meeting girls. He vividly remembered the sense of freedom when, for the first time, he could roam beyond the streets near his flat which he had, by then, already meticulously and exhaustively explored with his pushbike.

Not only did Gregory drive his moped to school, which allowed him to get up much later as he no longer relied on his mum driving him, but he very soon also ventured on his own onto the small roads in the nearby hill areas and forests of the eastern *Schwäbische Alb*, greatly aided by the fact that the estate in which their flat was situated bordered on forest and several easily accessible forest tracks. Gregory remembered the cool winter air in his face, the dusty-earthy scent of the forest tracks, and the intense sappy-pine-needle-smell stinging his nose, while zooming along on dark gravelly forest paths in the evening, with the headlight beam illuminating gnarled trees, juniper-clad banks, and muddy, murky and water-filled ditches on either side of the forest tracks. At times, he was tens of kilometres away from home, on small roads and forest paths he had never been to, occasionally getting lost, but increasingly beginning to find his way around the wider area with more and more confidence. The feeling of freedom this gave him was intense, addictive and unforgettable.

Hans also owned a small moped, a slightly more powerful two-gear chrome-blue *Herkules* which was the envy of all the boys in class. As soon as Gregory had received his moped, his relationship with Hans intensified further, while his other friends, especially Bill and Rufus, lost out because their parents did not want them to either ride mopeds before they were 15 (e.g. Rufus, who at 14 was about Gregory's age), or not at all because it was deemed to 'dangerous' (Bill's mum, who was such a worrier!). Now Gregory and Hans would not just meet up in Hans' room, where Gregory always felt stifled by the exaggerated cleanliness, sterile atmosphere, and claustrophobic and threatening presence of Hans' dad, but they could for the first time roam the streets of Heidenhausen and surrounding areas at will and at any time. To Gregory, it almost felt like the feeling conveyed in the movie *Easy Rider*, which came out a few years earlier (1969). Gregory had seen it in the cinema and it had left a big impression, conjuring up images of motorbike hippies with their long hair flowing, Steppenwolf's song *Born to be Wild* thundering away in the background, girls on the back seat (or so Gregory wished!), and wild orgies with bare-breasted girls under a starlit sky (dream on!).

While there were plenty of memories of Gregory driving along darkened streets behind Hans' always slightly more powerful moped, the most vivid memories of the time related to their jaunts to discos and nightclubs in the seedier parts of Heidenhausen located 'down below' in the valley previously inaccessible to them – places that, until, recently, had seemed mysterious, foreboding and out of reach. Of course, the gorilla-like bouncers of these venues never let them in, as they both were still well below the age limit of admission of 18 (and there the bouncers, unlike the traffic police, did check IDs for age). They never picked up girls either, at least not Gregory. But just the mere act of trying to get into these places, the attempt to pick up girls, often at what for them seemed to be quite late in the evening (although it was probably mostly still before 10pm), instilled in both of them a strong feeling of jocular camaraderie, intense friendship, and a feeling of conspiratorial male bonding, further sprinkled with a hint of the forbidden, a feeling of living a dangerous adventure together from which other kids such as Bill and Rufus were excluded.

Sitting on their mopeds outside these seedy venues, Hans did sometimes chat up girls, sometimes girls he knew (*where from?*, Gregory always wondered), sometimes new girls who, at times, seemed to be much older than Hans and, nonetheless, gravitated towards him like bees towards a beautiful flower full of nectar, or like flies towards an enticing and irresistible lump of sugar. Gregory could only watch in awe how Hans approached these girls, chatted them up easily and uninhibited with his big endearing smile, caught their attention with his deep brown eyes, and then waved over Gregory to join them. But Gregory was always weary of these occasions, almost afraid to approach these alien and unknown beings in their 'going-out' clothes, some with daunting mini-skirts, and almost all with heavy make-up that, Gregory always thought (but did not dare mention to Hans) made them look like tarts. Although he was not sure what kind of girls he liked yet, Gregory already inwardly knew that he was not attracted to these girls who looked like whores, who were 'tarting up' with make-up, glitzy jackets, and mini-skirts that showed their thighs and the rim of their panties. He preferred the demurer not-dressed-up girls, and almost certainly girls that were not attracted to these seedy-looking discos and nightclubs. There was, for example, that most beautiful slim, but very shy, blonde girl in the year below him that had recently caught his eye, but she seemed to be completely out of reach, and Gregory would have never dared approach her (he had never told Hans about this). The result of Gregory's rather mooted enthusiasm about the girls in front of these nightclubs was that, as soon as Gregory approached Hans and his huddle of female admirers and tried to say something smart or witty, the girls would quickly find excuses and scatter. While some of the girls were allowed into the venues by the bouncers, the two boys would be left standing there, hanging around and unsure about what to do next.

At this point, Hans often looked at Gregory with an unfathomable look on his face. It was not exactly a reproachful look, more like a look of pity or lack of understanding as to why Gregory was not showing more enthusiasm in their quest to pick up 'disco girls'. In return, although Gregory felt immense pride at being with Hans and pretending to chat up girls and to explore these inaccessible venues, he also felt very inferior to Hans. He thought he was still just a mere kid, a child, compared to this all-knowing flamboyant hunk who had a natural way with girls and who was maybe only taking somebody like Gregory on these outings out of pity.

These evenings out, therefore, always left a bit of a sour taste in Gregory's mouth – feelings of being constantly torn between daring and cowardice, courage and stupidity, allegiance and betrayal. He often felt emotionally drained after such 'Hans-moped-evenings', and was often happy to spend the next few evenings at Bill's house, which involved much more innocent, but equally rewarding, activities such as board games, or talking about their friends or (unattainable) girls, while listening to Bill's newly bought rock music records.

Maybe it was on these occasions that Gregory began to understand that there was a burgeoning rivalry between Hans and Bill, a rivalry that, to Gregory's astonishment, seemed to revolve around him, around their friendship with him, and about who would be his 'best friend'. At the time, this was mystifying to Gregory as he did not see himself as a particularly interesting boy of 14 or 15. Indeed, when compared to a star and flamboyant hunk like Hans, Gregory did not feel that he had much to offer anyone. And yet, he began to recognise that his friendship was highly valued by both Bill and Hans – by Bill possibly for gaining some access to Gregory's new-found freedom, 'wildness' and access to Hans' networks; by Hans for possibly getting closer to the more 'sophisticated' middle-class world of *Schweiss*-Kinder with parents, tastes and educational opportunities that were very different from Hans' own life. And yet, at this point in time, Hans' superiority was painfully obvious to Bill and Gregory: girls wanted to be *with* him and most boys wanted to be *like* him. At the time they thought that it would take a momentous shift to take Hans down from his pedestal and to change this unequal relationship between themselves and Hans. Little did they know then how quickly the complex permutations of friendships would change in the not-so-distant future, and how low Hans would sink soon afterwards.

The second vivid memory in Gregory's mind (not sparked by photos) was of an ordinary day sometime in late autumn 1975 – Gregory and Bill would have been just 14 and Hans just 15. Hans, Bill and Gregory were lying in the sun on the lawn above their school, half-way towards one of the new housing developments, where many of the *Schweiss-Kinder* lived, and the local cemetery. It must have been just after school, probably around 1pm, and for some reason they had decided not go straight home for lunch. Beyond the school, Heidenhausen could be seen in the distance in the autumn haze, with the new housing developments surrounding the nearby area of juniper heath where Hans' house was located; one of the Protestant churches puncturing the horizon of a nearby hill; further down, the centre of Heidenhausen in the valley with its narrow streets and the main church; a bit further off, the few remaining factories with smoke belching from their high chimneys; the brand-new retail park to the east; and the other new secondary school standing guard to the west with its squat, dominant and modern-looking buildings that oozed an arrogance and self-confidence that their own school, demurely tucked away into the hill, somewhat lacked.

Martina, Hans' 'official' girl-friend for at least the last 12 months, and another younger-looking girl Bill and Gregory did not recognise came up the lawn to join them. Hans introduced the unknown girl as Ursula. Martina and Ursula barely glanced at Bill and Gregory and walked straight towards Hans and lay down in the grass on either side of him. Watching the two girls with their short skirts, plastic bangles around their wrists, and unsubtly and unprofessionally applied make-up and painted fingernails, Gregory could not hide the thought that Hans always seemed to have a penchant for girls who were vane, flirty, indolent, fickle and somewhat irresponsive – 'wild girls' in other words who were not at all Greg's type. Greg had a sudden vision of a future Hans with money, driving a classy open-top Mercedes, sporting mirror sunglasses, elbow hanging out over the window ledge, and cruising along at night through Heidenhausen's seedier parts, tarted-up girls waving at him. Little did he know then that none of this would come to pass.

Hans was lying in the thick grass on his back, his upper body raised on his elbows, and chewing a long grass stalk in a way that made him look even cooler than usual. Hans looked utterly in control of the situation, and Gregory was not sure whether Hans had planned from the outset for the girls to join them in order for him to show off in front of Gregory and Bill. It certainly looked as if two attractive girls, simultaneously vying for Hans' attention, was a most natural and normal thing in the world to Hans. Hans nonchalantly pulled Martina towards him and they both kissed for a long time, their tongues playing with each other avidly and with audible sucking noises. Gregory and Bill looked at each other, a bit embarrassed and unsure whether they should stay in front of this unchained intimacy.

To their surprise, however – and this must be why this specific memory had suddenly surfaced in Gregory's mind – Ursula, the second girl, also started to kiss Hans on the mouth. Greg and Bill did not know Ursula, but assumed that she must be a friend of Martina's, as Martina let this happen without bashing an eyelid. Indeed, it seemed as if the three of them had done 'this' already before, that they were very familiar with each other, and that Hans had kissed Ursula in front of Martina before. While Martina was about Hans' age, i.e. about 14, Ursula did not look much older than 13, although it was sometimes hard to tell, as girls developed at such different pace. At this time, Gregory and Bill did not know anything about Hans' 14th birthday present and the fact that he had already been 'introduced' to making love to an older woman. But, from talking to Hans and other kids at school, they all thought that Hans had 'done it' with girls long ago, that he was lightyears ahead of Bill and Gregory who still did not have girlfriends at the time. They had certainly seen Hans and Martina hug and kiss at school before (Martina was in the same year as them), as Hans and her would meet up in almost every break between classes, and as it was impossible to avoid seeing them together in what was quite a small school with only a few places for couples to meet in secrecy. But for Gregory and Bill this was the first time they had seen Hans 'in action' with two girls simultaneously, and with one very young-looking girl at that. To Gregory at least, the scene unfolding in front of him came as a bit of a shock, and he looked at Hans and the two girls, kissing and hugging ever more intensively, with increasing awe but also apprehension. Hans must have felt his two friends glaring at him. He gently pushed Ursula aside, who had started kissing Hans' neck, and smiled back at Gregory and Bill.

It was Hans' smile that stood out in Gregory's memory of that scene in particular. It was a knowing smile, a smile that oozed superiority, an arrogant smile, a smile that seemed to say "Look at me! Not just one but two, at the same time! And look at you two, lying here and forced to watch! You two kids who haven't got a clue about anything and you probably never will!" Gregory hated it. He hated this whole situation, the fact that the two girls had not even looked at him and Bill, the fact that both girls did not seem to care one iota that there were other boys present watching them, the fact that they felt no shame doing a threesome in front of them. As if to sow salt on a festering wound, Ursula looked up at Gregory and smiled with a similarly arrogant and superior smile. Still staring straight at Gregory with her beautiful emerald-green eyes, daring him to continue watching, Ursula's hand made her way to Hans' crotch and started unzipping Hans' trousers. Gregory was even more shocked but could not take his eyes of what was happening. He remembered vividly thinking: *You won't dare! You can't do this in front of us!* At the same time, he rather embarrassingly felt his own penis stiffen at the thought of what Ursula was about to do and hoped that the two girls did not see the rising bulge in his pants. A hardening bulge was also clearly visible through Hans' underpants, but again this did not seem to bother either Hans or the two girls. Just when Ursula was about to take Hans' penis out of his underpants, Hans gently pushed her hand aside, looked into her eyes with a gentle smile and then turned his eyes towards Gregory and Bill who were still sitting there stock-still, shell-shocked and flabbergasted at what was happening in front of their eyes. Ursula nodded back, knowingly and smiling naughtily, glancing mockingly back at Gregory with a look that seemed to say "Okay, I understand. These two boys are still too young for this."

Gregory could stand it no longer. With an angry glance at Hans, he stood up and walked away as fast as he could, not looking back to check whether Bill was joining him. He remembered being deeply hurt that Hans had let the girls act like that in front of them, but he was also jealous ... very jealous. How did Hans find girls like that in the first place? And one probably barely 13! How could he get these girls to 'do things', and now with two of them at the same time? How did Hans manage to get these girls to do these things to him in front of each other, while kids like him ... and Bill ... struggled to even approach girls, talk to them, let alone kiss them?

11

1975-1977. It was becoming increasingly obvious to Gregory, that his feelings towards Hans had begun to be split since the specific incident on the lawn above school in late autumn 1975. On the one hand, he had been furious about the scene on the lawn, especially that Hans had so obviously enjoyed Bill and Gregory being shocked at what he was doing with the girls, and that he had so obviously flaunted his superiority when it came to girls. And yet, on the other hand, teenage Gregory also knew at the time that he still deeply admired Hans, that, in his deepest dreams, he wanted to be just like him. He was still very grateful to Hans for taking him on the moped rides, for showing him the seedy world of discos and nightclubs (even if only from the outside), for being out there with him at night in the 'adult world', even if what they did remained very innocent and relatively safe (as he kept telling his mum).

Gregory also knew at the time that Hans did not care too much about what Bill thought of him, and about what Bill had made of the recent scene on the lawn. Although Bill and Hans were 'friends', theirs was a different, much less intense, more detached friendship to that of Gregory and Hans. From the beginning, Bill had always been wary of Hans, had always managed not to be too enthralled by Hans' aura and had, therefore, remained a bit more aloof and, possibly, a bit more in control of his feelings towards Hans. Gregory respected Bill for that and, at times, wished that he could similarly leave Hans' spell, be more aloof himself and less in awe of Hans, and, in turn, see Bill and his other friends more often. In other words, often he just wanted to be a 'normal' 14-year-old and not somebody who was, stupidly and impossibly maybe, aspiring to be like Hans. And yet, Hans' world offered so many rewards with regard to meeting girls and living more flamboyantly, more daring, a world more visceral and rawer, something that was missing in Bill's safe and secure middle-class *Schweisser* world.

But Hans had maybe also realised at the time that he had gone too far with Martina and Ursula on the lawn in front of Gregory. Possibly to redeem himself and to make up for his behaviour, shortly afterwards Hans had introduced Gregory to Evelyn, a girl Gregory did not know at the time. Hans had told Gregory that Evelyn had just turned 14, that she was in the year below, 'ripe for the picking' and looking for a boyfriend, but that she was a bit shy and did not dare approach boys by herself. When Hans took Gregory to the corner of the school playing field where the meeting had been arranged, and where Evelyn was waiting nervously, Gregory realised that Hans had not warned him about one thing: Evelyn was not pretty. She was not ugly, but she certainly lacked the stunning beauty of girls like Martina, with her slim legs and pretty face, Ursula with her beautiful skin and piercing emerald eyes, or, indeed, that beautiful blond girl from school who had just recently caught Gregory's eye (but whose name he did not even know). Evelyn was a bit stocky, with freckled skin, rather large hips, and front teeth with a rather large gap in the middle. And yet, she greeted the two boys with the most endearing smile and looked Gregory deep in the eyes with her intense brown eyes, scrutinising every bit of his face. Gregory immediately liked her.

Evelyn became Gregory's first girlfriend. As Hans had rightly assumed, they were both well suited to each other, both shy, both inexperienced, and both ready for a partner. Gregory did not know how Hans had got to know Evelyn, and he thoroughly hoped that Evelyn had not already been one of Hans' many girlfriends. But it quickly became clear that, although Evelyn liked Hans as a friend, he was not 'her type' and, neither, it was fair to say, was Evelyn Hans' type at all. Hans' match-making appeared to be a purely genuine gesture of friendship towards Gregory, without any strings attached, possibly to make up for Hans' endless show of superiority and arrogant behaviour vis-à-vis Gregory.

Gregory was grateful to Hans for having introduced him to Evelyn and, for a while, it further cemented their friendship. However, Hans' goal to turn Gregory into a wild lover and 'sex maniac' like Hans himself proved elusive. Gregory and Evelyn went out together for over three years, but they approached their relationship with much caution and care. Although Gregory thought he was deeply in love at the time, in hindsight his relationship with Evelyn was more like an intimate friendship. Maybe it was because Gregory was never that physically attracted to Evelyn (or she to him?), or maybe it was just their shyness and inexperience, but it took them a long time to make love for the first time. Of course, there was a lot of hugging, kissing, fondling and petting, but it took at least two years for them to find the courage to have 'real' sex together. Contraception was an issue (how did Hans and his horde of girlfriends deal with it?), and it was not easy, even in liberal post-Hippie West Germany at the time, for a teenage girl to get the pill. Condoms were easily accessible, but neither Gregory nor Evelyn trusted them enough to try them. Pregnancy always remained a scary spectre, the sexual booby-trap, the thing that could finish you and your aspiring career as whatever off (in contrast, adult Gregory knew from his own son, who was 22, that, today, pregnancy and contraception were much less of an issue for young people and their sex lives).

The most annoying thing, however, was that, once he had matched them up, Hans was constantly curious about how Gregory's and Evelyn's relationship was developing. Hans seemed to have a lurid fascination about what Gregory and Evelyn 'did together', and especially whether they had 'done it'. Gregory thought that his sex life was his own private business, and got increasingly annoyed at Hans' prying questions. Adult Gregory remembered one occasion when he was sitting in Hans' room at his immaculately clean desk, while Hans was lying on his bed, his folded arms behind his head, asking, yet again, about whether Evelyn and Gregory had made love. At the time, Gregory had exploded with outrage and shouted: "Of course, we have done it! What do you think! But I don't think it is your business constantly asking me about it!" At this point they had, of course, not yet 'done it' and were only just experimenting with lying next to each other without their clothes on, but Gregory's outburst and constructive lie at least shut up Hans for a little while. Sometimes teenage Gregory was wondering whether Hans had just brought him and Evelyn together to obtain lurid details about other people's sex lives. A slightly unhealthy and strange aspect of Hans' inner life was possibly beginning to emerge.

Evelyn was a smart girl, and she quickly understood Gregory's complex, and at times antagonistic, friendship with Hans. She always seemed to understand when Gregory needed to be with his friends without her, either Hans or Bill, and occasionally Rufus and his friends, and she never applied pressure on Gregory to spend more time with her. Occasionally, Evelyn would join Gregory, Hans and his girlfriend(s), and Bill, in order to go out together into town or to the cinema, but, like Bill, she was also continuously weary of Hans. Maybe as a girl she saw much more *through* him, what Hans was *really* like, and that he could be very manipulating and calculating, especially towards other girls. At moments of intimacy with Gregory, Evelyn would sometimes try to steer the discussion towards Gregory's friendship with Hans, and warn Gregory that he was too much in awe of him, that he was in constant danger of being manipulated by his friend. Deep inside, Gregory knew that Evelyn was right, that Hans sometimes had a bad influence on him, that he was maybe even using him for some obscure and unfathomable reason. And yet, he could not let go of Hans. Hans had shaped him during this crucial phase in his life, he still greatly enjoyed going out on his own with Hans, zooming through the streets of Heidenhausen on their mopeds, with unforgettable feelings of being carefree, happy and on top of the world.

But at the same time Gregory was also beginning to distance himself more from Hans than in the past. One of the reasons was linked to school. Although they had tried to swat together for Maths before crucial tests, especially in Years 8 and 9 when they were 13 and 14, Gregory had quickly and pragmatically realised that Hans was simply not good enough in Maths to help him. Instead, Gregory's mother was now paying for a private Maths tutor and, although progress was slow and tedious, Gregory's Maths results were improving slightly, while Hans' results stayed either flat or deteriorated further despite of him receiving his own intensive private tuition.

But there was another school-related aspect that brought Hans and Gregory closer together again. Hans had developed a strong interest in French, greatly enjoyed French lessons, and got on very well with their (female) French teacher. Gregory sometimes thought that this was maybe one of the reasons for Hans' continued interest in his friendship with Gregory, as Gregory's mum was French and Gregory himself was a native French speaker (first language) and, inevitably, was very good in French lessons. Hans was also suddenly keener to visit Gregory in his flat, as he often used the opportunity to practice his French with Gregory's mum, who tried her best with her busy life to find some time for conversation in French with her son's friend. Was Hans, therefore, just using Gregory to improve his French? But Gregory knew that this was too cynical a view, and that Hans genuinely was interested in French language and culture, and, at times at least, Hans produced some good results in French tests, especially in oral tests where his excellent vocabulary and pronunciation were a real asset. Gregory was pleased that Hans managed to do well in at least one of his school subjects.

But in most other school subjects Hans was increasingly struggling – in particular Physics, Chemistry, Biology, English and German – while Gregory did just about all right in these subjects. Gregory was never a brilliant student, as he was rather lazy, but when he applied himself, and with the odd help from his mum (especially in French) or tutors, he somehow always managed to obtain reasonable grades (except in Maths). The result was that from Years 10 to 12, between the ages of 15 and 17, Gregory's and Hans' school results increasingly diverged. Hans' results became increasingly marginal with the constant threat hanging over him of having to repeat the year, while the performance of Gregory, and especially those of Bill and Rufus, improved. The German school system suited schoolkids like Gregory in particular, as pupils could start discarding certain subjects from Year 11 onwards and focus on subjects that were more interesting to them or where they performed better. Hans, on the other hand, struggled in almost all subjects and had, therefore, only limited choice about which subjects to focus on, or discard, in order to improve his grades. Very soon Hans' worsening school performance would prove to be one of the key reasons that further tore apart Hans' and Gregory's friendship and was, arguably, another factor that may have ultimately led to Hans' psychological meltdown.

At the age of 15 and 16, there were, therefore, several factors that were challenging Gregory's and Hans' friendship. Girls were both a binding and separating factor, the latter being particularly linked to Hans' endless prying into Gregory's sex life. Although Hans' interest in French bound them together more tightly, school results were certainly reinforcing pre-existing rifts between clusters of children (not only between Gregory and Hans), and maybe it was no coincidence that, as subject matters became more difficult from Years 9 and 10 onwards, *Schweiss*-Kinder did proportionately better than the other schoolkids. But there were some notable exceptions among the kids from Heidenhausen and neighbouring villages, as some rural kids turned out to be exceptionally gifted and bright, and excelled in many subjects.

There were, nonetheless, a few other key factors that led to Gregory and Hans drifting further apart, especially linked to diverging interests and hobbies, most notably linked to music. Although Gregory's first ever exposure to the fantastic world of rock music had been listening to *Deep Purple* in Hans' room when he was only 13 years old, Hans never showed the same enthusiasm as Bill in exploring new bands, buying the latest albums and chatting about rock stars.

One constraint for Hans would have been the high cost of purchasing vinyls – adult Gregory remembered dishing out over 20 *Marks* for some albums he bought (a sum probably equivalent to about $20 or €20 in today's money) – money Hans did not have, despite of the generous presents his parents would regularly give their only child. But it became quickly obvious that Hans did not have the same music taste as Bill and Gregory, as Hans started drifting increasingly towards French *chansons* – sparked by his burgeoning interest in French and French culture – a type of music which was completely uninteresting and 'uncool' to both Bill and Gregory. Listening to rock music albums and letting their hair grow long in the fashion of their rock music idols, thus, became increasingly important aspects of Bill's and Gregory's identities and intensifying friendship, leaving Hans somewhat out in the cold.

However, where music created the most important rift between Hans and Gregory/Bill was in relation to Bill's and Gregory's first rock band *Sidewinder* (named after a desert snake). Sparked by their interest in rock music, Bill had bought a cheap second-hand bass guitar, while Gregory had at first rigged up a drum kit made of old cardboard detergent boxes with cling film as drumskins and, a few months later, had received a full-set *Sonor* drumkit with cymbals, high-hat, bass drum, snare and two toms (paid again with money provided by his ever-guilt-ridden dad). Gregory's brother Max, aged 12 at the time, meanwhile, had received a relatively expensive electronic keyboard (through the same parental source of finance). While Gregory and Bill were mere beginners at their instruments, Max had already had piano lessons for years and was beginning to become a truly gifted and highly innovative musician. Together, the three of them formed *Sidewinder*, joined a bit later by Matthias, a fellow classmate and good electric guitar player, who also provided a (for the time at least) highly sophisticated *Leslie Box* amplifier with which they could perfectly mimic the then common floating *Hammond* keyboard sound characteristic for bands such as *Deep Purple*, *Uriah Heep* or *Pink Floyd*.

At the same time, Gregory, Bill, Matthias and Max also joined the school choir, led by a new glamorous, young, outgoing and interesting female school teacher called Heidi Blattmann. Although Gregory knew that joining a choir could be perceived as being a bit 'sissy, 'pufta' or boring to many of his other friends, including Hans, the fact that many of his friends, his brother, and also Evelyn and her friends, had joined the choir outweighed the negative sides. A particular allure were the infamous choir trips to nearby towns where the choir would perform in churches, town halls and other venues, sometimes staying overnight. Gregory remembered with very fond memories how boys and girls would surreptitiously mix together in the dorms (with smuggled-in alcohol), teacher-condoned pyjama-parties, and the overall satisfaction of singing together what were, at times, complex and ambitious classical choral pieces ranging from Bach and Mozart to more modern pieces such as *My Fair Lady*. The relationship between the schoolkids and Mrs Blattmann was so informal and enjoyable, that, even at school, Mrs Blattmann was just referred to as 'Heidi' by the kids – an arrangement that was almost unheard of at this time in German schools and that was deeply frowned upon and reprimanded by the upper school hierarchy. Indeed, to Gregory and his friends from the choir it almost seemed as if Heidi and them had entered a forbidden and secret alliance to subvert the school, which further cemented the already unusually tight bond between Heidi and her pupils. An additional benefit from having joined the choir was that Gregory, Bill, Max and Matthias were given unrestricted access for their rock band to one of the storage rooms adjoining the music classroom, where they could store their musical instruments and play music as loudly as they wanted after hours. Indeed, at age 15 they were the only schoolkids who had keys and access to the school building after hours, and they made ample use of it by practising at least two or three evenings a week. Sometimes Heidi Blattmann would listen in after work and give them useful advice and important moral support.

But both the choir and the rock band excluded Hans. Gregory could not remember whether Hans had shown an interest in joining the choir, and he could also not remember ever hearing Hans sing (or whether Hans could, indeed, actually sing). Apart from the odd occasions where sounds of dreadful Bavarian-style *Jodl* and um-pa-pa music were emanating from Hans' parents' room, Gregory also suspected that Hans' family were not much interested in modern or classical music or playing musical instruments. Hans himself, therefore, never showed any curiosity in playing an instrument and did not hide the fact that he thought the choir was for 'pussys' and 'fags'. Although they did not talk much about this, Gregory knew that Hans hated the fact that Bill and Gregory had joined the choir and now had their own rock band. Indeed, *Sidewinder* was quickly acquiring a good reputation at school, even soon elevated to the official 'school band', and asked to play at school events, end-of-year prize-givings, or even as a warm-up-act (together with the choir) at the yearly school ball. Hans never talked to Gregory about these relatively successful events (although, at one point, Gregory's bass drum fell of the stage while they were playing, to hilarious laughter from the audience), and Gregory secretly revelled in the fact that Hans was jealous of Gregory's new-found interest and circle of friends.

At this stage, pre-existing animosities between Bill and Hans particularly came to the fore. The constant jealousy between Bill and Hans was exacerbated by the music-induced rift, and the two began avoiding each other and, from about Year 10 onwards, they hardly spoke. Their fight for Gregory's time, while evident in the past, became more pronounced, with both criticising Gregory for spending too much time with 'the other'. Gregory was, therefore, constantly torn between his remaining allegiance to Hans on the one hand, and his commitments with *Sidewinder* and the choir on the other. As a consequence, he had less and less time to spend with Hans, sometimes only one evening a week.

The result was that – whether for revenge or genuine interest Gregory did not know – Hans had started drifting towards a new friend, Klaus Hintermaier. Klaus had always been somewhat in the background in their school class, lurking around and showing a keen interest in becoming one of Hans' friends. But for a while he was completely crowded out by Gregory's and Hans' intimate friendship. But as soon as cracks became evident in the Gregory-Hans alliance, Klaus pounced. Klaus was from the 'rural kids' group at school and had a lengthy and complicated commute to school. Possibly for this reason it had been difficult for him as a younger kid to join in with after-school activities of the Heidenhausen kids. However, at age 15 Klaus got a moped which gave him independence from his tightly-scheduled bus commute. Although barred from driving his moped to school by his parents when it was snowy or icy (in those pre-climate-change-days days the *Schwäbische Alb* still had pretty harsh winters with circa 4-5 months a year with snow cover at higher altitudes and in rural locations), this now gave Klaus the opportunity to do things with Hans after school for most of the year. As a result, Klaus began to replace Gregory on moped outings. This annoyed Gregory, especially as he was not sure what Hans and Klaus did on their joint jaunts, and whether Hans took Klaus to the same places he usually went with Gregory. It was as if some sacred ground had been breached and invaded, which left a slightly sour taste in Gregory's mouth and a strong feeling of having been betrayed by Hans.

One of the reasons Hans was drawn to Klaus, was that Klaus was also very good at French. Indeed, Gregory had to admit that he admired Klaus for pronouncing French excellently, despite of Klaus' very broad *Schwäbisch* dialect which proved such an obstacle in French and English pronunciation for all the other *Schwäbisch*-speaking kids. But, overall, Klaus was seen as rather weird by most kids in their school class. Not only was he subject to the cruel discrimination evident against kids from rural provenance – *Bauernkinder* (peasant kids) as they were nastily referred to, often wearing poor 'peasant garb' characterised by rough stitched-up trousers with leather patches on the knees and battered moth-eaten jerseys (German schoolkids do not wear school uniforms) – but he was also teased for the fact that he spoke so incredibly fast (both *Schwäbisch* and French) that nobody could understand him. When he introduced himself, for example, trying to say "Hallo, ich bin Klaus Hintermaier", it sounded more like "Hloibinklaushnmr". This problem was further amplified by a tick he had, jerking the right side his mouth upwards when he spoke. This earned him the nasty German nickname of 'Rucki' (after *Ruck* or jerk, equivalent to 'Jerky' in English).

Bill, Rufus and Gregory, therefore, found it rather puzzling why an adored and flamboyant womanizer such as Hans would suddenly associate himself with 'Rucki'. Yet, it seemed to exacerbate a trend that had already become apparent at the beginning of Year 10 – they would have been about 15 years old – when Hans had begun to lose his position as flamboyant class idol and womanizing hunk. This was undoubtedly linked to the fact that most other kids had now 'caught up' with Hans in terms of their voices breaking, muscle development, height, and maturity. Hans had always been one of the older kids in class and had, therefore, had a substantial advantage and head-start when they were young teens. But now that many other boys began to have their own girlfriends – including Gregory and Bill – and were quickly gathering sexual experience, Hans no longer seemed exceptional. Indeed, it became increasingly evident that Hans had lost his early 'first-mover advantage'.

But Hans was also increasingly marginalised with regard to his poor school results, in what had always been a high-achieving and ambitious school class environment. Many other classmates now performed better than Hans, leaving Hans increasingly desperate. Although there was a general trend that most kids in their class did better from Year 10 onwards, when unpopular subjects could be dropped, the eternal clash of class-worlds at *Franz-Bosch Gymnasium* became apparent once again. On the whole, *Schweiss-Kinder* did better, propped up by better educated parents and better, more expensive, tutors to help them at a time when exam results were more important than ever. Although Gregory did not like to see Hans struggle, he, also felt securely tucked into his own little better-performing *Schweiss*-world bubble, shared with kids such as Bill and Rufus. Indeed, Gregory's advantage of being fluent in French particularly came to the fore from Year 10 onwards, when many of his schoolmates, who had kept French as a subject, often struggled with the increasingly difficult subject matter, while Gregory cruised through the French tests without much effort and work. This allowed him to concentrate more on subjects he was struggling with, such as Maths and Physics. Gregory's mum, who also taught English, could also greatly help Gregory with English tests. Indeed, at her school she had access to a copy of a book of short stories that was also the basis of many English tests at Gregory's school (a fact, luckily, unknown to their English teacher), which greatly helped Gregory in test preparation (and was not seen at all by Gregory as a form of cheating but, arrogantly, as his entitlement for having the privilege of an English teacher as a parent). Hans had none of these advantages, and instead school became more and more of a grind for him.

Gregory could see that Hans felt immense and increasing pressure to perform better, and yet neither Gregory nor Bill were inclined to help Hans with schoolwork and exam preparation at this stage. They key reason was linked to Klaus Hintermaier. Klaus did not like Gregory and Bill, and he never hid the fact that he despised them. Gregory never fully understood why this was the case, but suspected that it was linked to Klaus being jealous of Hans' friendship with Gregory, the fact that Bill and Gregory were part of the group of kids who continuously teased 'Rucki' for his unfortunate tick, and the fact that Gregory and Bill had never hidden their (largely unjustified and arrogant) feelings of superiority as *Schweiss*-Kinder over the group of rural kids in their school class. As a result, Gregory and Bill had the impression that Klaus was actively trying to wrench Hans away from them, and they increasingly left Hans to fend for himself when it came to school tests and exams.

This increasing rift between the two groupings of Gregory/Bill and Hans/Klaus became particularly apparent in two ways. While Gregory had sat next to Hans in Years 8 and 9, relegating Bill and Rufus to the side-lines, from Year 10 onwards Gregory had begun sitting next to Bill, usually in the front row, while Hans was now sitting with Klaus towards the back of the classroom. Sometimes Gregory felt Klaus' intent stare of hatred boring into the back of his head, but when Gregory turned around Klaus pretended to look elsewhere, while Hans looked embarrassed and rather apologetically back at Gregory with an unfathomable look that may have suggested regret and a yearning for old times.

Gregory remembered several occasions when he and Bill had great times together during lessons, with a lot of fun and laughing. On one occasion, Gregory was bored (again) during a French lesson and doodling (again) in his schoolbook. In a chapter on Paris and its parks, a photo depicted a young couple on a bench leaning amorously towards each other. Gregory had erased the bloke's head and had redrawn the head as a large alien's head with pointy ears and globular eyes. As the picture emerged – which looked even more hilarious than Gregory had intended – Bill and Gregory could not stop laughing. This began to distract their teacher – Herr Achter who was much liked and very popular with Gregory and his school class (but who, unfortunately, had been head-hunted by one of the new Heidenhausen schools and due to leave the next school year) – who had stood in front of them while giving a lengthy harangue in French about his life in Paris as a young trainee teacher. Herr Achter stopped talking and looked at the cause for Bill's and Gregory's jocular outburst. But instead of telling them off (as he was an excellent and shrewd pedagogue), Herr Achter started laughing heartily himself, saying in French that Gregory's drawing had definitely improved the picture, which, of course, aroused the curiosity of the other kids. Herr Achter waved Gregory's classmates to come forward and look at the drawing, which caused a lot of laughter, a few snide comments, and many pats on Gregory's back congratulating him on the sublime modification of what most of them had seen as a rather naff and uncool picture. Surrounded by the throng of kids and briefly revelling in his short moment of fame, Gregory looked behind him towards the back of the classroom. Hans and Klaus were the only ones still sitting in their seats, Klaus with a look of fierce hatred and determined disinterest on his face, while Hans looked away sheepishly and guiltily and evidently curious about what the commotion in front of the classroom was all about.

The second instance where the animosities between Gregory and Klaus came to the fore was linked to table tennis. For some reason, their main classroom (where most but not all of their lessons were held), had a tennis table at the back, with generous space to run around it and play *Rundlauf*, in which a large group could play at the same time, hitting one shot each while running around the table. As more and more players were eliminated by losing a shot or by being outplayed, one had to run faster and faster to get to the ball. Sporty kids like Gregory and Klaus did well at this and often ended up playing for the 'final' together, which consisted of a brief best-of-5 match where they stayed at their respective ends of the table. Although for most kids, the table tennis matches merely provided a welcome break between lessons and, for the less fit ones a bit of welcome exercise, for Gregory and Klaus, in particular, the regular table tennis sessions became an issue of intense and fierce competition. Almost mirroring his jerky mouth tick, Klaus' table tennis style could best be described as 'jerky', with an incredibly fast flick of the bat generating, at times, ungettable smashes from the most complicated angles. As Klaus' style was so unorthodox, it was rather effective and, to be fair, Klaus was a very fit player with excellent hand-eye coordination. Gregory, on the other hand, was a more 'conventional' player with a solid backhand and an excellent forehand smash which, based on the application of large amounts of spin, could generate difficult shots that were hard to return. In addition, both had vicious serves with a lot of spin that could, if not returned properly, spin off opponents' bats by as much as 90-degree angles.

Often Klaus' and Gregory's 'finals' were characterised by long drawn-out rallies, with ever intensifying smashes, angles and returns, watched in awe by the other less-able kids who would often cheer and clap at the end of particularly gruesome exchanges. Although Gregory wanted desperately to win against Klaus, he also had to admit that he admired Klaus for his skilful handling of the bat and his dexterity around the table. Klaus, on the other hand, never hid the fact that he wanted to *annihilate* Gregory, *smash* him to pieces, and *push* him into the back wall with ever more vicious smashes. At the end of their 'finals' – won probably evenly between Gregory and Klaus – Gregory sometimes had the impression that Klaus wanted to continue the fight off the table, to smash Gregory's jaw, or kick him in the stomach. There seemed to be so much hatred in Klaus' stare that Hans often had to hold Klaus back from assaulting Gregory or Bill. It often took Klaus several minutes to calm down after they had played, and Gregory was always a bit worried about meeting Klaus on his own somewhere in a dark and remote corner of the school. Although he was much taller and stronger than Klaus, Gregory was not sure whether he could muster enough hatred to really want to hurt Klaus.

Yet, and in hindsight to adult Gregory, this emerging rift between Hans and himself, and the evident hatred and jealousy of Klaus, seemed rather petty and trivial. Ever since Gregory could remember, their school class had always been riven by factions, changing allegiances, and ever-shifting friendships, often driven by a cruel and crude Darwinian 'survival-of-the-fittest' approach that did not leave much room for inclusivity or acknowledgement of difference. The worst example beyond Gregory's and Hans' immediate group of friends related to the continuous, persistent and, at times, outright nasty and xenophobic ostracism by the whole school class of the only openly gay boy, Xaver, in their midst. Despite of desperate attempts by teachers to counteract this brazen xenophobism, Xaver was prevented by the kids from joining-in during group sports, was rarely invited to parties, and had no friends in class. Sadly, adult Gregory had heard in 2015 that Xaver had committed suicide after having lived on his own for a long time in Berlin and falling into a deep depression – a piece of news that had instilled in adult Gregory a strong feeling of guilt and that suggested that German society as a whole had continued to do to Xaver what they, as schoolkids, had done to him without thinking about the future repercussions of their actions. *How can schoolkids be so brutal to each other?*, Gregory thought from his adult vantage point, reminiscing about what they had done to Xaver. Compared to this, the rift between Gregory/Bill and Hans/Klaus was indeed rather trivial, but, again in hindsight, it turned out to be yet another small cog in the unfolding story of Hans' psychological meltdown.

12

1st August 2019/early and late summer 1978. Adult Gregory went through the scanned photos of Hans again on his laptop, and the photos taken with his own (at the time brand new) camera during their London school trip in the early summer of 1978 stood out again from the rest. Gregory was nearly 17 at the time and Hans almost 18. Gregory particularly stared at the pictures of Hans looking at the camera with a sheepish grin and a lost-puppy-look in his brown eyes, and the other photo where a hint of jealousy was perceptible in Hans' facial expression as he – again seemingly caught unawares of being photographed – stared askance at Bill who smiled at the camera with a confident, almost arrogant, look on his face. The latter photo seemed to confirm the new power constellations in Gregory's complex relationships with his friends from Year 12 onwards, with Bill now firmly installed as Gregory's 'best friend' and Hans relegated increasingly to the side-lines.

As had so often been the case when Gregory – from the vantage point of an old and retired person – had started thinking about specific episodes in his and Hans' lives, long-

hidden memories suddenly came flashing back. Hans'
increasingly strange behaviour during their London school
trip was one such memory. For some reason, Klaus had not
gone on the trip (his parents probably could not afford to pay
for it), and Hans was left without Klaus' support. Throughout
the trip, Hans had desperately tried to regain Gregory's
attention and to lure him away from Bill's protective
clutches. Gregory remembered Hans constantly hovering
next to them, be it on the plane, in museums they visited,
over lunch, or when walking in London's busy streets. But,
to Gregory at the time, Hans' attempts felt increasingly
desperate and clumsy. Hans knew that he had long lost his
earlier advantage with regard to girls and his 'savoir-vivre'
flamboyant demeanour, and that Gregory and Bill were now
sharing many new interests and hobbies – especially linked
to their rock band and the choir – which were increasingly
out of reach for Hans. Unlike Bill, Hans could also not
impress Gregory with much knowledge about English
culture and history relevant for their London school trip or,
indeed, about the English language. In contrast, Bill was a
fluent English speaker due to his American upbringing, and
he evidently shone in London, being able to converse
fluently with people they met and even outclassing their
teacher who was herself a fairly competent English speaker.

As a result, Hans must have realised during the trip that
he had few trump cards left to impress Gregory. Yes, Hans
was still good looking and a flirt, and many of the girls on
the trip responded well to Hans' approaches, but to Gregory
and Bill this all seemed increasingly less important. Hans
certainly could not impress them with his academic skills, as

it was more than obvious at this stage how much Hans was struggling at school. Possibly because of this, and maybe also as a last straw to impress both Gregory and Bill, Hans had suddenly and unexpectedly told them about his infamous 14th birthday present. Hunched over the photos of the London trip on his laptop screen, adult Gregory remembered the scene when Hans had told them the shocking story about him and Elke Schmidt and his 'birthday present'. At the time, Bill and Gregory had been sitting in the common room of the London youth hostel where their group was staying, chatting about the day over cans of Coke, when Hans had come over to them. So far during the trip, Hans had avoided disturbing Gregory when he was with Bill, which meant that there had been few opportunities for the three of them to be together and chat. By casting a rather nasty look back at Hans approaching their table, Bill had tried to tell Hans that he was not welcome at their table. But Hans was again in one of his funny belligerent moods and appeared not to see Bill's stern face. Hans had sat down next to Gregory and had looked at him intensely.

"I never told you about my 14th birthday present, have I?", Hans had said, addressing Gregory directly and rudely interrupting the discussion Gregory was just having with Bill.

Gregory looked at Bill with a bemused look. *Where has this suddenly come from?*, he thought at the time. *What is Hans trying to do? To get my attention with another one of his stories about female conquests?*

Bill smiled back with a superior smile. Neither of them was very interested in what Hans had to say. But that did not stop Hans from talking. Hans must have felt that he was not welcome at their table and that Bill preferred to be alone with Gregory, but in his belligerent mood he started telling them the uncensored story about how his father had arranged for him to make love to Elke Schmidt on his 14th birthday. Initially, both Gregory and Bill had thought that this would be another one of Hans' stories about past girlfriends, but as Hans began giving them lurid and explicit details of what had happened on that fateful day, Gregory and Bill could not prevent themselves from getting more and more drawn into the story. After a while, they had both listened with open mouths at what Hans' father had made him do on that fateful day, how Hans had enjoyed what Elke had done to him, and how, overall, he thought it had been a fantastic experience. While Hans was recounting the lurid details of the sex he had with Elke Schmidt, Gregory could not stop thinking that Hans had achieved what he set out to do by picking this specific place and time to tell them the story about Elke Schmidt: he had indeed impressed both Gregory and Bill, he had found a story they had not heard of before, and he had entranced them to listen to him at least for a few minutes.

While Gregory could see that Bill was increasingly sceptical about the veracity of the story as it unfolded, Gregory had never had any doubts that what Hans recounted about Elke Schmidt was true. It was difficult to explain, but, despite of all of Hans' foibles, he was not a liar. There were no occasions when Gregory could remember that Hans would have exaggerated a story about his love-making prowess or how he had persuaded young and inexperienced girls to fall into his clutches. But when Hans had finished recounting the story of his 14th birthday 'present', it nonetheless left a very sour taste in Gregory's mouth. Of course, adult Gregory mused, Hans had told them this story at that time in the London youth hostel because Gregory had blatantly neglected and ignored Hans, because Gregory had spent all his time with Bill, and because Hans had felt desperately side-lined and saw this story as the only way to impress Gregory and Bill, and to lure Gregory back towards him and away from Bill. In this sense, Hans' plot had worked. But, on the other hand, the lurid details about his experience with Elke Schmidt had also added another piece of evidence about the weird world of Hans Schlesier, where it seemed 'normal' for parents to give their 14-year-old child a sexual encounter with an adult woman as a 'birthday present', and where it seemed normal for Hans to subsequently brag about such abnormal behaviour.

In the long run, therefore, Hans' telling of the story about Elke Schmidt backfired and further increased the rift between Hans and Gregory/Bill. Indeed, after Hans' desperate attempt to recapture Gregory's attention during the London trip, Hans' constant clumsy and cloying hunger for Gregory's attention became so annoying that Gregory had to tell Hans off during the trip and ask him not to bother him anymore. Gregory remembered that this was the first open rebuke he had given to Hans, and – as it all happened at the time in front of Bill and a few other schoolmates standing nearby – it evidently hurt and embarrassed Hans. Hans did then indeed stop harassing Gregory for the remainder of the trip, but the whole situation had left a sour feeling and a widening rift in their friendship. The whole episode was yet another chink in Hans' position as idol and role model, not just for Gregory but for all the schoolkids on the trip. Gregory now increasingly felt that he could look right through his former friend, that Hans' armour of self-assuredness, maturity and cocksure arrogance had crumbled to reveal that all of Hans' bluster and supposed sexual achievements had just been platitudes, sad stories of early sexual encounters, shallow showing-offs of an insecure bully, and possibly even early signs of a narcissistic personality disorder.

As a result, after the London trip Greg and Bill found it harder and harder to take Hans seriously. While observing Hans' increasingly odd behaviour among their London fieldtrip group, what suddenly struck Gregory was that, like all show-offs, Hans loathed being alone. Indeed, it suddenly struck Gregory that there was nothing self-sufficing or self-sufficient about him. Hans was in constant need for company and he had felt lost in London without Klaus and without Gregory's close friendship. Indeed, his ascetic and sterile room back home was testament to the fact that he had no hobbies, nothing that would keep him occupied in the few instances he was alone. Apart from chasing girls, Hans had no interests. It dawned on Gregory that Hans had always been afraid, very afraid, of solitude, of being alone, with an overwhelming need to win his schoolmates' esteem. Indeed, on his own, Hans was just a shadow, a ghost, who needed both a constant stream of girlfriends as a mirror for his own life and as a constant comparison with his schoolmates to bolster his feelings of macho superiority, to self-elevate himself to this image of a person he was not and never would be. Without Gregory and Bill as counter-images of schoolmates who, in the past, had been inferior to him, Hans was nothing. And if Bill and Gregory truly abandoned Hans as a friend, what would be left of Hans Schlesier as a person and human being? Was it, therefore, also at least partly Gregory's fault that Hans soon began to struggle psychologically, that Hans was beginning to show signs that 'things were not quite right'?

Adult Gregory continued to scan the Hans Schlesier photo folder on his laptop. While the London school trip had undoubtedly been another key moment in their gradually disintegrating relationship, the next set of photos, from a trip to Brittany in France, reminded Gregory that he and Hans were still doing many things together, and that some aspects of their friendship had not yet greatly changed by then. The Brittany trip took place in the summer of 1978 at the end of Year 12, a few months after their London trip. Hans had just obtained his driving licence and his uncle, who was also involved in the family plumbing business, had kindly lent Hans his van to take on the holiday trip as an 18th birthday present.

There were several reasons why Hans had asked Gregory to come with him to Brittany. Most likely, Gregory thought, Hans had wanted to use the trip to patch up things between them, and that Hans saw the trip as an occasion to be alone with Gregory just like during the heyday of their friendship. The second reason was possibly more pragmatic and calculated: Hans had planned a stop-over of a few days in Paris and Gregory's uncle (his mum's brother) lived in Paris and could, therefore, offer them free accommodation.

Gregory was happy to come with Hans to Brittany, but he saw it less as a way to patch up their friendship but rather as an interesting trip to a part of France he did not know. Gregory's mum had been a bit worried about Hans driving such a long distance in a foreign country just after having passed his licence, but, as it turned out, Hans was a reasonably competent driver and there were no problems with regard to Hans' driving abilities during the trip.

Hans' decision to go to Brittany had not come out of the blue and was linked to the fact that he wanted to see his new French girlfriend, Monique, who he had met during a recent Year 12 school exchange between *Franz-Bosch-Gymnasium* and the *Lycée Martine Bénédicte* in Rennes, Brittany. Gregory had, again, been impressed how quickly Hans had been able to pick up a new girlfriend among the group of vivacious and attractive French schoolkids visiting their school in Heidenhausen (and how quickly he dumped Heike, his German girlfriend at the time). As it happened, Monique had stayed with Evelyn during the school exchange, and it was Evelyn who had introduced Hans to Monique in the first place. Hans and Monique immediately hit it off, and adult Gregory remembered vividly how they became inseparable during the visit of the French school children, despite the fact that Hans was still somehow with Heike during the first few weeks of the school exchange.

In many ways Hans' relationship with Monique, who was very much liked by everybody, at least briefly reinstated Hans' status at school as a womanizer and flamboyant romantic. But the fact that Hans wanted Gregory to go with him to Brittany left Gregory in a quandary. He certainly did not intend to end up as the 'third wheel' when Hans was meeting up with Monique in Rennes, where they would be staying in Monique's parents' house. As a result, Gregory insisted on bringing Evelyn on the trip, aided by the fact that during Monique's stay with Evelyn, Monique had become good friends with her. Gregory remembered that it took some cajoling to persuade Evelyn's parents to allow a 16-year-old girl on such a lengthy trip with two teenage boys, but with the help of Gregory's mum and some firm assurances that they would be 'careful', Evelyn was allowed to go. As a result, Evelyn's presence on the trip scuppered Hans' plan to rekindle his friendship with Gregory, as Gregory, inevitably, wanted to spend a lot of time with Evelyn on what was their first holiday together.

Despite the unalleviated tension that had existed between Hans and Gregory since their London trip (and before), their trip to Brittany was a success. The three of them had a great time in Paris, and everything worked out more or less as planned when they met up with Monique in Rennes and stayed in her parents' house. Although Monique's parents put the girls and boys in separate rooms, very quickly secret arrangements were made for the two couples to sleep together in their own rooms during the night. Gregory remembered furtive and secretive scrambles back into their 'allocated' rooms early in the morning before Monique's parents woke up, and they thought that Monique's parents never suspected anything.

But timing the changeovers back to their allocated rooms in the middle of the night proved difficult, as whoever needed to move room had to set their alarm clocks at exactly the same time so as not to disturb the others. It was during a rather botched changeover towards the end of their visit (a changeover that occurred earlier than planned as Evelyn was tired and wanted to sleep), when Gregory was making his way as quietly as possible back to the room he was sharing with Hans, that Gregory obtained proof of Hans' and Monique's always bragged about, but so far never hitherto proven, very active sex life. Without knocking he walked in on them and surprised Hans making love to Monique from behind, thrusting his penis deeply inside her and caressing Monique's swaying breasts – a sexual position Gregory at the time did not even know existed (Evelyn and him had still not started making love then).

Hans saw Gregory come in, but Monique had not seen him as she had her eyes closed while Hans was thrusting his penis deep inside her. But instead of stopping his love making and taking his penis out of Monique immediately, Hans looked at Gregory with an arrogant smile and pushed his penis deeper inside Monique. Worst of all, he continued to look at Gregory with a defiant look on his face, and, while increasing the cadence of his thrusts, he raised his arms behind his head so that Gregory could get a better view of Hans' penis thrusting in and out of Monique's wet vagina. Monique must have suddenly realised that Gregory was standing there – dumbfounded and with his mouth wide open – and, when seeing Gregory staring at them, she emitted a loud and embarrassed cry, quickly pushed Hans' penis out of her, and awkwardly crawled backwards towards the top of the bed, while desperately clutching the bedsheet to cover her private parts. Hans had stayed on his knees, his large erection standing naughtily upright, still covered in Monique's vaginal fluids. He still looked straight at Gregory with an arrogant, superior and knowing smile, as if taunting Gregory to acknowledge what a great lover he was. Gregory was so embarrassed that he did not know what to say or do. After what seemed like an eternity, and desperately trying to avoid Monique's reproachful gaze, he quietly shuffled backwards out of the room and closed the door. For a long time afterwards, the vision of the kneeling figure of his friend, with his large throbbing erection thrust deeply into Monique from behind, was uncomfortably etched in Gregory's mind.

Although Gregory had not enjoyed Hans' behaviour and seeming arrogance when he barged in on them making love, and although Monique had looked at him askance for a few days after having been caught unawares in the act of making love, Gregory nonetheless thought that he and Hans had grown a bit closer again during the trip. Gregory was pleased to see Hans' continuing enthusiasm about anything to do with France and French culture, and although Brittany was different from most of France with its Celtic idiosyncrasies and rural quirkiness, Hans made ample use of their stay to practise his French. He made a point of only speaking French with Monique, which partly excluded Evelyn from discussions, as her French was still relatively poor (despite of regular 'French-speaking sessions' with Gregory), and he also made ample use of Monique's parents' willingness to speak French over breakfast and dinner.

The most vivid memory of the Brittany trip for adult Gregory was, however, not Hans' raunchy love-making, the intimate times he had with Evelyn on their first holiday trip together (despite of them not yet making love), or the joys of speaking French with Hans, Monique, and her parents, but a memory linked to one evening when Gregory and Hans had a rare moment of being alone together with time to chat.

13

28th July 1978. Gregory and Hans were sitting together on the porch in front of Monique's parents' house. They had glasses of French *Kronenbourg* beer in their hands and were looking at the stars that were only faintly visible over the flicker of street lights of suburban Rennes. Gregory thought that Hans was unusually quiet and pensive, and he wondered whether there was a problem between Hans and Monique, and whether Gregory's barging in on their love-making had anything to do with it. After a while, Hans had turned towards Gregory with a stern face.

"I wanted to tell you something", Hans said with a voice that evoked dread and gloom.

"What is it? Is it about me?", Gregory replied fearfully.

"No, no, not all", Hans reassured Gregory. "It's … it's about my parents and school …"

Hans was still for a while, but Gregory did not want to prompt him further. He felt that Hans was about to tell him something important.

"They have decided that I should repeat Year 12", Hans eventually said, hanging his head.

Gregory wondered whether Hans was trying to hold back tears. "Why would they do that?", he asked surprised.

"It's … it's my father", Hans admitted, looking back at Gregory with an almost pleading look. "He says that my results have not been good enough, and that if I continue like this in final Year 13 my results will not provide me with much opportunities to go to university or to find a good job".

For several years, Gregory had watched Hans' school results worsening. Even bright science-and-language-whizz-kid Klaus Hintermaier had not been able to help Hans improve in subjects such as Maths, Biology, Chemistry, Physics and English. But Gregory also immediately felt guilty at the time, as he had quickly abandoned swatting for Maths school tests with Hans when he realised that Hans knew and understood even less of the subject matter than Gregory did. Gregory also realised that for a long time he had avoided asking Hans what his plans were after school, especially whether Hans was interested to go to university, maybe to even study French. For Gregory it was clear that he himself would go on to study, and he had his eyes set on Geography, a subject that had always fascinated him even as a kid and that he had greatly enjoyed in Year 12. Gregory wondered whether Hans really wanted to go to university, or whether he rather intended to follow in his father's footsteps and help with the family plumbing business.

To Gregory the fact that he had not even discussed these crucial questions with Hans over the past year or so had further confirmed how much they had drifted apart. Indeed, at that moment it dawned on Gregory that, with all the activities around their rock band, the choir, and the increasing time he spent with Bill and Rufus, he had less and less time to be with Hans, to think about Hans, and to be interested in Hans' desires and wishes. Gregory almost felt as if he should put his arm around his friend who sat hunched over and rather downcast next to him, but he was not able to muster the courage to do it. Even a year earlier, he would not have hesitated to show Hans his affection, that he still cared, that he wanted to help Hans. But now, sitting on the porch with Hans in Rennes, Gregory only sat there, not quite knowing what to do or say. Deep inside, Gregory was also annoyed that Hans had not told him earlier about the momentous decision to repeat Year 12.

"But that will mean that you will be separated from all of us, from all your friends?", Gregory found the courage to say, but he also quickly realised that this did not greatly help Hans' situation.

Tears had welled up in Hans' eyes, but rather than turn away in shame, Hans looked Gregory straight in the eyes, as if to imply: *Exactly! See what my father is doing to me, and all of this because you no longer helped me at school!*

Hans wiped his tears and snivelly nose on the sleeve of his shirt, leaving a long trail of snot clearly visible in the dim porch light. "That's exactly what I told my father", he replied with a voice that betrayed utter desperation. "I don't want to go down one year! I am already older than most of you kids,

131

and now I will be almost two years older in a school class where I barely know anyone. Imagine! I will be in Evelyn's year group surrounded by young kids!", Hans said while sobbing, with his face in his hands and his body shaking uncontrollably.

Hans' desperation was so great that Gregory was no longer able to hold back. Tears also welled up in Gregory's eyes, and he finally mustered the courage to lean over towards his friend and gently put his arms around him, hugging him tightly. Hans responded immediately by gently leaning towards Gregory, his loud sobs abating slightly. Gregory looked at the illuminated windows fringing the porch, hoping that neither Monique nor Evelyn, who were in the house chatting with Monique's parents, would see Hans in this state. But, to Gregory's relief, all seemed quiet.

"There must be something you can do", Gregory said trying to console his friend, but having met Hans' father he knew that any attempt to sway Bernhard's decision would be futile. "Look! It's not the end of the world! We will still be friends and see each other as often as possible", Gregory continued, trying to sound reassuring, but realising all the while that Hans leaving their year group would probably be the death-knell for their already flagging friendship. The last year had clearly shown that Gregory's allegiances now firmly lay with Bill and their rock band, and that Hans had lost most of his earlier allure and flamboyance. Sure, Gregory still admired Hans for his way with girls, including the highly impressive love-making from behind with Monique. But Gregory also knew that Hans repeating Year 12 would be another brick in the wall of disengagement, separation and disentanglement that had already characterised their relationship over the past year or so. Little did Gregory know at the time, that Hans' father's decision to make his son repeat Year 12 would be another contributing factor in Hans' psychological meltdown.

14

1st August 2019. Gregory had not realised at the time that their Brittany trip would be the only holiday he would ever take with Hans (and with Evelyn to that effect). As Gregory had predicted on that fateful evening on the porch, during Year 13 Gregory gradually lost touch with Hans and got ever closer to Bill and Rufus. Sure, Hans and him occasionally saw each other in the school corridors or the playfield between lessons, but long gone were the days when they would roam the streets of Heidenhausen carefree with their mopeds, or when Gregory would go back with Hans to his house. In fact, looking back, adult Gregory could not even remember when he had last been in Hans' house. Probably in 1977 when they were still in Year 11?

It quickly became evident that the decision to take Hans out of their school year had been disastrous for Hans. Not only had it completely severed the link between Hans and Gregory, but it had also led to Hans losing touch with Klaus

Hintermaier. During their occasional meetings, Hans would reluctantly reveal to Gregory that he had not made new friends, and that the kids in his new year group were much too young and immature to be of any interest. The only person who was nice to Hans was Evelyn, although she was too busy with both Gregory and her own circle of friends to be able or willing to help Hans much. Adult Gregory suddenly remembered that in one of Gregory's and Hans' more intimate meetings between lessons at the time, Hans mentioned that he greatly missed Gregory and the others and that he was deeply unhappy. Hans also admitted that he still struggled with his school subjects, although he knew that he *should* do better, as he had already heard it all and had done the tests and exams once before. In hindsight, therefore, the decision by Hans' parents to make Hans repeat the year had clearly been a mistake and undoubtedly also contributed to Hans' psychological deterioration. In the end, Hans completed school with only a medium *Abitur* result, probably not much better than if he had stayed in his old year group, while Bill, Rufus and Gregory all ended up with very good (Bill and Rufus) and good (Gregory) final results.

Immediately after completing school, Gregory left Heidenhausen to study Geography in Freiburg in the south-west of Baden-Württemberg, about 300 km from home. Because Evelyn was still at school and both Gregory and her agreed *not* to embark on a complicated long-distance relationship, they decided to split up and go their own ways. Gregory had not realised it at the time, but he understood now that part of the attraction of leaving Heidenhausen for Freiburg was that he wanted a clean break from his relationship with Evelyn, and that he had lacked the courage to tell her directly. Gregory remembered that, for him at least, the decision to split up with Evelyn did not seem too difficult at the time. To him, and in hindsight, this had further confirmed that their relationship had never been that intensive and that he probably had not loved her as deeply as he thought when they first met. *Maybe Evelyn had felt the same?*, adult Gregory still wondered after all these years. After all, their relationship had been a match-up orchestrated by no other than Hans.

Gregory still went back from Freiburg to Heidenhausen regularly, mainly to see his mother and his brother Max, and to meet up with Bill and Rufus who were doing two years of *Zivildienst* (social service) in nearby towns in lieu of military service (Gregory, as a British citizen was exempt from German military service). At the time, West Germany had compulsory military service for German nationals, and young men who had finished school had three options: join the military on a fully paid basis for two years (with the chance to also climb in rank during that time and join the professional army thereafter); join the military for only 18 months for 'basic service' with only board and lodging paid (with no promotion possible); or to be a conscientious objector and do a (highly questionable) 'moral and ethics' aptitude test in front of a draft board which enabled those who passed the test to do two years of *Zivildienst* in lieu of military service. The rather arbitrary and highly subjective questions in the aptitude test to which there simply could be no 'correct' answers included questions such as "What would you do if an assailant with a knife assaulted your grandmother in front of your eyes and you were in possession of a knife yourself?".

Not unexpectedly, with little prospect of obtaining a place at a good university based on his rather poor *Abitur* results, Hans had chosen the two-year fully paid military service, and had been assigned to a military base near the small town of Göggingen in north Baden-Württemberg about 100 km from Heidenhausen. When Gregory heard about Hans' decision to join the military for the full two-year option, he suspected immediately that Hans' macho father had probably also greatly influenced Hans' decision.

During one of his visits to Heidenhausen from university, and while in their favourite pub with Bill, Gregory remembered running by chance into Hans. It must have been sometime in late 1981 or early 1982, adult Gregory wondered, but he was not entirely sure. While Gregory was chatting with Bill about how much he enjoyed studying Geography in Freiburg, Hans had suddenly come into the pub. Hans was alone and immediately spotted Gregory and Bill and, after a brief moment of hesitation in which Hans appeared to judge whether it would be wise to join Gregory with Bill at his side, Hans joined them while waving at the barman to bring another round of *Hefeweizen* (the delicious yeast-based *Weissbier* typical for southern Germany).

It had been a while since Gregory had seen Hans, and Hans looked different from the last time Gregory had seen him when they were still both at school. As Hans had been at school one year longer than Gregory and Bill (as he had repeated Year 12), this meant that their last meeting at school was well over a year ago. Hans had short cropped hair typical for the military, revealing an already receding hairline. He wore a neat cream-coloured shirt which looked as if it had been recently ironed (by Hans' assiduous mother, Gregory assumed), and polished black leather shoes. Gregory thought that Hans looked incredibly dull and boring, more like a car salesman or an accountant fresh from the office. But, with the rift of time now between them, Gregory did not want to openly show Hans what he thought of his attire. Gregory and Bill, on the other hand, in tune with the early 1980s Hippie fashion prevalent among university students and social workers at the time, had let their hair grow even longer than at school, wore t-shirts (Gregory's had a left-wing motto emblazoned on the front betraying his budding political activism), baggy flared jeans full of holes, and tattered trainers that had seen better days. In other words, while Hans looked rather prim, Gregory and Bill were rather proud of looking utterly dishevelled and hippie-like. Their different attires, thus, immediately set Gregory and Bill starkly apart from Hans.

Both Hans and Gregory felt uneasy at seeing each other in such an unplanned way. As a result, during the first few minutes of awkwardly standing together they only managed to exchange platitudes about being pleased to see each other. They asked each other polite questions about how military service was, and how Gregory liked university. But Gregory could not hide the fact that, since the issue of military service had surfaced for his friends at the end of school, he had adopted a rather extreme left-wing pacifist view on militarism and military service. Indeed, Gregory, and Bill to a lesser extent, had begun to severely criticise a society that

137

forced young men into serving for the military and to be trained to kill people. Gregory felt particular contempt for those who, like Hans, had volunteered for the two-year fully paid option, thinking that they were the most hypocritical of all, selling their souls for the sake of a full salary and the possibility of a military career. Gregory felt more respect for those who did the basic military service, as some of these may have failed the *Zivildienst* aptitude test, but he held most respect for conscientious objectors like Bill and Rufus who had outright refused to do military service and who, luckily maybe, had passed the aptitude test by answering the stupid questions about avenging grandmothers from assailants the 'right' way. *Had they said that they would not kill the assailant, or was, counter-intuitively, the answer that you would kill the assailant the right one?*, Gregory had always wondered, but nobody could ever tell him what the 'correct' answer was. Since going to university, Gregory had not met many who had done the full two-year military service, and Hans was one of the first of this strange bunch he had encountered for a while. Gregory's and Hans' worlds were, therefore, not only increasingly separated by attire and the way they presented themselves, but also by attitudes towards militarism and military service.

But after two rounds of *Weizenbier* that had made them relax a bit more, Gregory and Hans had increasingly warmed to each other again, while Bill had stayed a little more in the background and was still eyeing Hans with suspicion. Gregory told Hans that Evelyn and he had split up with mutual consent and no hard feelings, and that Gregory had met a new girlfriend at university who also studied

Geography. Hans was immediately very curious about this girl and asked Gregory several, rather intimate, questions that reminded Gregory of Hans' prying questions about him and Evelyn several years ago. But Gregory was pleased to hear that Hans was still going out with Monique, although he thought that Hans' plan to move in with Monique and maybe even get married after his military service was rather 'bourgeois' and not in keeping with the laissez-faire attitudes towards relationships among his new university friends. Indeed, marriage was seen by Gregory and his new friends as rather old-fashioned, outdated and 'uncool', but politeness, and the distance that had grown between Gregory and Hans over the past years, again made Gregory refrain from expressing his thoughts too directly to Hans' face. Although Gregory was pleased to hear that Hans and Monique were still together, he was also worried that the macho environment of the military could be a very bad influence for Hans, and that this could negatively influence his behaviour towards Monique, but again he kept his thoughts to himself. He was simply not close enough to Hans any more to embark on a deep, and possibly problematic, discussion about such issues.

Certainly, the way Hans spoke, the way he now dressed, and his whole demeanour during their impromptu meeting in the pub, suggested to Gregory that Hans had already been greatly influenced by the idiotic, sad, macho and bigoted military way of life and thinking. Little did Gregory realise at the time how right he was in his assumption that military service and the macho environment surrounding it would be a further nail in the coffin for Hans' psychological wellbeing.

15

20th June 2019. Hans opened his eyes. Where was he? He looked around, but could only see a wall of white in front of him. The pungent smell of stale food, urine and faeces around him made him retch, but his stomach was so empty that nothing came out. He was so thirsty! How long had he been here? He could not remember. Certainly days, maybe even weeks? He had lost all sense of time.

Hans tried to prop himself up on his elbows, but he was so weak from lack of food that he could not manage to raise his heavy bulk from the urine-sodden bedsheet. He started crying in desperation. *I will die here!*, he realised, looking around him for a way out. Could he crawl along the sofa, through the narrow gap on the side? But then he remembered why he was here in the first place. The intruders! They must still be in his flat. He lay perfectly still for a few seconds, only his heavy lumbered breathing audible. There! There was a noise! He could definitely hear a key turning in a lock. Somebody was coming into his flat! Had the intruders gone out briefly and were coming back? Maybe they had grabbed a few things from his flat to sell and were now coming back for more? To fondle his clothes and underwear, to sit in his kitchen and eat all his food, maybe even to sleep in his bed?

Hans could clearly hear footsteps, the door to his bedroom opening with a creaking sound, steps going down the hallway towards his kitchen, and then approaching the living room where he was hiding behind the sofa.

"Herr Schlesier? Are you here?", a voice belonging to an elderly woman could be heard shouting.

Hans froze. There was definitely somebody very close! He tried to hold back his breath.

"Herr Schlesier …?"

The footsteps came closer, they were now very near to the sofa.

A sudden gasp was audible. "My oh my … Herr Schlesier! What are you doing behind the sofa? Oh, my oh my!"

Stephanie Müller, the care worker who visited Hans once a month, was leaning over the back of the sofa, holding her nose to ward off the indescribable stench.

"Good Lord, Herr Schlesier! Are you alright? How long have you been lying here? And all this … all this filth? Oh, my Lord!", Frau Müller said, holding her hand in front of her mouth, not fully understanding what she was seeing.

Hans slowly turned his head and looked straight into Stephanie Müller's anguished face. *Is she real, or is she a figment of my imagination?*, he wondered. Frau Müller seemed real, but then so had all the noises coming from the 'intruders'.

Stephanie Müller had made her way around the sofa and only now saw the extent of dirt, faeces (some squashed, some smeared into the bedsheet), urine puddles and discarded food wrappers. Hans was lying among this mess on his urine-sodden bedsheet, his clothes covered in piss and shit. He

141

looked grimy, dirty and very tired, and did not seem able to move.

"Oh my God, Herr Schlesier! What have you done this time?", Frau Müller gasped, while gently grabbing Hans' arms and pulling him out slowly from behind the sofa. Hans was very heavy and it took Stephanie Müller all her strength to drag Hans a few metres away from the mess and stench.

What about the intruders?, Hans wondered while being gently dragged into the middle of the living room. But he was too tired, too worn out to care anymore. May the intruders get to him, it did no longer matter! But at the same time, he was also immensely relieved to see Frau Müller. Although his mind was still hazy, he nonetheless realised that Stephanie Müller was real, that she had come to rescue him, like she had done before not so long ago.

"Oh my, Herr Schlesier!", Stephanie sighed again, trying to supress tears. "You must have had another one of your episodes? You probably forgot to take your pills?"

Pills? What pills?, Hans wondered. Somewhere in the distant recesses of his fogged-up brain he remembered that he had been told by his doctors and Frau Müller to take his medication regularly. The pills that prevented him from seeing things, from hearing things. Yes, he must have forgotten to take them.

"Frau Müller …", Hans whispered almost inaudibly.

"Yes, it's me, Herr Schlesier. Frau Müller ... I have come to check on how you are doing, like every month. But I see that things have not been good for you … My oh my! Thanks God that I was due to come today. God knows what would have happened if I had come a few days later."

Hans tried again to prop himself up, but Frau Müller, seeing how weak he was, told him to stay where he was lying. She went to his bedroom and came back with a pillow and his duvet. She gently placed his head on the pillow and covered his reeking body with the duvet.

"Don't move, Herr Schlesier. Don't move ...", she said, her voice still shaking. "I will call the psychiatric clinic immediately and we'll get you out of here. You just stay here".

Hans still did not have the strength to move. He heard Frau Müller take out her mobile phone and talk to the clinic. *It must be Bad Schlossenried where I have been before*, his numbed mind realised. Maybe everything would be alright again? They would look after him like they had before. They would take him away from this wretched place, they would take him away from the intruders.

Part 3

Meltdown

16

15th March 1982. The souped-up battered VW Golf stopped with screeching tyres and squeezed into a tight parking space between a shiny new Mercedes and a rusty old BMW. The five young men, who had been squashed together in the small car, extricated themselves from it through the two doors and stood up to stretch their limbs after the hour-long drive. Hans Schlesier was the last one to emerge. He looked around him, trying to get his bearings. They were in front of a dimly lit entrance of a large building in one of the seedier parts of central Stuttgart, the capital of Baden-Württemberg.

"C'mon, Schlesier!", bellowed Frank the driver. "Get your ass up here so that we can finally sample some pussy!", he continued, eliciting raucous laughter from his fellow car passengers Sascha, Gernot and Bernd, who were all looking at Hans expectantly. "Your dithering has already cost us enough time!", Frank continued to admonish Hans.

Hans looked self-consciously at the four young men standing in front of him. They were all roommates of his at the *Fritz Heidenreich Military Base* at Göggingen, about an hour's drive from Stuttgart. All five of them had enlisted for the full two-years of military service and were sharing a room in one of the barracks. Frank and the others had already tried several times over the past few months to cajole Hans to join them on their regular trips to the brothel, but Hans had, so far, always resisted. He looked at the building in front of them, with its faded charm of architecture typical for the *Wilheminischer Ring*, built when German cities were expanding rapidly during the frenetic industrialisation phase of the late 19th century. Hans saw the peeling plaster, the cracked porticos and the faded drawn curtains that suggested a place that had seen better days. A dilapidated and faded sign next to the door read *Eros Centre – Für Jugendliche unter 18 ist der Zutritt verboten* (adults only).

Hans felt very uneasy about all this. He knew that it was peer pressure that had compelled him to come along on this trip, but he did not really want to be there. He had now been at the *Fritz Heidenreich Military Base* for about seven months, and had found it very difficult to adjust to this new environment after leaving school and home. At the time he joined the base, he was still stunned by how poorly he had performed in his school exams. He would never forget the day when, just after receiving his final results, he had gone back home, tail between his legs, and admitted to his father that his final Abitur results were not as good as he had initially thought. He knew that he had deluded himself during Year 13 that he could rescue his final grade by doing well in the final exams (which counted for about one third of the overall grade, the rest was continuous assessment through tests and essays during Years 12 and 13 in which he had done poorly). But despite working hard with his tutor and pouring over books and notes at his desk at home, he had done even worse than he feared. While his final *Abitur* grade in French was acceptable (9 points out of 15, equivalent to a C+), his performance in German was only 7 points (C-), and was even worse in Physics with 5 points (D) (which he had to take as his compulsory 'natural science choice'). In Biology, which he thought would interest him and which he had voluntarily selected despite of warnings by his parents, he obtained a very disappointing 3 points only (Fail) based on the fact that he had completely misinterpreted one question and had run out of time to answer the last two out of five questions. His father greeted Hans' poor results with an outburst of shouting and stomping about, culminating with Bernhard hitting Hans in the face. At the time, Hans was too stunned to respond or react to his father hitting him again, but he somehow understood his father's reaction at his failure to perform better. In the end, repeating Year 12 and losing contact with all his former friends had not helped at all, and Hans increasingly begrudged his parents for having forced him to repeat the year.

It was partly to placate his father that Hans had agreed to join the military for the full two years, 'to make a proper man out of you' as Bernhard had called it. But Hans also had to admit that with his C/C/D/Fail *Abitur* results, his chances for a place at a good university were nil, as were his chances of obtaining a place as an apprentice in a good business. Although he was pretty sure that he did not want to join his father's and uncles' plumbing business, Hans did not know at all what he wanted to do, and he also felt that the two-year military service option would give him a bit more time to think about his future. He envied Gregory for knowing what he wanted to study, for having secured a place at a good university, and for having several years of studying before being forced to think about a job or a career. But when he decided to join the military, Hans also had to admit that the

147

good salary and promotion prospects had appealed to him. For the first time in his life, he would earn his own money and would be able to live independently and away from his over-domineering father.

But Hans quickly realised that military service was not what he thought it would be like. Images in his mind of tough outdoor training, where his sportiness and fitness would be an asset, quickly made way to the reality of drab and repetitive courtyard exercises, dull rote-learning in class about menial issues such as military rank, equipment and management, and very little freedom to go out and spend all that money he was earning. But most difficult was living in one cramped room with bunk beds with four other blokes. Although Hans had always thought of himself as being very social and adaptable, he quickly realised that his self-assuredness was of no great help in an environment that had attracted young men who were even more arrogant, self-assured, macho and domineering than Hans himself had been at school. Indeed, he quickly came to realise that he was one of many, not so 'special' at all, and that he had been very lucky at home in Heidenhausen with a large room of his own, no other siblings to share everything with, and with naïve, parochial small-town schoolmates who had looked up to him for most of the time.

Even his perceived prowess with regard to girls seemed to vanish in the haze when compared to the eagerness with which his fellow roommates used their spare time to go to the brothel in Stuttgart. Although Hans was certain that neither Frank, Sascha, Gernot or Bernd had made love to an adult woman like he had when just aged 14, they nonetheless seemed even more self-assured with girls – or at least pretending to be in their endless boasts – than Hans himself. Yes, there were subtle differences between the five of them, with Frank clearly the dominant one who was able to claim the only single bed in their room while Hans and the others had to sleep in the cramped and creaking bunk beds. Frank was also the only one with a car, which gave him special status as they often relied on him if they wanted to go further afield than just the small town of Göggingen where their military base was located. But what annoyed Hans most was that the four others appeared to see him as rather conventional and 'boring' after he told them, proudly at first, that he had been going out with Monique for over three years now and that they intended to marry eventually. Although the four others all claimed to have girlfriends 'back home', none of them seemed to worry about cheating on their girlfriends by going regularly to the brothel in Stuttgart. Initially at least, this seemed like anathema to Hans, and his loyalty to Monique was the key reason he resisted joining the four others on their sex trips.

However, his continuous refusal to join the others on their trips to Stuttgart made Hans increasingly feel like an outcast in his dormitory. The other four started teasing him not only when they were in their room, but also when they were out exercising and in class. They began to call him *prüde Jungfrau* (prude virgin) whenever they saw him, and this nickname seemed to proliferate among the rest of the military base, where fellow military trainees would chuckle with a knowing smile when they passed him. This particularly jarred with Hans who had come to the military base with a reputation from his school as a flamboyant hunk and successful womaniser adored and envied by all his schoolmates. Sure, Hans knew that from about Year 12 onwards his reputation as a great lover and magnet for girls had been reduced as the other schoolkids had grown up and were themselves going out with girls and gathering experience. But even by the end of school, Hans could still feel an aura of envy and jealousy among many of the other (admittedly younger) boys in his new year group. This all seemed to be dashed in an instant at the *Fritz Heidenreich Military Base* where Frank, Sascha, Gernot and Bernd treated him increasingly like an immature kid, like a conservative country bumpkin keen to get married, and like somebody not equal to themselves who were regularly 'sampling' hookers in the Stuttgart brothel. The pressure mounting on Hans to either concede defeat and be forever branded *prüde Jungfrau*, or to agree to join his roommates on one of their sexual outings, therefore, had reached boiling point. As a result, and although reluctant, Hans had finally agreed to join the four others on their next trip to Stuttgart.

Standing in front of the brothel, Hans, therefore, was well aware that the other four had been there several times before, and that they had already 'sampled' several of the girls on offer. During their drive to Stuttgart, Frank and the others had explained to Hans the range of girls available, and which ones they would recommend. Hans, thus, knew that most of the prostitutes were West German girls, with a few from other countries such as France, Italy and Spain. While Frank was raving – rather primitively, Hans thought – about a French girl he had fucked several times in various positions,

Sascha insisted that a girl from Yugoslavia was the most attractive and 'did everything you asked her to do'. It was with mixed feeling about which girl he would choose that Hans followed the others towards the *Eros Centre* entrance.

Frank rang the buzzer and a rough older female voice was audible through the crackling intercom. The woman seemed to recognise Frank and buzzed the door open. The five young men walked through the door and were greeted by a scantily-clad girl in a maid's costume who led them to a lounge with a well-stocked bar and blood-red armchairs and sofas in which several almost naked girls were sitting while smoking and chatting. As soon as the five young men entered the room, the girls' demeanour changed and they presented themselves in ever more lascivious and sexually explicit postures to entice Frank and the others to pick the most alluring one over the other girls. A young girl got up, walked towards Frank and put her arms around him. *She must be the French girl he mentioned*, thought Hans. Soon after, Sascha was united with his Yugoslavian girl, and Gernot and Bernd were also rapidly paired up with girls they obviously already knew. While the others went upstairs led by their girls, Hans was left standing there, feeling uneasy and unsure about what to do.

An old woman, probably the one who had talked to them on the intercom, and who was possibly the owner or the manager of the place, came from behind the bar to greet Hans. "Welcome stranger!", she said, sensing his insecurity and placing a hand gently on Hans' arm. "It is good to see a new face", she said with a smile that accentuated the heavy wrinkles around her mouth and eyes that even her thickly applied make-up could not hide. Her breath had a heavy, pungent and unpleasant smell of nicotine and alcohol. "My name is Lolita and I look after this place."

God, I hope she will not take me with her upstairs!, Hans feared, looking at Lolita. *She may have looked good a long time ago, but she can't have many men attracted to her now!*

"Oh, don't worry", Lolita replied as if reading Hans' mind. "I am too old for these things now. I am just the manager of this place. Come with me and we will find you a nice girl. Is this your first time, lad?"

Hans was not sure whether Lolita meant the first time with a hooker or the first time with a girl ever. Did he really look that virginal? She took Hans gently by the arm and ambled with him between the armchairs and sofas where the girls were lounging around, lasciviously fondling their breasts, throwing him kisses with their heavily lip-sticked mouths, opening their legs and placing a hand on their scantily-clad crotches with fake rubbing motions and pretend-feelings of extasy on their faces, and looking expectantly up at him. Hans began feeling aroused with all these half-naked girls lounging on the furniture in front of him, some smacking their lips at him even more fervently as he passed them, and with some rubbing their crotches with ever more intensive luscious sighs. But Hans was not interested in these women who behaved like cheap and ordinary hookers. Instead, one girl, sitting a bit apart, caught Hans' eye. She seemed a bit demurer and shyer than the others and did not appear to want to catch his attention. Lolita noticed Hans looking at the girl with interest.

"Oh, this one is pretty new", Lolita said. "I am not sure whether that's what you want if this if your first time. Why not try our beautiful Heidrun there? She would give you your money's worth!", she said while trying to gently push Hans towards a rather fat girl with platinum-blond dyed hair who was fondling two huge breasts that looked like gigantic balloons filled with water and ready to burst.

But Hans resisted Lolita's gentle push and continued to walk towards the 'new' girl. Lolita realised that Hans had made his choice. "Well, ok then", she said with a slight hint of disappointment that Hans had rejected her 'offer' of Heidrun. "This is Nadia. She has only recently joined us from Czechoslovakia. It's hard to get girls from the 'East', with the Iron Curtain and all that", Lolita sighed. "But they are good workers and keen, so I am sure Nadia will give you a good time."

But Hans detected a reluctance in Lolita's voice. Maybe there was something about Nadia that was not right? But it was precisely the fact that Nadia may not have been 'tarnished' as much as the other sex workers in this establishment that attracted Hans to her, maybe also that Nadia did not see the need to explicitly flaunt and fondle her wares in front of Hans. Lolita nodded to Nadia, and Nadia took Hans' hand and led him upstairs, where individual bedrooms were located. Hans could hear muffled groans, shrieks of pleasure and heavy panting while Nadia and him walked past the closed doors, and he imagined Frank, Sascha, Gernot and Bernd entangled with their girls in different sexual positions.

Nadia led Hans to one of the rooms. It was rather spartan, with just a bed, drawn faded curtains, and a naked lightbulb hanging from the ceiling. But at least the bed looked freshly made with what looked like clean sheets. Hans realised immediately that Nadia had not done this often before. She seemed to be almost as nervous as he was, but this fact aroused Hans. While he had initially feared that he would not be in control enough with one of the experienced hookers, with Nadia he felt that he could be on top of the situation, that making love to her could feel like making love to a girl he had just met at a bar or disco like in the good old days back in Heidenhausen before he had met Monique.

Nadia took off the flimsy dress she was wearing and stood naked in front of Hans. Hans immediately felt his penis stiffen. He was very horny as, after all, it had been a while since he had last been with Monique, and jerking off was not easy in the narrow confines of their room at the military base. Without waiting for Nadia to help him, he took off his shirt, trousers and underpants, his erection thrusting upwards like a Mercedes hood ornament. He looked at Nadia and found her very attractive, with long brown hair framing a very pretty face, dark brown eyes, small slender hips, long thin legs and small breasts that stood in sharp contrast to Heidrun's monstrosities downstairs. Her pubic hair had been shaved off, except for a thin sliver of hair around her vaginal lips, which turned Hans on even more. Apart from porn magazines, he had never seen in real a shaven pubis before. Hans had to admit that Nadia was the most beautiful girl he had ever seen, more beautiful than Martina and cute Ursula when they were 14, and more beautiful than Monique who

154

was, Hans conceded, rather heavy around the hips and who, like many French girls, never shaved the thick tufts of pubic hair around her vagina. Nadia was even more beautiful than Elke Schmidt, whose body Hans still remembered fondly.

Like Elke at the time, Nadia lay back on the bed and invited Hans to join her. Hans knelt between Nadia's legs, staring at her breasts and vagina. Nadia gently took Hans' penis in her hand and started caressing him gently. She then took his penis in her mouth, moving up and down with her wet lips and touching the most sensitive parts of his glans with her tongue. Although she did not seem or act experienced, Hans had to admit that Nadia was sucking him more expertly than any of the many other girls he had known. Nadia seemed to sense immediately when he was about to come and then slightly slowed down the motion of both her lips and tongue. For what seemed like an eternity Nadia held Hans' penis in her mouth in a state of exquisite pre-orgasm. When he felt that he could hold on no longer, Nadia stopped briefly, took his penis out of her mouth, spread her legs wide and motioned him to move on top of her in the missionary position, and then inserted his penis slowly into her vagina. Hans felt immensely aroused looking at Nadia's slim legs, her shaven pubis, and how his penis was gliding slowly in and out of her wet vagina. Again, she seemed to sense perfectly when he was about to come and would then stop her hip movements for a while, just leaving him inside her without moving.

After a while of exquisite near-orgasmic thrusting in the missionary position, Nadia then turned around and kneeled in front of him, inviting him to come inside her from behind.

Looking at her small and tight bottom and the shaft of his penis going in and out of Nadia's vagina from behind, Hans thought that he had never been so aroused in his life. It felt as if he was in an eternal pre-orgasmic state. When he was about to come, Nadia changed position again, this time straddling Hans from atop. At first, she did not move at all, just feeling him inside her and looking intensely into his eyes. Then she started moving her hips, at first slowly, then gradually increasing the cadence. She then moved her upper body up and down, so that Hans' penis almost left her vagina on the upward thrust, while being plunged deep inside her during her downward push. This motion seemed to last forever, again keeping Hans in that perfect all-consuming pre-orgasmic state. Nadia then increased the cadence and lurched her upper body and shoulders backwards, her hands holding Hans' knees, threw her head back, and emitted a loud and intensive moan. Hans did not know whether Nadia had really come or whether she had faked an orgasm, as the girls were probably instructed to do in this establishment, but he did not care. Nadia's thrusting had reached a frenetic stage and Hans could no longer hold back. While watching his glistening penis glide in and out of Nadia's vagina at ever more frantic pace he came inside Nadia with what felt like a giant explosion, with an orgasm that seemed to last forever. Her hip movements took him in as far as possible, sucking the last bit of sperm out of him. Her movement gradually eased and for a while she sat astride of him, eyes closed and not moving at all, both of them panting heavily from the exertion.

After a while Nadia allowed Hans' now flaccid penis to slip out of her, sperm oozing out of her vagina onto Hans' belly. She leaned forward and kissed Hans for the first time on the mouth. *It almost seems as if she enjoyed this as much as I did!*, Hans hoped, but he was not sure. He looked into Nadia's eyes, but he could not detect whether this had been a genuine act of pleasure and delight or simply another 'job' for her. Whatever, she had made him feel great, and Hans was sure that he would want to see Nadia again.

They quickly got dressed and went downstairs where his four roommates were already waiting. They looked at him with curious and knowing smiles, and Hans' return smile quickly showed them that bringing him along had been a 'success'. Hans certainly felt vindicated for having decided to come with them, and maybe his position among their group of five was now finally settled. No more *prüde Jungfrau*, he hoped.

They each paid 400 *Marks* to Lolita in cash, and Hans began to understand why the others never seemed to have any money left at the end of the month, in spite of their respectable salaries. He glanced back at the room, trying to catch Nadia's eyes. But she was again sitting apart from the other girls, with a slightly dreamy and demure look on her face that did not betray anything about what they had just 'done' together. *Maybe I am just another customer for her after all!*, Hans thought sadly as they made their way back to Frank's old battered VW.

17

6th April 1983. Hans looked out of the train window at the French landscape rushing by. He did not know exactly where he was, just somewhere in north-western France between Rennes and Paris. But he could not focus on the fields, copses, hedges and farm buildings of the *bocage* landscape visible in the dusky twilight. He knew that something had happened to him. It felt as if something had broken inside him, not physically broken, but something mental, something in his brain, something affecting the way he thought. His world had suddenly collapsed around him, as if he had lost control over his life. Although he had felt a little depressed before, even before going to the military, with violent mood swings ranging from total elation to complete sadness, this new emotional abyss was something new both in its intensity and magnitude. Something had snapped inside him, something had irrevocably changed, never to be healed again. In his current state, he was not even sure whether he would make it back in one piece to his military barracks in Göggingen. He did not even know whether he would survive the trip to his next stop at the *Gare Saint Lazare* in the West of Paris and, even worse, whether he would manage to make it by tube to the *Gare de l'Est*, where he needed to catch his connecting train to Germany. Tears welled up in his eyes which he tried to hide from the only fellow passenger in his six-seat compartment, and old lady sitting diagonally opposite him clutching an old battered handbag. He turned his face away from her and pretended that he was looking out of the window. Hans felt immensely tired like never before in his life. He could barely hold his head up. He felt utterly empty, he had nothing to look forward to. He was desperate.

I am so stupid, stupid, stupid!, he thought, clenching his fist until it hurt. *How could I be so dumb? What came into me?*, he cursed, thinking about the last few days he had spent in Rennes with Monique. He had so looked forward to seeing her over the Easter break when he had been on the train from Göggingen to Rennes, via Stuttgart and Paris, only a few days ago. After all, it had been nearly four months since he had last seen Monique at Christmas. Hans clenched his fists even harder at the memory of their ardent love making on Christmas Eve, when Monique was so keen and so much in love with him. *And now I have thrown it all away!*, he sighed, unable to supress a loud sob which made the old lady opposite him turn her head and wonder what was going on. Hans sent her an apologetic smile back as if to indicate that all was fine, but he knew that nothing was fine. He had completely messed up, he had utterly misjudged Monique's reaction to what he had admitted to her.

Although it felt like an eternity, it was only a few hours ago, the morning of this same day, when Monique and him had breakfast together in her bedroom. They had made love when they woke up – gently on Monique's insistence – and Monique seemed to be in an excellent mood. Indeed, she had been in high spirits throughout his visit, and Hans had the impression that there was something up in the air with Monique, something unspoken but positive between them, something that made Monique even happier and keener on him than usual. But in his stupidity he had completely misread the signs and had, instead, utterly messed up.

Looking back at this fateful morning, Hans could not understand his own reaction. Of course, he and Monique had had their run-ins and little fights over the years, but they loved each other and they had always managed to sort out whatever problems they had. Sure, living apart had never been easy, and the fact that Hans could only take a few weeks holiday per year from his military service to visit Monique had not made life easier for them over the past 20 months or so. And yet, they had regularly phoned, and Hans had frequently sent Monique ardent love letters in French which, she said, she had always enjoyed reading. Maybe it was precisely this feeling of utter happiness, the nice breakfast after their gentle love making, and particularly Monique's positive mood, that had compelled Hans to do the most stupid thing in his life.

Sitting in the railway carriage zooming back through the French countryside towards Paris, Hans did not know what had gotten into him that morning. With immense sadness he recalled the fateful discussion he had with Monique while they were munching away at their breakfast in Monique's bed. Holding a croissant in one hand, Hans had cuddled up to Monique and was gently nibbling at her right ear. He felt so in love with her at that moment that he thought that there should be absolutely no secrets between them at all.

"You know that I love you very much", Hans had said to Monique in French, "that you are everything to me".

Monique had looked back at him, wondering why Hans was saying this at this moment in time. She had heard so often from him how much he loved her, but this time it felt a bit out of place.

"I think there should be no secrets between us, don't you think?", Hans probed further.

Monique just looked back at him, but did not answer. She wondered where this was going.

"I love you so much that I feel I need to tell you what I have been up to recently", Hans continued, gaining further encouragement from Monique's inquisitive look. "I just wanted to tell you that I have seen a hooker. I have seen her a few times, but don't worry. It was only sex. It meant nothing. I never stopped loving you. But I thought it was only fair I should tell you."

As Hans was speaking, Monique's jaw had begun to drop. Just as Hans was finishing his sentence, he realised that this was a big mistake. A totally stupid mistake! Monique's demeanour had changed in a flash from curiosity to outright horror. She spilt her coffee over the bedsheet.

"You did … what!?", she screamed.

Hans had completely underestimated Monique's reaction. He saw how angry and hurt she was, and it shocked him.

"Don't worry, my love. It was nothing …", he tried to explain again, but he knew it was too late.

Monique stood up, spilling the entire breakfast tray onto the bed, but she did not care. She stood in front of him, hands on hips, purple in her face and struggling to speak.

"Nothing? It was nothing? I guess you fucked her? Of course you fucked her, why else would go to see a hooker?"

"Well, yes … I …", was all Hans could stammer. He tried to touch Monique who had begun crying uncontrollably, but she abruptly whisked away his hand.

"Don't touch me, you bastard! How could you! One instant you tell me you love me, the next you tell me that you fucked a whore! What kind of a sick person are you?", Monique shouted, walking up and down her bedroom in anger, breathing hard and sending angry looks back at Hans.

"Well, I'll also tell you something, but this is not the way I wanted to do it …!", she continued, sobbing even more loudly. "You stupid prick! You have destroyed everything. I was about to tell you that … that …", she cried even more desperately, "that I am pregnant!"

This was the moment when it really hit Hans how idiotic his admission to Monique had been. What in hell had made him tell her about Nadia the hooker? What had gotten into him? Monique was pregnant, she was carrying his child! That was the reason why she had been so happy at seeing him. Hans instantly realised that this must have been the result of their ardent love making at Christmas, maybe Monique had realised then that she was in her fertile phase, maybe she had wanted to become pregnant then? It suddenly dawned on Hans that Monique was already nearly four months pregnant. But why had she not told him before? Panicked thoughts were racing through Hans' head. Was Monique not certain about their relationship, and was that why she had not told him earlier? Had she even thought about abortion? But it was too late for this now! Or had she

162

just waited for what she thought would be the most opportune and intimate moment to tell him? Had she told him earlier, he would have never told her about Nadia. He would have asked her to marry him there and then. But, sitting on Monique's bed, Hans had also immediately realised that he was having these thoughts to placate his guilt, the immense guilt he now felt for having admitted to his adultery at this most inopportune of moments.

"Yes, I'm pregnant, you stupid idiot! We are having a baby ...", Monique cried, while unable to stand up any longer in her misery. She stooped down and sat down on the floor, hiding her sobbing face behind her hands. "But this changes everything!", she shouted at him. "I never want to see you again! I will get rid of this baby and I'll never see you again!".

Hans was unable to move. He realised again that he had completely mishandled the situation. For the first time he did not know what to do faced by a woman crying in front of him. Monique was so angry, so hurt, so desperate, that he did not dare go to her, touch her, console her.

"Go! Just go!", Monique shouted, while getting up and walking unsteadily towards the door without looking back at him.

Hans sat on the bed for a long time, utterly miserable. *Idiot! Idiot!*, he kept thinking, shaking his head at his stupidity. *What have I done? Why? Why? Why?*

He was listening out for footsteps, for Monique to come back, to hug him in understanding and reconciliation. Or maybe for her parents to come in and talk. Even if it would have been angry, scalding talk from an irate mother or a desperate father, Hans would have welcomed it at this moment. Anyone who he could admit his terrible mistake to, anyone who may help him to assuage Monique's anger, to make her come back to him, to hug him and to forgive him. But there was nothing. No sound, no footsteps. It was as if he suddenly was all alone in this world, basking in the cesspool of his own thoughts. After what seemed like an eternity he got up, but he felt like a robot, as if somebody else had taken over his body. He got dressed mechanically, stuffed his passport, wallet and clothes into his backpack with an absent look on his face, and opened the door to the hallway. His legs felt wobbly, he could barely walk straight. The house was eerily quiet. Where was Monique? Hans could not remember whether her parents were in the house that morning or not. Had Monique left the house in desperation? Had she gone to her friend Sybille who lived not far away? What should he do? Should he wait for her, hoping things would calm down? Could their relationship ever be the same after this? His body felt heavy and tired. It was at this moment that Hans felt that something had changed, that something had broken inside him, that something had cracked inside his head.

He walked through the house trancelike. Nobody seemed to be there. He opened the front door and walked out, not even realising that it was raining hard. In a daze he walked towards the railway station, drenched but not caring, and he somehow managed to re-book his ticket, as he had originally been due to stay with Monique for another three days until the end of the Easter break. Then he sat for hours on a bench on one of the station platforms, waiting for the train and staring into the void. Should he go back? At moments his mind was empty, at others it was racing with memories of his fateful discussion with Monique. But he could not formulate a clear thought, everything was confused. He barely noticed his surroundings, did not look at people coming and going, trains arriving and departing. He managed to get onto the right train destined for Paris, and somehow one part of his brain was still working as if on remote control.

Hans was still looking out of the train window. It was getting dark now and only indistinct shapes could be made out on the horizon silhouetted against the last vestiges of daylight: a row of lampposts, a large barn, distant houses, low hills, and scraggly trees. He had stopped crying, but his mind was empty. It seemed as if a lifetime had passed since his dreadful and fateful admission to Monique that same morning. He thought now that he had done the right thing to leave as Monique had asked him to do, not to insist, not to pester her further. *But what will happen to our child now?*, Hans wondered. *Will Monique now get rid of it as she said in her anger? Will she ever want to see me again? Will she calm down and maybe contact me in the next few days? It was only a hooker, after all!,* Hans tried to console himself, remembering the five or six times he had seen Nadia overall. Yes, the sex had been great, but Nadia had always remained aloof and professional, just like the first time, so no feelings were involved. Although he found Nadia very beautiful, he had never loved her. After all, he had only come along to see her because of Frank and the others. *Yes! It was all their fault after all. So, what does Monique get so worked up about a hooker? It really meant nothing, why could Monique not see that?*

Anger began to well up inside Hans, anger against Monique and the fact that she had completely misunderstood what he had tried to do this morning. Why could Monique not understand that him telling her about his visit to the hooker was his way to show Monique that he had no secrets to hide from her, to show her how much he loved her by being so damn honest? Why had Monique so completely misinterpreted what he wanted to tell her? But he knew that this reasoning was wrong, that of course it mattered, it mattered immensely to a woman who was pregnant with his child, a woman he had planned to marry, and who had planned to marry him, before all this. *Oh dear, oh dear!*, he thought while tears welled up again in his eyes. *There is no solution to this! I've done it, I've messed it up totally. There is no way back!* Hans closed his eyes, too tired and exhausted to think further …

18

1st August 2019. At the time of the incident between Hans and Monique, Gregory was living his own life, studying in Freiburg, enjoying moving into a flat and living for the first time with his girlfriend, and meeting new friends. Only occasionally did Gregory come to Heidenhausen for weekends to visit his mum. That is where he heard bits and pieces from friends and acquaintances about what had happened to Hans. Gregory heard, for example, that Hans had had what his friends called a 'nervous breakdown', or what some referred to as a 'psychotic break', but nobody seemed to know the reasons why. Neither Gregory nor any of his friends were psychologists, so the story that emerged through the Heidenhausen grapevine was one that had been endlessly recounted, twisted around, and forever distorted. Some people said that Hans was still completing his military service and was still going out with Monique, but others mentioned in hushed voices and behind cupped hands that Hans had been referred to the closed psychiatric unit at the clinic in nearby Bad Schlossenried.

Of course, Gregory was worried about his old schoolfriend, and he remembered thinking whether he should go and visit Hans if he was, indeed, a psychiatric patient at Bad Schlossenried. But Gregory, aged only 22 at the time, simply did not have the maturity or the time to deal with something complicated like this. His visits in Heidenhausen were always busy, with demands from his mother for Gregory to do things with her, and with meeting up with his various friends who wanted him to go out with them, drink beer and have a good time. Having to deal with somebody who may have lost his mind simply did not fit in with Gregory's mindset at the time. This was, admittedly, also influenced by negative comments tinged with envy, anger and jealousy from those who knew Hans, such as 'He had it coming anyway', 'I thought he was always a bit nuts',

'Look at what all this womanising has done to him!', or even 'Serves him right!'.

The result was that a myth began to emerge in Heidenhausen around what had happened to Hans Schlesier. There were a lot of rumours, but nobody seemed to have the eagerness or willingness to check whether any of the facts were true, nobody seemed inclined to actually visit Hans, or, indeed, to check the facts with Hans in person. Gregory remembered also thinking at the time that maybe Hans had brought on all this by himself, through his arrogant behaviour and feelings of superiority, through his macho decision to join the military, and through his poor decision to repeat Year 12. Sometimes it almost felt that Gregory agreed with his friends who thought that Hans' nervous breakdown had been inevitable, even deserved. Indeed, Hans' breakdown had occurred at one of these key moments in the tree of life, at the point where the childhood and early teenage pathway of the main trunk branches off into one of the key branches that defines the future life pathway. Evidently, most of Hans' acquaintances thought, Hans must have taken the wrong decisions at this crucial point in his life, propelling him on a branch of madness from which there was, possibly, no return.

Gregory only heard directly about what happened from Hans a long time later, during his first visit to see Hans in 1993. But until then the ever-changing rumours, swirling around conspiratory huddles over endless pints of beer in various Heidenhausen pubs, coalesced around three stories: the belief that Hans had not been able to complete his military service as he had to go into psychiatric care at Bad

168

Schlossenried; that, for unknown reasons but possibly linked to his breakdown, he had broken up with Monique; and that he had been diagnosed with either paranoid schizophrenia, or bipolar (manic-depressive) disorder, or both together. Gregory often shook his head in disbelief at the time when his friends raised the 'issue of Hans' again and came out with ever more ludicrous rumours and diagnoses that were unlikely, especially as nobody had seen, or talked to, Hans in person.

And yet, these rumours had forced Gregory at the time to think back about his relationship with Hans when they were younger. Had there already been hints in Hans when he was young about manic-depressive behaviour, even about schizophrenic traits? Gregory did not know enough about schizophrenia and its symptoms, but thought that some of Hans' behaviour when they were out chasing girls, Hans' strange behaviour at the time with Martina and Ursula, his hunger for attention, and, in particular, his endless need for confirmation that he was the flamboyant school hunk and womaniser, may have already been signs of manic behaviour. But had Hans also been depressed at times? Gregory could not really tell. There were times at school when Hans had seemed more withdrawn, where he just wanted to be left alone, but Gregory had always thought that these episodes were linked to Hans' poor performance at school or during times when he had particularly bad run-ins with his dad. Gregory could not recollect that he had ever seen Hans in a truly depressed state, and he had to admit that this would have been difficult to spot anyway as a teenager constantly concerned with his own problems and issues. As a result, even Gregory, as Hans' best friend for years and as somebody who knew Hans well, could not tell whether there had been any prior warning signs about whatever psychological illness was now affecting Hans.

These discussions about 'the issue of Hans' were severely skewed by the fact that, by the mid-1980s, nobody seemed to know whether Hans was still in psychiatric care, whether he had moved back in with his parents, or whether *Heidenhausen Social Services* had allocated him a flat. One rumour stipulated that Hans had been declared unfit to work, and Gregory wondered what, if this rumour was true, Hans would then be doing all day. It was hard to imagine Hans sitting in a council-appointed flat, fiddling his thumbs. What was more disturbing was that there was talk about people having seen Hans roaming through the streets of Heidenhausen, looking dishevelled, fat and ugly, mumbling to himself, and having lost all the womanising allure that had made him so famous at school.

Sitting at his living room table, scratching his stubbly chin, adult Gregory tried to remember why he did not make an effort in the mid-1980s to check out for himself what had happened to Hans? Was it peer pressure from his friends, from Bill, Rufus and others, who kept telling him that 'Hans has lost it', 'Forget it, Hans is beyond rescuing', 'Who cares about Hans anyway?', that kept him from making an effort to visit Hans and finding out what had really happened? Was it the old jealousies, the old and complex power relationships within his circle of friends, that showed their ugly faces again, the fact that friends like Bill and Rufus did not want Gregory to be close to Hans again? Was it his own weak personality, the fact that he could not go beyond these peer pressures, assert himself more, that made him stay away from Hans? Or, more disturbingly, was it simply that he did not want to see his old friend because he was not interested? Or maybe, more likely, because he did not want to see Hans in his current state, so changed from the Hans he had idolised in his youth? Yes, Gregory had to admit, he had been afraid at the time to see Hans in his diminished state, and he was still afraid even now, to see Hans whose condition had probably not improved since he had last seen him all these years ago. *In the end*, adult Gregory kept repeating to himself, *I am not a psychiatrist, I am not trained to look after people such as Hans, I don't know how to react towards them, how to respond to their incredibly complex needs!* But he also knew, yet again, that he was only trying to alleviate his guilt, this incredible guilt for having failed Hans, for not having been there when he was most needed. *Maybe next summer, when Amelia and I are back In Germany I should pay a visit to Hans?*, he mused.

19

16th **August 1987.** Hans did not feel well at all. He was lying on his bed in his room back home. As so often in summer, it was swelteringly hot in his room under the roof. Although he had taken off all his clothes, he was still too hot. He looked down at his sweaty body, but the sight of rolls of fat around his tummy and his chunky thighs made him look away in disgust. He had gotten so fat! *What has happened to me?*, he sighed. *Ten years ago I looked great, I was tanned, played a lot of tennis, and had beautiful girls vying to be with me. And now? Look at me! I am so ugly!* He tried to remember when he had last made love to a woman. *It was … it must have been … no, that could not be true! It was when he had last seen Monique, on that fateful morning back in Brittany, sometime in … sometime in early 1983. That is so long ago! Over four years without a girl!*, he moaned. But he knew that it had been all his fault, that he had completely misjudged the situation with Monique at the time, and that everything had gone pear-shaped thereafter. *This stupid admission to Monique that I had slept with a hooker!* Hans could still not believe why he had mentioned it to Monique. *And then she had said that she was pregnant!*

As had happened so often over the past few years, at the very thought of Monique's utterly desperate face when she had given him the news about their child, Hans could no longer hold back his tears. He lay there on his bed, naked, sweaty and crying, his obese body convulsed by rhythmic sobs. *And then she aborted our kid!*, Hans thought angrily, burying his face in the pillow. *She did what she had threatened on that fateful day, and went ahead and aborted our kid! In her fourth month of pregnancy!* Hans did not know how Monique had managed to get an abortion so late in her pregnancy, but maybe French law was different? He had never seen Monique again since their fateful row. It was

172

her mum who had written to him in May 1983 with the sad news, and in a very condescending tone, that Monique had had an abortion. In her letter, Monique's mum blamed Hans entirely for what had happened. *And she was right!*, Hans conceded for the umptieth time.

When he received the letter from Monique's mum he was already at the psychiatric clinic in Bad Schlossenried. Hans shuddered as he thought back at the dreadful few weeks and months after his visit to Monique in Brittany in April 1983. He had felt increasingly poorly on his journey back by train from Rennes to Göggingen. He knew that something had happened in his head, as if a switch had been flicked and extinguished part of his brain. He could barely remember getting to his barracks, being teased by his roommates for how awful and tired he looked, lying down in bed more tired than he had ever felt before, and then … nothing. There was a gap in his memory spanning several days. He was told later, when he woke up in the morning in his bed at the military base, that he had been completely incoherent and unable to get up. His roommates had become so worried at his strange behaviour that they called the military base doctor who immediately had asked for Hans to be transferred to the local hospital in Göggingen. The doctors there had undertaken a psychological evaluation and, seeing the babbling and incoherent mess of a person he had become, had declared him 'temporarily insane' and had immediately referred him to the psychiatric clinic at Bad Schlossenried. Again, Hans could not remember anything about that time. His first memories were about waking up, tied up with straps around his hands and feet in a spartan room in Bad Schlossenried.

Apparently he had become violent and had injured a nurse so that the doctors had tied him to his bed.

Bad Schlossenried! He knew nothing about the place before his incarceration there, other than it had been the butt of jokes at school where kids would tease each other by shouting 'careful how you behave or you'll end up at the loony-bin in Bad Schlossenried!' *Bad Schlossenried is for nutcases, for weirdos, for psychiatrically severely ill people! Why am I here?*, he had wondered at the time.

The first weeks at Bad Schlossenried had passed in a haze as he was under heavy medication and sedation. He remembered vaguely his parents at his bedside at one point, his father stern and angry and not saying much, his mother demure and small, desperately clutching a handkerchief and looking at him with desperation and deep sadness in her eyes. Hans could not remember anybody else visiting him. He vaguely remembered doctors and nurses going in and out and, occasionally, because he was too weak to walk, wheeling him in a wheelchair to some obscure room for further tests and endless questions and consultations. He also remembered constant feelings of deep unease and unhappiness. Doctors gradually revealed through his medically-induced haze that he must have had a sudden psychotic shock, probably on the day he had last seen Monique. His doctor, a small, arrogant and vane man with a white coat and glasses hanging down his neck on a golden chain, tried to explain to him that a traumatic experience, such as the one with Monique, could trigger a psychotic shock, and that it was difficult to tell what other psychological effects this could have in future. The doctor talked at length about some of the symptoms Hans had been having since, either witnessed by the doctors and nurses themselves or reported by Hans during their meetings, including depressed mood, sadness, hopelessness, guilt, lack of motivation, loss of interest in activities and other things (the latter easily said, Hans remembered thinking at the time, if you are tied to a bed!), mood swings and violent outbursts (which was the reason in the first place they had tied him up), emotional numbness, sleeplessness, loss of appetite, lack of self-care, and extreme fatigue. Because all these symptoms he was experiencing were real, were affecting him on an hourly basis, Hans clearly understood that something was wrong with him. He was at Bad Schlossenried because he had gone mad! He belonged in the loony-bin!

What was more difficult to accept for Hans were the sudden hallucinations he had begun to experience while lying strapped to his bed. He often thought that there was somebody else in the room with him, although he could never see anyone. The nights were particularly horrendous as he constantly heard noises, shuffling, whispering and moaning. Often, he would wake up, bathed in sweat and unable to get back to sleep for fear of the 'intruders' who he thought were hiding somewhere in his room. This was all new to Hans, never had he experienced anything like this before, and it made him afraid, very afraid. But his doctor kept saying that such paranoia or auditory and visual delusional thinking was not untypical after a psychotic shock, although it was difficult to say how long these delusions would last. The doctor clearly tried to allay Hans' fear, but when Hans heard the final diagnosis he knew that he was in for the long haul, that this was not something that would simply go away like a bruise or a cold. The diagnosis which the doctor had uttered one day with a stern and sombre voice, and several months after Hans had been admitted, was that Hans was suffering both from paranoid schizophrenia and bipolar disorder. The doctor also argued that both of these conditions may have been already subliminally present long before and that they may have just been exacerbated by the shock Hans experienced on that fateful day with Monique. Worst of all, the doctor said that, for his own safety Hans would have to be kept in a closed psychiatric ward probably for at least two years, with regular evaluations to check on changes and progress with his condition.

Hans remembered having been utterly shattered at the time of receiving this 'formal' diagnosis about what was wrong with him. He had never heard of bipolar disorder and did not know what it meant (although the doctor had tried to explain it to him). But he knew anecdotally that his other condition, paranoid schizophrenia, was very serious and that this really put you towards the extreme end of psychiatric illnesses, that this would most definitely classify you as 'mad' and a 'loony'. Of course, there were no electric shock therapies, no lobotomies, none of the ever-more horrific 'treatments' offered up in B-rate psychological thrillers or horror movies set in lunatic asylums. But, from a social starvation and loneliness perspective his incarceration at Bad Schlossenried was as bad as anything he had seen in B-rate movies about mad people in lunatic asylums. Apart from the hospital-based psycho-therapist whom Hans had to meet regularly, he had nobody to talk to, no friends coming to see him, no nurses taking him out into the hospital gardens in a wheelchair covered in a fluffy blanket to ward off the cold like in the movies. None of that at all! Instead, Bad Schlossenried was an ascetic, spartan and sterile place where patients were often left for hours on end to fester on their own in their spartan rooms, devoid of any sensory stimulus and allowed to wallow in their own psychotic hell. What made things even worse for Hans was that, after the formal diagnosis, the visits from his parents became more and more sporadic. His father had stopped visiting altogether, and Hans knew that Bernhard would have wanted nothing to do with his 'loony' son, while his mum was always so distraught when she visited him that Hans suggested that she should not visit him anymore.

Although Hans was kept in a medical haze for most of the time, there were nonetheless moments of lucidity when he realised in what a predicament he was. Apparently because of his violent outbursts (which Hans never seemed to remember), the medical staff had to keep his room as spartan as possible, with only a bed where he could lie in and sit on during the day, and to which he was tied during the night. His room was a 'padded cell' with a padded floor and walls so that he could not hurt himself in his angry uncontrolled outbursts. But this meant that he had nothing to do when he awoke from his pill-induced wooziness, other than think … think about his past, about Monique, about Gregory, Klaus, school … But often all this thinking, and going over and over all the mistakes he had made over the past few months and years led to further psychotic episodes, which, in turn, led to more medication. It was a vicious circle, a seemingly never-ending horror from which Hans, at the time, could not see any escape.

Hans looked up at the Velux window in the ceiling of his room at home and shuddered again at the thought about the awful time he'd had at Bad Schlossenried. Somehow he got better, the seemingly endless discussions with the hospital psychiatrist – 'talking therapy' as he called it – must have borne fruit, his angry uncontrolled outbursts and verbal and physical attacks on staff gradually abated, his medication was eventually reduced and, in turn, his lucidity improved. But, as his doctor had predicted, it had taken about two full years for Hans to be finally released in the summer of 1985. The military base had a policy that anyone who had suffered a severe mental breakdown like Hans could never re-join the army, so Hans never returned to Göggingen, never saw Frank, Sascha, Gernot or Bernd again, and wondered whether they were still regularly whoring and how they got away with it vis-à-vis their girlfriends. Life was so unfair! While he was incarcerated at Bad Schlossenried Hans had been declared unfit to work (at least for the time being, with regular re-evaluations), and the only place he could go to was back to his parents' house, to his old room which, either by coincidence or cunning ploy to lure him back again, his parents had left unchanged from when he was still a young kid at school.

Hans was not worried about going back to his time-warp room with his old schoolwork still neatly laid out on the table, his faded posters of past rock music legends on the wall, and the bed bought for him when he must have been about 12 years old. The familiarity of his surroundings indeed gave him some comfort, some reminder of a time when he was a star, a flamboyant teenage womaniser, and when he had felt great and invincible. But he was also worried about living back home again, especially about being in the same house with his father. Bernhard had only agreed to allow his son back into their house if Hans meticulously stuck to his strict medication regime, and on the understanding that Hans would not 'bother' his parents too often by coming down to their floor. Hans could clearly feel that his father had lost all interest in him, indeed that Bernhard did not even regard him any more as a human being but just as a weird 'thing' that happened to live with them. Although this had not been unexpected, it had deeply hurt and completely shattered Hans and had increased his sadness and his feelings of being unloved and unworthy. He found it very difficult to cope with, and his sadness was exacerbated by the fact that his mother had, so far at least, not been of great help and support either. Something big had changed in his relationship with his parents since he had been declared mentally ill. His parents did clearly not cope well with the new situation.

Hans looked towards the several small pill containers standing on his table. The dreadful *Lithium* tablets trying to control his manic-depressive states but which made him so tired and 'not with it', complemented by mood stabilisers that had to be carefully tailored to whether he felt more manic or more depressive. And then there were the pill containers with *Clozapine* and *Chlorpromazine* and other anti-psychotics for his hallucinations, paranoia and delusional thinking. The side-effects of this cocktail of pills were horrendous, causing shaking, trembling, pains, nausea, headaches, drowsiness, extreme tiredness and the feeling of being completely withdrawn from the world around him. He hated it!

And he did not enjoy the bi-weekly meetings with his psychiatrist at Heidenhausen hospital. He felt that the man was prying into his innermost secrets, his childhood, his (now non-existent) sex life, his most inner thoughts and feelings. They frequently talked about Hans feeling detached from himself or his environment, his almost complete social withdrawal and isolation, his difficulties with focussing, concentrating and thinking clearly. Although this sometimes seemed to help Hans, he also mentioned to his psychiatrist that his worries and anxieties never really went away, but he never had the impression that the psychiatrist was helping him much in that respect. The psychiatrist rather concentrated on trying to find the reasons for Hans' psychotic break, although to Hans it was pretty clear that it had been directly linked to the fateful morning with Monique back in Brittany in April 1983. Yet, the psychiatrist often insisted that while a psychotic break may seem to come on suddenly, chances were good that this crisis had been building for some time, and that the healing process was, likewise, very gradual and extensive. For these reasons, they seemed to talk endlessly about Hans' youth, his relationship with his father, mother, friends and girlfriends, and his most inner thoughts – discussions Hans found very difficult. Hans did not want to talk about his past and about what may have triggered the psychotic break, he did not want to talk about his father or his friends. He just wanted to be left alone. He did not want to face the ghosts of his past. He did not want to admit that his life had completely and irretrievably changed.

As a result, Hans often felt more depressed after having seen his psychiatrist than before. Worst of all, the discussions with his psychiatrist and the cocktail of pills he was taking still did not curtail the constant flashbacks of past and traumatic experiences or the horrendous nightmares Hans was regularly having, nor did his violent mood swings appear to be under control. Worst of all, thoughts about self-harm or suicide Hans had been getting lately were worsening, but he had not dared mention this to anyone, especially not his psychiatrist. Hans was well aware that he did not help himself much by holding back what was probably crucial information about himself and his feelings from the person who was meant to help him most. But he did not trust his psychiatrist enough to completely open up, to divulge his innermost angsts and suicidal feelings.

Lying on his bed, Hans was very weary of constantly rehashing the dreadful time he'd had at Bad Schlossenried. He had been told by his psychiatrist that he needed to move forward, not be constantly embroiled in his past. Very slowly Hans moved the heavy bulk of his body, stood up and put on his clothes. He looked at the plastic containers with his various pills on the table and smiled. Because of their dreadful side-effects, he had recently decided to stop taking his mood swing and *Lithium* pills. He was proud that he had managed to hide this from his parents for several days now, although he had to admit that he had felt increasingly depressed over the past few days. Would he be able to continue without pills? He put on his slippers. He hated them as they made him look like an old man, but he had to admit that they were comfortable as he shuffled out of his room, through his parents' party and disco room, and down the stairs to the first floor where his parents lived.

He entered his parents' flat without knocking. In front of him, the dining room table was laid out as usual with a typical Swabian breakfast assortment: *Laugenwecken* (pretzel rolls encrusted with delicious lye salt), small rolls adorned with various assortments of seeds (including poppy seed rolls), slices of ham, liver sausage, various cold cuts, salami, pickled gherkins, an assortment of jams and marmalades, and the typical incredibly strong German coffee in which you could almost stand up a spoon. Hans' mum Sigrid briefly greeted her son and busied herself as usual around the kitchen and breakfast table, making sure that everything was laid out the way Bernhard liked it. Bernhard came into the room, and sat down at the table while unfolding his linen napkin, not looking at his son once or uttering a word of greeting. Ever since coming back from Bad Schlossenried, Hans was used to his father's refusal to acknowledge his presence. They had not talked much, and not once had Bernhard enquired about how Hans was feeling or how Hans' time had been at Bad Schlossenried. Hans sat down at his end of the table and did not dare look his father in the eyes. He grabbed a *Laugenwecken*, buttered it and placed some salami and a pickled gherkin on his plate.

"Are you too proud to even say hello now?", Bernhard bellowed from his end of the table.

Hans was taken aback by his father's sudden outburst, as he usually did not speak to his son over breakfast.

"I said hello to mum", Hans replied meekly.

Sigrid Looked pleadingly at Hans not to talk back to his father. But Hans was not willing to take the hint. Why should he allow himself to be insulted by his father who had treated him as if he did not exist since he came back home? Why should he always be the one to cede ground?

"You also never greet me when I come in", Hans continued, with more anger in his voice. The fact that he had not taken his mood-control medication for a while seemed to spur him on to be bolder and more daring than the medically-subdued zombie he usually was.

Bernhard stopped eating, placed his spoon back in his coffee cup, and looked baffled at his son. He had obviously not expected a reply from Hans.

"How dare you insult me?", Bernhard shouted, clutching his fists.

Hans looked up at Bernhard and saw the swelling anger in his father's face, his clutched fists, and the red painful blotches of psoriasis on his face, neck and arms. But this time Hans did not yield. Maybe it was the fact that he had not taken his medication, or the simmering anger linked to his worsening depression, or maybe it was just that Hans had enough of how his father treated him. Tears began welling up in Hans' eyes as he shouted back at his father: "I am sick and tired of being treated by you as if I don't exist, of constantly being told off even when I have done nothing wrong!"

With a very worried look on her face Sigrid placed a hand on Hans' arm and looked pleadingly at him to stop, but Hans brushed his mother's hand away and stood up, spilling the coffee from his cup over the freshly ironed white tablecloth.

"Not once have you told me that I am welcome back home!", Hans continued shouting, "you make me feel like a complete stranger. It is as if … as if … I am no longer your son! You probably see me as a complete nutcase, as somebody … somebody … who should be locked up! I hate you!"

During Hans' stammering insults, Bernhard had shot up from his seat and had rushed over to Hans with astonishingly quick speed, taking half the tablecloth with him and spilling the whole breakfast table contents crashing onto the carpet. Bernhard had reached Hans who stood by his chair, surprised at his father's sudden reaction. Without warning, Bernhard slammed his fist into Hans' face, making Hans fall over his chair and banging his face hard on the carpeted floor. Sigrid let out a cry and covered her mouth with her hands in surprise. Hans' nose was bleeding profusely, it was probably broken. Bernhard towered over his son and began to kick him hard in the ribs and side with his fists and feet. Hans felt a sharp stab of pain as one his father's kicks hit Hans' testicles.

"This will teach you, you ungrateful bastard!", Bernhard bellowed, kicking Hans even harder. "Look at you, you fat blob! Look at what you have become … you … you… weirdo, lunatic! I want you out of my house … back to the loony-bin where you belong!"

Hans was trying to shield his face with both his hands as Bernhard was increasingly concentrating his blows towards

184

Hans' face, not hearing his wife imploring him to stop. But although Hans was slow due to his heavy bulk, he was still young and reasonably agile. Hans rolled onto his side, avoiding his father's foot which was about to stamp heavily on his chest. While he rolled, Hans propped himself up on his elbows and heaved his aching body up, just like he had learned during his brief military training. Now he was standing in front of his father, holding his elbows in front of his face and chest to ward off the heavy punches his father was trying to land. Hans could feel the strength in his father's blows, punches his father would have used a thousand times as a boxer in his youth. Several heavy blows made Hans stumble, but he managed to stay upright, in spite of the seething pain in his face and torso.

At one point his father stopped his punches briefly to catch his breath. Hans looked at his father through the slit between his protective elbows and seized the opportunity. With all the force he could muster, Hans punched his father in his unprotected face with his right fist, just as they had practiced with punch bags at the military base. Hans could hear the crunch of his father's nose breaking as he landed his blow in the middle of his father's face. Bernhard was so stunned at Hans hitting back that he just stood there for a moment, mouth and eyes wide open, nose bleeding profusely, and looking at his son in utter surprise. Hans did not hesitate a second and landed a second hard blow in the middle of his father's face. Hans had aimed his punch well, making Bernhard sway. While moving backwards to recatch his balance, Bernhard stumbled over a chair behind him, fell over backwards and hit his head hard with a loud crunching sound on the edge of the radiator mounted on the wall below the window. Both Hans and Sigrid had watched Bernhard fall as if in slow motion. Up to then, they could not imagine this mountain of a man, this former boxer, falling and hitting his head. Now Bernhard lay there, unconscious and with a puddle of blood oozing out from the back of his head, soiling the carpet.

"Oh my … oh my!", Sigrid cried while bending down towards her husband. "What have you done?", she said while holding a hand in front of her mouth in surprise and disgust and looking at Hans through tears that left ugly smudged make-up trails on her cheeks. "You have killed him!"

Hans stood there, flabbergasted at what he had done. With just two punches he had knocked out his father! Rather than being worried about how badly injured his father was, he thought that he had finally done it. After all these years, he had finally found the courage to hit back, not to take his father's bullying any more. He had knocked him out!

But a moan from his father brought Hans back to reality. His father opened his eyes and tried to move, but his head was too painful and he felt too dizzy. He was not dead, but Hans saw that his father was severely injured after knocking his head on the radiator.

"Quick! Call an ambulance!", Sigrid shouted, looking very worried at her husband's ashen face and the puddle of blood on the carpet.

Hans tore himself away from the scene, went to the kitchen and phoned for an ambulance. Although he was worried about what he had done to his father, he could not supress a smile.

20

20th July 1993. Gregory had, yet again, been oblivious to what was happening in Hans' life. At the time, he continued to hear snippets of news through the Heidenhausen grapevine, rumours about Hans' renewed incarceration in the psychiatric ward at Bad Schlossenried, stories about a fight Hans may have had with his dad. But like most people in their late 20s and early 30s, Gregory had been very busy. He had lived in New Zealand for four years from 1988 to 1992 to complete his PhD during which time (before internet, e-mail and mobile phones) he only obtained sporadic information about what was happening in Heidenhausen. He then got his first academic job at a London university and got married to Amelia whom he had met when he started his job in London. All of this left little room for his former schoolfriends from Heidenhausen.

By July 1993, Gregory's hectic life had calmed down a bit and he was back in Heidenhausen to visit his mum for the first time since he had left for New Zealand in 1988. Although he had only been away for five years, many things had changed since his last visit. Germany was reunified, and the mood in the country was one of cautious optimism tinged with worries about the future, especially about how former East Germans would integrate into this newly-constituted country. But, as with many political and socio-economic changes that had affected Germany since Gregory was born,

Heidenhausen seemed surprisingly oblivious to what had happened, by-passed by the vicissitudes of globalisation, cocooned in its *Schwäbische Alb* naïve remoteness. To be sure, people and friends he met talked about reunification, but more in an abstract way how it affected the rest of Germany, rather than about how it had affected Heidenhausen itself. Not much seemed to have changed in the town. The people were still more or less the same, there had not been an influx of East Germans into the town as had occurred in other, more economically booming, conurbations. The shops were still more or less the same (and struggling), the town was still gradually oozing population to the more buoyant centres in and around Stuttgart, the schools were (as far as Gregory could tell) still broadly the same as when he had been a pupil in the 1960s and 1970s.

But something had changed within Gregory himself at the time. Gregory was not sure what it was, maybe the fact that he was married and was, for the first time, carrying some responsibility for another person, or maybe it was just his stint in New Zealand and the fact that he had finally, at the age of 31, got a permanent job? Whatever it was, Gregory remembered vividly feeling a compulsion to see his old friend Hans again for the first time since their unplanned encounter in one of the Heidenhausen pubs so many years ago, at a time when Hans had just started military service. Of course, Hans, together with Gregory's other school friends Bill and Rufus, had always been at the back of Gregory's mind. But Gregory knew that Bill and Rufus were okay, pursuing careers of their own, getting married themselves and, in the case of Rufus, having his first (unplanned) child.

Gregory had been in regular contact with Bill and Rufus by mail and occasionally by phone, even when he was in New Zealand. But it was different with Hans, partly because of the rumours that were swirling around, partly because Gregory had an inkling that his friends, who always had a problematic relationship with Hans, were probably not telling him the entire truth, or, indeed, did not really know what had happened to Hans. Gregory had to admit, therefore, that an element of curiosity had also come into his sudden decision to visit Hans. How was Hans doing and was he as bad mentally and psychologically as his friends made him out to be?

But 'visiting Hans' was easier said than done. Hans was apparently no longer living with his parents and had been allocated a flat by the *Heidenhausen Sozialamt* (*Heidenhausen Social Services*). However, enquiries at the council about Hans' address and phone number led nowhere, as the female clerk at the council informed Gregory that she was not allowed to give out details of persons who had been allocated social housing due to mental illness. The only source of information was, therefore, Hans' parents. But Gregory, wary of how long it had been since he had seen Hans' parents, and feeling guilty that he had not been there for Hans when things had started to break down, was reluctant to pick up the phone and ring Hans' parents. In particular, he did not want to speak to Bernhard who Gregory had never liked. But even Sigrid would be difficult to talk to.

As a result, it took Gregory several days to muster up the courage to pick up the phone and ring Hans' old number. Were the parents even still living at their old address?

Gregory had picked a time in the middle of the day in the hope that Bernhard would be at work. It was indeed Sigrid who picked up the phone.

"Hello Frau Schlesier, this is Greg …"

"Greg?", Sigrid asked hesitantly.

"Yes, hello, Greg … you know … Hans' old friend from school."

"Friend from school…?", came the indistinct reply.

"Yes, remember Frau Schlesier. Hans and I went to school together up to Year 12. I came to your place several times …"

A deep sigh could be heard at the end of the phone. "Ah yes, Greg! I remember. How are you?", came the unconvincing and unenthusiastic reply.

"I am well, Frau Schlesier. But I heard that ... that … Hans has not been so well these last few years …"

There was a long pause at the end of the phone. Gregory could hear Sigrid breathing heavily. He was afraid she would hang up. After a long time, she said: "Yes … well… things have not been good for Hans lately. He … he … he has had some problems."

Gregory could hear how difficult it was for Sigrid to talk about her son, and he wanted to keep their conversation as short as possible. "Yes … I heard … That is why I thought I would like to visit Hans … you know … to see how he is … to talk to him about … about us and memories of the past …"

"Memories of the past …", came the parroted answer from Sigrid after another long pause. "I don't know … Greg … whether this is a good idea … Hans has been so poorly …"

Gregory could hear the audible struggle in Sigrid's voice. On the one hand she felt impelled to protect her son, but Gregory also thought that he could hear relief in Sigrid's voice that one of Hans' old friends was showing an interest in her son.

"I was wondering whether you could pass me Hans' phone number so that I can contact him?", Gregory persevered. "I guess he can then decide whether he wants to see me …"

Another long pause, but after a while Sigrid replied with a hint of resignation in her voice: "Well, I guess so … It is really up to him whether he wants to see you. He has not had many visitors these last few years, you know …"

Gregory wondered whether this was another subtle reproach. But he also understood if Sigrid felt that all of Hans' former friends had abandoned him as soon as his mental problems began. Again, a long time seemed to elapse, but Gregory thought that he could hear Sigrid rummage in a drawer or handbag. *She does not know her son's phone number by heart!*, was his immediate thought, but he did not dare challenge her for fear that she may change her mind. Sigrid gave Gregory Hans' phone number, Gregory thanked her, promised her that he would be very careful with Hans, and put down the phone.

For a long time, Gregory played with the piece of paper with Hans' phone number in his hand, without being able to make up his mind whether to ring or not. Was he ready to see his old friend? Would his visit open a door he did not really want to open? Was he willing to take on interacting with Hans again, when all the other friends had obviously decided not to? Did they know something Gregory did not know? And was he mature enough to take on the responsibility ensuing from such a visit? And, on a more practical level, was it even possible to stay in touch with Hans from London? All these thoughts swirled through Gregory's mind as he dialled Hans' number.

21

20th July 1993. Gregory stood in front of Hans' flat and looked up at the peeling paint on the façade, the flaking render on the balconies, the leaking drainpipes hugging the front of the apartment block. Although Heidenhausen had its share of drab districts, mostly built in the 19th century to house poor textile workers and often in poor state of repair, this part of Heidenhausen was particularly dire. Gregory had never been to this district before, which was hidden behind the small red-light district near the railway station. He felt unsafe even in the middle of the day among the human debris littering the streets near the station: tramps in tattered clothes lugging plastic bags with what looked like rubbish; whores in skimpy dresses and tarted up with too much make-up; pimps with golden rings on their fingers, fur coats, and golden chains oozing from their frilly shirts; and young drug addicts with haunted and gaunt looks of death on their haggard faces. It was a different kind of city around here, darker, poorer and older, oozing a decrepit working-class feel, a world away from the bourgeois districts with middle-class *Schweiss* employees and their well-educated, privileged and arrogant self-entitled kids.

Dirty looking *Ausländerkinder* (immigrant children), probably of Turkish, gypsy or Eastern European origin, had started congregating near where Gregory stood, boldly holding out hands towards Gregory for a small offering of coins. Gregory knew that such pockets of poverty, vice and deprivation existed in Heidenhausen, and he was ashamed that he had not paid more attention to these blatant economic inequalities in his own home town. But what could one do but to avoid these places as best as possible? *I hope my car will be alright*, Gregory thought with a worried look towards the side street where he had left his rental vehicle. The begging kids were edging closer, uttering unintelligible words in a foreign language. But Gregory was still hesitating as to whether to ring the doorbell labelled 'H. Schlesier.' The bell was among a whole row of doorbells, suggesting that there were at least ten flats in this apartment block. He finally mustered the courage and rang the bell. A few seconds later the buzzer was activated and Gregory pushed the entrance door open, leaving behind the begging and chattering children.

On the phone, Hans had explained that he lived on the fifth floor and Gregory made his way up the stairs. On every floor, noises could be heard behind the closed doors he passed, loud music of Balkan origin, a couple shouting at each other or at their kids in a language unknown to Gregory, stomping feet, the flushing of a toilet, and the faint sounds of a creaky and mistuned violin playing a slow tune that oozed Eastern European sadness, lament and gypsy melancholy. When Gregory reached the fifth floor, Hans stood on the landing. Seeing his old friend, Gregory was at first speechless. Hans looked like a wreck. He wore an old t-shirt which was much too short, wide baggy pants, and black slippers which were more befitting of an 80-year-old. Hans had lost most of his hair, with a large bold patch at the front, and the remainder of his greasy and unwashed hair hung down the sides of his head in lumpy strands. His face was pasty and pale, his brown eyes, which had attracted all these girls in the past with their lost-puppy-eyed-look, had relinquished all their lustre and shine and looked rather rheumy, red, swollen and inflamed. But what shocked Gregory most was how fat and bloated Hans become. Bulges of fat were not only visible on Hans' cheeks, face and neck, but Hans also had a huge tummy which was hanging out his much too short t-shirt like a giant water-filled bag. Gregory stared for a long time at Hans' bulging tummy which reminded him of one of these exotic hanging-belly pigs he had seen in a zoo when he was a kid. Obviously the days of Hans' svelte and trained tennis-playing body were long gone.

Hans did not seem to worry at all about his appearance and greeted Gregory with a large smile, evidently happy to see him. "Greg …", Hans said, holding out his arms.

For a brief moment, Gregory did not know what to do, but after a brief hesitation he moved towards Hans and they hugged intensively. Gregory could smell Hans' unwashed skin, an evil stench wafting up from his armpits, and an even more pungent smell emanating from further down, but he held Hans' embrace for as long as possible.

"Greg ...", Hans repeated with a big smile, using the familiar and intimate short form of Gregory's name. "So good to see you, it's been such a long time!", he said with a hoarse voice as he led Gregory into his flat.

The flat was nothing like Hans' sterile and perfectly clean and tidy teenage room back home Gregory still remembered so vividly. Hans' flat was very crowded, full of junk, with old papers piled almost ceiling high, discarded clothes on the floor, and piles of dirty dishes in the small windowless kitchen. There was a smell of rot and unwashed clothes in the air. Gregory felt very uncomfortable but followed Hans into the living room towards the only chair that did not have piles of junk on it. Despite the disorderly state of the flat, Gregory had to admit that the flat itself, allocated to Hans by *Heidenhausen Social Services*, was, after all, not too bad. It was not very spacious with only one bedroom, a kitchen, bathroom and living room, but the living room had nice large south-facing windows and a balcony. The sun was shining through the windows, casting the mess on the floor and chairs in an eery white, almost surreal, glistening light. Glancing out of the window, Gregory surmised that the balcony had a nice view of this part of Heidenhausen and the distant wooded hills towards the east.

"I cleared up the flat a bit for you", Hans said while shoving newspapers from a chair and sitting down heavily. "It was such a mess!"

Gregory could not imagine the flat being messier than it was, but refrained from commenting. The whole situation felt awkward, and he still was not sure whether it had been the right decision to come here and see his old friend. Evidently, Hans was no longer the same person he had known when they were younger.

"So, how have you been?", Hans tried to break the ice, realising that Gregory felt uncomfortable. "You said on the phone that you are now married and that you live in London?"

Gregory briefly told Hans about his time in New Zealand and how he got a job at a London university where he had met his wife. Hans mentioned how pleased he was to have received regular postcards from Gregory while he was in New Zealand. He pointed with his chubby hand towards a row of postcards on the windowsill, all sent by Gregory from New Zealand (to Hans' old home address) and showing pictures of kiwis, keas, tree ferns, South Island west coast temperate rainforest, and the volcanoes of central North Island. Hans explained that these had been passed on by his mum to this new address, and that he was always amazed at the exotic places Gregory had visited on his various trips to and from New Zealand, such as Hawaii, the Cook Islands, Fiji, Tahiti, Oregon and Washington State, and how he felt that Gregory had already had such an exciting life. Embarrassed, Gregory had to admit that he had almost forgotten about all these postcards he had sent to Hans and other friends. He looked around him and could not imagine how drab and dull Hans' life must have been over the past years compared to his own, with Hans stuck in this flat in this god-awful part of Heidenhausen. *Hans has probably not left Heidenhausen, with the exception of his spells at the clinic at Bad Schlossenried, since his psychological problems had started*, Gregory thought dismayed. Gregory continued the brief account of his recent life and how he had met his wife Amelia while working in his new job. Immediately Hans enquired about how Amelia looked, how she was as a person, what her interests and hobbies were, immediately reminding Gregory about Hans' intrusive inquisitiveness a long time ago about his first girlfriend Evelyn. In that sense, Hans did not seem to have changed at all.

But Gregory wanted to hear about how Hans was, about what had happened to him, so he gently tried to steer the discussion away from himself and Amelia. "Enough about me", Gregory said cautiously after he had addressed the barrage of questions from Hans about Amelia in the most perfunctory but polite manner. "What about you? Your mum said that you had not been too well lately?"

"You spoke to my mum …?", Hans asked with a worried look on his face.

Gregory realised that maybe he should not have admitted talking to Sigrid. "Well yes … social services would not give me your phone number, so I had to ask your mum."

Hans scratched his stubbly chin, he was evidently not happy that Gregory had spoken to his mother. But then he seemed to relax a bit and smiled back at Gregory. "Yes, things have been a bit rough lately … to say the least", at which point he let out a very strange hysteric laugh which took Gregory by surprise. *Was this laughter a sign of nervousness or is he making fun of me?*, Gregory wondered. But Hans did not even seem to notice that he had emitted such a strange sound. "You have probably heard that I … that

I was at Bad Schlossenried for a few years?", Hans enquired, scrutinising Gregory's face for how he would react to this admission.

"Yes, I heard rumours … but you know how it is", Gregory replied, "people just don't know the facts, so they make up all kinds of stories."

Hans nodded. Obviously he had heard about the rumours swirling around about him and his time at the 'loony bin'. He looked rather embarrassed back at Gregory. "I guess some of the rumours are true, but I am sure there is also a lot of bullshit floating around … People are so nasty sometimes", and Hans let out this strange hysteric laugh again that took Gregory aback. Was it a nervous tick or something deeper, indicating that Hans could no longer control his emotions?

Gregory did not know how much he could probe Hans to tell him about the past few years. He rather wanted Hans to speak freely about what had happened, without feeling pressured. Hans was kneading his hands, evidently nervous, occasionally glancing up at Gregory. "Well, you know … I have done some pretty stupid things …", Hans began to admit. "I … I … I completely messed it up with Monique. You remember Monique?"

"Yes, of course", Gregory replied, "I remember our trip to Brittany well. I liked Monique. I thought the two of you were well suited to each other." Gregory realised that his last sentence sounded a bit naff and gratuitous, but he did not know what else to say at this point.

"Well, I thought so too … but I … but I really messed it up with her", Hans said, kneading his hands more forcefully. Tears began welling up in Hans' eyes.

Here we go!, Gregory thought. *This is what I feared would happen and the kind of situation I didn't really want to get into. Maybe we should have just kept the discussion about myself and my own life, but then what would be the point of the visit? Poor Hans has probably not talked to anyone except for his shrink about this for years. Will I be able to react the right way with what he is about to tell me?*

"When I was at the military ... you know in Göggingen ...", Hans continued, "we went to see hookers regularly. All the blokes in the barracks did it, it was just normal. I resisted at first, but then I met this girl ... Nadia ... from somewhere in the East ... you know ... she was not like a normal hooker ... she was ... nice ... she was good looking. I saw her several times."

Hans stopped and looked up at Gregory to see how he was digesting this news. Gregory kept his face as implacable as possible, trying to encourage Hans to continue. Based on Hans' behaviour with his various girlfriends in the past, Gregory had to acknowledge that Hans' admission about seeing a hooker did not unduly surprise him.

"But my mistake was not seeing this hooker ...", Hans carried on, trying to control his sobs, "but that I then told Monique about it."

This came as a shock to Gregory. What was Hans thinking at the time? Why admit to Monique that he had seen a hooker? It did not make sense.

Hans saw Gregory's frowning face but continued nonetheless. "I don't know why I admitted this to Monique at the time. Everything had been so perfect during my visit, we got on well, I enjoyed being in her parents' house, we loved each other … We had talked about getting married … I felt so happy that maybe I thought … I thought that I could tell Monique anything … that nothing could come between us, no matter how bad. That we could be totally honest with each other. But as soon as I had said it, I immediately realised that it was a huge mistake … Monique's reaction … and then she told me that she was pregnant!", Hans said letting out an almost inhuman cry of despair. His hand-wringing intensified. "Pregnant! With my child! What a fool I was! She had just been about to tell me, when I told her about seeing a hooker! Can you imagine that?"

Gregory could indeed not imagine the scene. Hans' stupidity was too much to fathom.

"Monique broke up with me there and then and I heard later that she had an abortion … she killed our baby!", Hans said, breaking down completely and holding his face in his hands.

Gregory did not know what to do. He knew that the right thing to do was to go over and hug Hans, comfort and console him, but there was such a huge gulf between them now, a rift of both time and a new lack of familiarity that prevented Gregory from getting up and hugging Hans as he would have done in the past.

Hans looked up through glazed eyes. "Something broke in me after that, Greg. I don't know what happened … but I have not been the same ever since. The doctors at Schlossenried called it a psychotic break. I am still not sure what this really means. And they diagnosed both a bipolar condition … you know 'manic-depressive' as it's more commonly called … and also paranoid schizophrenia. I have been on this heavy medication since … this medication which makes me really drowsy, tired and ill, and I just can't do anything these days. Look at me …", and Hans pointed at his fat belly hanging unappetisingly over his trousers, "I can't muster the energy to do anything because of this medication. It makes me feel like a zombie …"

Gregory froze at the mention of paranoid schizophrenia. Although he had heard various rumours through the grapevine about Hans' mental condition, and although these rumours seemed to be, in hindsight, surprisingly accurate, to hear the formal diagnosis of Hans' mental problems directly from Hans' mouth was quite different. Gregory did not know much about either of these two conditions, but from various movies he had seen that involved paranoid schizophrenics he knew that this was a very serious illness. Should he be worried about his own safety, sitting here opposite a person who had been diagnosed as paranoid? Could this mean that Hans could become violent? Thinking beyond Hans' mental problems, Gregory also thought that Hans' admission about what had happened between Monique and him was even worse than the rumours he had heard. But, at the same time, Gregory realised that he felt privileged that Hans still trusted him enough to divulge such intimate information.

"Greg, you must promise that you won't tell anyone about Monique", Hans implored as if reading Gregory's mind. "Nobody knows about this, not even my parents. My doctor at Bad Schlossenried knows, of course, but that's about it …"

"Of course, Hans", Gregory replied with a lump in his throat. "This will stay entirely between us." Gregory was flattered that Hans had chosen him of all people to tell him about his secret. Maybe Hans felt that, even after all this time, they were still intimate friends?

"The rest of the story you probably know", Hans continued. "Two years at Bad Schlossenried, with a lot of medication, talking to psychiatrists, and hardly any visitors."

Gregory was sure that the latter comment was a reproach targeted specifically at him. He did not dare look Hans in the eyes, feeling immensely guilty that it had taken him so long to see Hans. But then he was at least here now! None of the other friends had even made an effort to contact Hans or to find out about what had really happened to Hans. Or maybe they knew more about Hans' condition after all, and were just plain worried to be in a room with a paranoid schizophrenic?

"And you probably heard about the fight I had with my dad a few years ago?", Hans looked at Gregory inquisitively. But Gregory had, again, only heard vague rumours, snippets of information distorted by the endless rehashing of half-truths and misinformation through the Heidenhausen grapevine.

"Well compared to what I had done to Monique this did not feel like much", Hans continued, "although I apparently had another breakdown afterwards, with another two years at Schlossenried. I can barely remember what happened to me after I hit my dad, it is still kind of a blur. My doctor said that it must have been … must have been another psychotic shock. I felt worse than ever! But it had felt so good to hit back at my dad … after all these years of abuse, when he beat me up for my bad school grades, taunting me, and constantly harassing me. Dad was not badly injured after all, but he used our fight to prevent me from going back home after my second spell at Schlossenried. Both my parents abrogated all responsibility and had me declared a ward of the state. Can you imagine that! Even my own mum would initially not want anything to do with me after I beat up my dad. And on top of that my dad had managed to get a court order against me which prevents me from coming within 200 metres of their house, and which also prevents my mum from seeing me."

Gregory could not believe what he heard. Yes, there had been rumours that Hans had beaten up his dad, but when Gregory first heard this a while ago from his friends he thought that Hans had actually done well, that he had finally gathered up the courage to hit back. This asshole and bully Bernhard deserved it, especially after the way he had always treated his son! But Gregory had not heard about the court order before. It seemed unbelievable that parents would do something like this to their severely mentally ill son. *Who were these people? They should never have had children!*, he thought with disgust.

"But my mum nonetheless visits me occasionally", Hans continued his account with a mischievous grin on his face. "She sneaks out without letting Bernhard know and comes here occasionally, to clean up a bit, chat, and check that I am OK and take my medication. But it's been a while since she's been here ... maybe two months ...", Hans suddenly seemed to realise, looking out of the window with a distant and pensive look on his face and scratching his chin.

Well at least his mum has not completely given up on her son!, Gregory thought relieved. *But what a weird situation it is nonetheless, where the mum has to sneak out to see her son!* Gregory felt immensely sad about what Hans was telling him.

"I also have a carer appointed by *Heidenhausen Social Services* who comes here about once a month to look after me and to monitor my medication. She is nice and does not interfere too much with how I live …", Hans said, looking around him as if realising for the first time how messy his flat was.

"But where are my manners?", Hans suddenly changed the topic. "I have not offered you anything to drink! What would you like?"

Judging from the state of the kitchen and the pile of dirty dishes, Gregory was not sure whether he wanted to risk drinking from one of Hans' glasses, but politeness compelled him to accept the offer of a glass of apple juice. While Hans rummaged in the kitchen, Gregory used the opportunity to look around the living room. Visible behind the sofa, a disorderly pile of sheets and what looked like discarded food wrappers caught Gregory's attention, and he wondered what was going on there. Was this a stash of something Hans had prepared? Why would he do that, in his own flat? Gregory was caught unawares looking at the strange mess behind the sofa, when Hans came in, holding two glasses with apple juice in his hands.

Realising what Gregory was looking at, Hans looked embarrassed and let out his inhuman hysteric laugh that again caught Gregory by surprise. "I have been hiding behind my sofa the last few days as there were intruders in my flat ...", Hans said almost matter-of-factly, while placing the two glasses on a stool in front of Gregory.

"Intruders? What intruders?", Gregory asked worryingly. "How did they get in? Have you called the police?"

But Gregory realised immediately that there was something strange about this story, as the way Hans' eyes darted back and forth between the pile of stuff behind the sofa and Gregory suggested that Hans himself was not sure about what was happening.

"I don't know how they get in ...", Hans mumbled, "but I am really scared ... They go through my stuff, they sleep in my bed, they sit in my kitchen ... I really want them out!"

Gregory was now even more worried. Evidently, Hans was imagining things. There were clearly no intruders in his flat, otherwise social services, Hans' carer, or his mum, would have seen them and called the police. This was evidently a sign of Hans' delusional paranoia. But Gregory did not know how to react to this. Should he play along with it and pretend that it was normal for intruders to come in and take over a flat? That it was normal for someone like Hans to hide behind a sofa for days on end?

"Eeeemh ...", Gregory replied, unsure what to say. "Have you told your carer about this?"

"Of course, I have", Hans replied with another inscrutable gaze back at his pile of stuff behind the sofa. "But she doesn't believe me. She thinks it's in my head."

Well, join the club!, Gregory thought. Hans was evidently completely bonkers, but Gregory did not know how to react to this. Dealing with Hans' admissions of mistakes he had made with Monique, of beating up his dad or of feeling depressed, Gregory could somehow cope with. But delusional paranoia was at another level, something so deeply psychological and so unfamiliar to Gregory with his all-too-normal life that he simply did not have the mental and emotional repertoire to respond appropriately. What could you say to somebody who imagined that there were intruders in his flat? So, for a while, Gregory said nothing, averted his gaze from the mess behind the sofa, sipped his tepid apple juice while trying to avoid the patches of encrusted dirt on the rim of his glass, and hoped that the discussion would turn back towards slightly more mundane, and manageable, matters.

Hans looked back at Gregory. It seemed as if Hans knew Gregory well enough to realise that any talk about intruders was making Gregory uncomfortable. A smile suddenly appeared on Hans' face. "Remember the good old days, Greg?", Hans said trying to sound cheerful, "when we used to zoom around with our mopeds, exploring the nightlife of Heidenhausen without a care in the world?"

Gregory was taken aback at Hans' sudden change of topic, but Hans' comment had immediately conjured up images of the two of them whizzing through Heidenhausen's back alleys when they were 14 and 15, Hans chatting up girls in front of the nightclub near the railway station (*not far from this flat*, Gregory thought with a shudder), the two of them speeding through deserted streets in the rain yelling as loud as they could at passers-by and not caring whether it woke up sleeping residents in the houses adjoining the streets. The thought left a nice warm feeling in Gregory's gut, indeed they had great times together when they were young.

"Or do you remember how I introduced you to Evelyn? You were so shy at the time", Hans continued.

Again, the image of the day when Hans had first introduced Evelyn to him sprang to Gregory's mind. Shy but nice Evelyn! Had he loved her after all? And yes, Hans had been instrumental in Gregory and Evelyn getting together. Suddenly Gregory felt that he was slipping back into his old role vis-à-vis Hans. Despite of Hans' mental breakdown, despite of his awful appearance with his greasy hair, his dishevelled looks, his fat tummy hanging out of his trousers, despite all this Hans still cast a spell over Gregory. Hans could still exude a feeling of being in control, of being the one who was guiding Gregory's life. Gregory was utterly taken aback at how easily he slipped back into this old role. Suddenly it seemed as if nothing had changed at all, that they were back in Hans' tidy old room and chatting about girls and school.

Gregory smiled back at Hans. He did not need to say anything. Hans saw that his comments had conjured up images of the past in Gregory, pleasant and warm images of their former friendship. For a short moment they both just looked at each other and smiled. At this moment, Gregory was glad, after all, that he had come to visit Hans.

But, at the same time, this forced remembrance of their more glorious past made Gregory also feel guilty that he had not seen Hans earlier. He felt immense remorse that he had not been there for his friends at his time of greatest need, when he had his psychotic break, when he was incarcerated at Bad Schlossenried. Why had he not seen Hans earlier? But, Gregory also rationalised, Hans had brought on most of this by himself. It was certainly not Gregory's fault that Hans' life had taken such a nasty turn. Sure, the fact that Hans' parents made him repeat Year 12 was stupid, and they all, including Hans and Gregory, already knew it at the time. Gregory was also convinced that Hans' decision to join the military service was not only due to his macho father's insistence, but that there was also something within Hans, about his personality, that made him rather suitable for the idiotic, simplistic, male-dominated military life that somebody like Gregory, or Bill, or Rufus, hated so much. And then Hans' idiotic decision to tell Monique that he had seen a hooker! What was he thinking? How could anyone be so stupid? And on top of this, Hans' fight with his father! In Gregory's mind, Hans' life unfolded as a series of wrong decisions taken at key intersections of Hans' life pathway. Going to the military already propelled him towards one of these thick branches of life from which it was more difficult to escape, exacerbated by his poor school results (despite repeating Year 12), his breakup with Monique, and beating up his father. Hans had himself chosen the branch of life he was currently on, and his poor decision-making and misjudgements had simply made it more difficult to veer off this chosen pathway.

But it was also clearly the mental illness that ensued from all this that kept Hans trapped on his life branch from which, Gregory feared, there may be no return. Hans was now firmly locked-in and path dependent on a self-destructive pathway, and there was not much somebody like Gregory could do about it. Looking over at Hans sipping his apple juice, Gregory wondered not for the first time whether there had already been signs of Hans' mental illness when they were kids. Hans constant hunger for attention, for wanting to be in the centre of things, for revelling in being adored as a flamboyant hunk and womaniser by his schoolmates. The fact that he constantly needed Gregory, and to some extent Bill, as mirrors, as counterparts, to show Hans how superior he was, at least for a few years when they were teenagers.

Were these already signs that things would go wrong later on in Hans' life?, Gregory wondered not for the first time. Seeing Hans in person again had evidently urged Gregory to think more deeply about what may have gone wrong with Hans. *But then all kids were like this at that age!*, Gregory conceded. *Ok, maybe there were hints of manic-depressive behaviour already at that time, but Hans' behaviour was certainly nothing out of the ordinary, compared to many of the other schoolkids. We were all somehow mad in our pubescent world, each one of us had weird things going on at the time. But the paranoid schizophrenic part of Hans' mental illness may be more difficult to account for. Clearly it must have something to do with the psychotic break Hans mentioned, and that seems to have been brought on by the self-inflicted episode with Monique. But again, was this just the tip of the iceberg? Did the other issues Hans had to deal with already predispose him towards such mental illness? Was Hans' weird experience with Elke Schmidt on his 14th birthday, for example, one of the many issues that would propel Hans on a pathway of deteriorating mental health? Or did the fact* *that he brushed the incident with Elke Schmidt aside as something 'normal', when Hans had first told me about it during our London trip in 1978, indicate that even at age 14 Hans was already psychologically scarred? Was the fact that Hans had boasted to me and Bill about the incident with Elke Schmidt, rather than being worried about what his father had made him do at the time, a sign of mental problems to come? But I certainly don't think that there was anything evident when we were kids that somebody like Hans would become a paranoid schizophrenic.* But Gregory also knew that he could no broach the topic of the incident with Elke Schmidt at this point in time. Obviously Hans would remember that he had told Gregory and Bill about it when they were in London, but this was not the time nor the occasion to embark on complex psycho-analysis.

"It has been so great seeing you", Hans said, jolting Gregory back from his sombre thoughts into reality. Hans was again kneading his hands. Gregory looked up at Hans. Maybe there was something else Hans wanted to tell him?

"I … I …", Hans stammered, looking pleadingly at Gregory, tears welling up in Hans' eyes again. "I often think about killing myself …"

There it is!, Gregory thought. *The cat is out of the bag!* He realised immediately that he had feared that Hans may be suicidal from the moment he had seen Hans, the messy flat, the pile of stuff behind the sofa. But why was Hans telling him this? Surely he must have mentioned this to his health carer, to his psychiatrist? Why should Gregory now carry the burden of this admission, the knowledge that he would now constantly have to worry about the fact that his friend could kill himself at any moment? Why was Hans doing this to him? This was precisely why Gregory had been so reluctant to visit Hans in the first place, and the reason why all their friends had shied away from seeing Hans.

Gregory again did not know how to answer, but both his own helplessness and the awkward position Hans was putting him in began to greatly worry Gregory. "But Hans …", he said after a while, "look … people care about you … you seem to have good support from the social services and your doctors … I … I am sure they can work something out …" But he also immediately realised how hollow his words must sound. Of course, Hans' life was miserable, he could not even properly and openly see his mum, he had no friends left, no social network to fall back on to, and he was suffering from severe mental illness and paranoia. And Gregory had been one of the many people who had abandoned Hans. But worst of all, Gregory knew that he did not want to get embroiled with Hans' problems. He had other things to do, he had a wife, a new university career which was very demanding, and he and Amelia wanted kids, which would, in turn, further curtail the time Gregory would have to help Hans. He could not spend time travelling back-and-forth between Britain and Germany to look after his friend. That was not his role. Surely, there must be others in the system, better trained and able than him who should look after Hans?

Gregory suddenly felt a strong urge to leave. It had been a mistake to come here after all. Hans' mental state was so bad that he did not need a friend, he needed urgent medical help. At that moment Gregory did not want to see Hans again. Hans was psychologically too unstable, and Gregory was not in a position to offer any solace, to help Hans. He was not a trained nurse, the demands were simply too great. Gregory knew that Hans had expected something different from their meeting, maybe a reconnection to their youth, to their 'golden years' together, to a time when Hans was still healthy and had his whole life still in front of him. But at this point in time Gregory knew that he could not offer that. Talking about the past may have opened more wounds than provided healing, and conjuring up ghosts from a long time ago was not always the wisest thing to do, especially with mentally unstable people. But Gregory was also utterly dismayed by his own cruelty and indifference. Here he was, with his delusional friend sitting opposite him, admitting that he had suicidal thoughts and was seeing intruders, and yet Gregory's reflex was one of escape, fleeing this difficult situation, like a coward with his tail between his legs.

Hans looked back at Gregory and must have seen the fear, worry, and possibly even disgust, etched in Gregory's face. He realised that no help could come from his friend, at least not this time. Gregory limply asked whether they could ring somebody from the health services to help Hans, but Hans tiredly waved the thought aside. They both knew that they had said all that could be said, discussed all that could be discussed, that they had reached the limit of what Gregory could, or could not, do for Hans. Leaving his half-full dirt-encrusted glass of apple juice on his stool, Gregory slowly got up, awkwardly looking at his watch and pretending that he had another engagement. They both knew that this was untrue, but the tension was left unspoken. They still knew each other well enough that they both understood that nothing else needed to be said. Gregory could not help Hans, and Hans could, in turn, not expect more from Gregory.

While Hans led Gregory slowly back to the front door they exchanged platitudes about how great it had been to see each other, and Gregory wished Hans best of luck and suggested again that he should contact his carer if his depression continued. Hans, in turn, wished Gregory best of luck with his job and to say hello to his wife. A last sad look, a brief raise of the hand, and Gregory rushed down the stairs, feeling Hans' looming and overpowering presence on the landing above him, but Gregory did not dare look back. *Out, out, out!*, was all Gregory could think. *Don't get embroiled with a suicidal paranoid schizophrenic!* Gregory darted through the main door of the apartment block, sped through the throng of begging kids, who had obviously waited for him, and made his way to his car, parked in one of the side streets. Back to his mum, his normal life in London, his wife, his job, away from this mental abyss, this psychological dead-end, this nightmare!

22

15th **December 2009.** Hans entered the bookshop. He was looking for a birthday card for his mum who was turning 72 in a few days' time. He had already bought flowers for her in a nearby shop, a bunch of red roses that had cost him a chunk of his monthly social allowance. He was hoping that the flowers would last until he saw his mum next. Hans steered his heavy frame along bookshelves towards the rows with birthday- and greeting-cards. He found it increasingly hard to move about these days, and he knew that he had grown morbidly fat over the years through lack of exercise. But then there were all these pills he had to take to keep his mental problems under control. They made him so lethargic! And Hans was convinced that the pills also made him fat, but he had long ago resigned himself to the fact that he had to take the pills. When he tried to live without them, the consequences had always been catastrophic, often landing him back in the psychiatric ward at Bad Schlossenried. Hans' feet were aching and his knees were hurting. The excess weight he was carrying around was beginning to take a heavy toll on his body.

Scanning the cards, Hans felt somebody standing in the aisle next to him. He slowly turned his head and realised that a young Turkish-looking girl was standing to his left. Hans glanced over towards her. She couldn't be much more than 18 and was the most beautiful girl he had ever seen. It had been an eternity since he had looked at a girl, let alone kissed or made love to a girl. Was Monique really the last girl he had sex with nearly 30 years ago? After all the young girls he'd had when he was a teenager this was almost unthinkable. Looking at the Turkish girl Hans started to become aroused, and a bulge became clearly visible in the baggy pants covering his fat legs. *Wow, this is still working!*, Hans thought looking down in astonishment at his bulging penis. The Turkish girl had not noticed him, nor his erection, and flicked through some of the birthday cards in front of her. Hans could not take his eyes of her, she was so beautiful!

"You are the most beautiful girl I have ever seen!", Hans blurted out while moving closer to the girl.

It took the Turkish girl a little while to realise that this utterly obese and ugly old man was talking to her. She turned around and looked at Hans.

Hans looked straight into her face and smiled. He took one of the red roses destined for his mum out of the bunch and held it towards the girl. "This is for you, you most beautiful apparition", Hans said.

The girl did not know what to do and looked around her in confusion to see whether anyone else was witnessing this embarrassing scene, but they were alone in the aisle. "Was willsch, olter Mah?" (what to you want, old man?) she asked in broad *Schwäbisch*.

"I just want to give you this rose because you are the most beautiful woman in the world", Hans replied, still smiling and holding out the rose.

"Fuck off you bloody creep!", the girl shouted back, grabbed the rose out of Hans' hand, threw it on the floor and trampled it in disgust. "Piss off!", she shouted again and stormed away.

A few customers standing in the other aisles turned their heads to see what the commotion was about, but quickly lost interest. Very sad, Hans looked at the trampled remains of the rose on the floor. So much for his bumbling attempt at flirting with a girl for the first time in many years! He looked around him embarrassed, but as nobody in the shop had reacted to what he had just done, Hans turned back at the row of cards and tried to find a suitable one for his mum. After a few minutes of searching, he spotted a card with a nice flower on it, which he thought his mum would like, and made his way towards the cashiers.

As was often the case with his ailing body, Hans felt the sudden urge for a piss. "Excuse me, have you got a toilet here?", he asked the cashier while paying. The cashier said that unfortunately they did not, but that the pub next door had a toilet. Hans thanked her, left the store and spotted the pub next door. He briefly looked at the sign which read *Zur Post*, with a smaller sign below indicating 'Döner Kebab served all day'. Although the pub looked rather ramshackle and run-down, Hans' bursting bladder forced him to go inside quickly. His urge to piss came on so suddenly these days – Hans guessed that it may be linked to the medication he was taking – that he had to hold his crotch to prevent him from wetting himself. With one hand on his crotch, he stormed up the few stairs into the pub, quickly looked around him to locate the *WC* sign and, after a brief glance at the young barman cleaning greasy glasses behind the bar who nodded that it was ok to use the toilet, Hans rushed to the toilet and relieved himself into the dirty and grimy urinal with an audible sigh of relief. The pungent smell of stale piss, together with the acrid stench of blue chlorine balls that congregated in a jumble near the urinal drain, made him wretch.

He zipped up his trousers, grabbed the bunch of roses he had placed on the toilet floor, and made his way through the pub towards the exit. Suddenly he felt a hand on his shoulder.

"Is that the guy?", a voice said behind him. Hans turned around to see who was holding him back. A tall young Turkish guy was holding him, looking back at a group of teens standing around a pool billiard table in the smoke-filled room. At first, Hans could not make out the shapes and faces in the foggy cigarette smoke mist, but a young girl peeled herself from the group of people and walked towards Hans. "Yes, that's him", said the young Turkish girl from the shop. "That's the fat old guy who gave me a rose and made a pass at me".

It took a while for Hans to grasp what was happening. He realised that he had walked straight into a pub frequented mainly by Turkish teens. The girl he had accosted in the bookshop was one of them. He had walked straight into the hornets' nest!

"Why did you give my girlfriend a rose?", the young tall Turkish boy asked in a German heavily tinged with a Turkish accent. "Have you two got something going?"

It was suddenly eerily quiet in the pub. The other teenagers had stopped talking and playing pool. They began moving closer towards Hans.

"I … I … Look …", Hans stammered, not knowing what to say. This was a rather unfortunate situation. "Look, I didn't mean to offend anyone … I … I …"

"What?", the Turkish boy shouted back. "Are you fucking my girlfriend, you fat old slob?", and he started to shake Hans violently.

Hans began to feel dizzy. "What? Fucking your girlfriend? No … I … I just thought she looked so beautiful that I wanted to give her a rose."

"What is going on, you fat ugly turd?", the Turkish boy replied, grabbing the bunch of roses out of Hans' hand, throwing them on the ground and trampling the roses to pulp. "What do you want with my girl?"

Seeing her boyfriend's anger, the Turkish girl had edged backwards. Her friends were still standing stock still behind her, nobody dared say a word.

"Look, I … apologise", Hans stammered. "I didn't know she had a boyfriend. I … I didn't mean anything by it. Honestly … it was just a … just a …"

But the Turkish boy did not let Hans finish his sentence. He grabbed a billiard queue and smashed it down towards Hans. It would have hit Hans square on the head had Hans not put his right forearm up to protect himself. Hans could hear the bones in his arm being crushed to pieces, he felt an indescribable pain shooting through his elbow, and he crashed to the floor in agony. The Turkish boy lashed out even harder at Hans who was trying his utmost to protect his head from the heavy blows from the billiard queue. Every time he was hit, Hans could hear more bones being shattered in his arm. He did not know how much longer he could hold up his broken arm to protect himself. Just when Hans had completely collapsed onto the floor and could no longer hold up his arm, the friends of the Turkish boy had finally mustered the courage to hold him back. But even three of them found it hard to constrain the Turkish boy who, red in the face and foaming at the mouth, continued to try to lash out at Hans. It was only when the young barman came rushing to the scene that they managed to disarm the Turkish boy and take the queue out of his hands.

Hans lay on the floor, whimpering with agony. His right arm felt like it had been torn to pieces.

"What have you done, Recep?", the barman looked reproachfully at the young Turkish boy. "You nearly killed him! And all this for a bloody flower!"

Recep just stood there, still breathing heavily and red in the face with rage. His girlfriend had retreated to the back of the room, her right hand cupped in front of her mouth in disgust, sobbing loudly and utterly dismayed.

"Well, someone call an ambulance quickly!", the barman shouted, trying to cajole the shocked group of youngsters into action.

23

3rd **June 2010.** Gregory took a big swig from the tall *Hefeweizen* beer glass in front of him. How he missed the yeasty taste of this wheat beer back in England where all you could get in most pubs were stale luke-warm ales and mass-produced tasteless lagers. Bill, Rufus, and Matthias, the guitar player from their old rock band, were sitting at the table with him in their favourite pub in Heidenhausen, each with a different brew in front of them. The pub was slowly filling with patrons, but Gregory did not recognise anyone. *How young everybody looks!*, Gregory realised with astonishment. *It feels like only yesterday that I was sitting here, when we were just finishing school. How quickly time has passed and how much has happened since in all our lives!* Bill still had his long hair and had become an academic like Gregory himself, Rufus had gone into banking and was doing very well financially (as evidenced by the pricey Rolex watch on his wrist), and Matthias who, with his passion for music, had gone into the music business managing a moderately famous southern German rock band called *Spiritual Meltdown*. With a nostalgic look, Gregory glanced at his three friends, thinking back at the time when they were all much younger, more innocent, more carefree.

But Gregory could not fully enjoy the meeting with his friends. The reason he had come to Heidenhausen was that his mother had unexpectedly been diagnosed with terminal bowel cancer. Not knowing how much time she had left, upon hearing the diagnosis Gregory had immediately rushed to Heidenhausen to see his mum. She was still at home but in much pain and under heavy medication, and it was only a matter of time until she would have to go to hospital. Gregory had always been very close to his mum, and he felt very sad about her condition, although he knew there was not much he could do other than just be by her side. Coincidentally, the time of his visit had fallen on a public holiday which Bill, Rufus and Matthias had also taken advantage of to see their families in Heidenhausen. Gregory could not remember when the three of them had last been together in the pub. Indeed, this may have been the first time that they had gone to the pub in this specific constellation of four friends. While Gregory, Bill and Matthias had often gone for a pint after practice sessions with their rock band, Rufus had not been part of their band and had never much mingled with either Bill or Matthias.

They had started their evening with the usual platitudes discussing their jobs and their families. Rufus talked for a while about his recent divorce and how difficult it was for him to see his teenage son. Bill had mentioned his recent academic sabbaticals to Hawaii, eliciting jocular teasing from the others about the 'hard life' of academics, while Matthias had talked at length about some of the things happening off-stage with *Spiritual Meltdown*, especially the frequent sexual encounters with young female fans and groupies which seemed to confirm all the clichés associated with a touring rock band.

Looking back, Gregory could not remember exactly at what point their discussion had turned towards Hans Schlesier. Possibly it was linked to them chatting about school and former friends, or maybe one of them had just mentioned the latest Heidenhausen gossip involving people they knew. What Gregory did remember was that, despite each of them having to drive home later, they had by then been at least on their third pints, with Rufus possibly on his fourth, and that they were, therefore, getting rather inebriated.

"Did you hear the latest about Hans Schlesier?", Rufus had started the ball rolling, slurring his speech which made the others wonder whether he would still be able to drive home. "Apparently he's been in a fight."

After his fateful last visit to see Hans in his flat in the decrepit part of Heidenhausen so long ago in 1993, Gregory had not seen or heard much about Hans. It was not that he had forgotten about Hans. He knew that Hans and his sad story would always be somewhere in the back of his mind, but Gregory's life in England had completely taken over any free time he may have had and had kept him too busy to constantly think about Hans. Indeed, his job kept him busy, but it was also that Amelia and he now had a son who was 12 and the greatest joy of Gregory's life, and on top of all this they were travelling a lot both for work and pleasure. As a result, Gregory's visits to Heidenhausen had become rather sporadic – a fact his mum was constantly complaining about. And yet over the past 17 years or so there had always been a feeling of guilt in Gregory's mind, guilt that he had abandoned his former best friend Hans after their last meeting, guilt about his weakness of not being able to help a friend who had been evidently suicidal at the time and at the brink of another mental breakdown. As before, Gregory had only heard the odd snippets of gossip about Hans, the odd bits and bobs about Hans' strange behaviour, about further spells at Bad Schlossenried, and about Hans' overall inability to cope with life. Although he was not sure whether the pub after three or four pints was the right time and place to talk about Hans with his friends, Gregory had to nonetheless admit that he was curious to hear the latest gossip about Hans. What had his former friend done this time?

"Yes, I also heard something, I think it was my mum who mentioned it", Matthias replied, taking a large swig from his beautifully frothy and smooth *Bitburger Pils*. "Apparently he accosted some young Turkish girl in a shop and was then beaten up by her boyfriend."

222

"Yes, another weird story about this lunatic Hans!", Bill chipped in. "I don't know what it is about him, but he always seems to be looking for trouble. I heard that he was beaten up inside that Turkish pub by the station, God knows what he was doing there."

"Apparently he got badly injured", Rufus continued the story, "and had to be stitched up in hospital with multiple fractures. I heard that he went back again to the loony bin in Schlossenried after that."

This was the first time Gregory had heard about the latest mishap that had befallen Hans, and he felt immensely sad about it. Was this latest crisis linked to yet another of these weird decisions Hans had taken that propelled him further down his unsustainable life pathway? What was Hans doing? Had he not learned anything from his past mishaps? Were these wrong turns he took in life solely explicable through Hans' mental condition?

"Have you heard anything, Greg?", Bill enquired. "After all, you're the one who was always closest to Hans."

Could Gregory detect a hint of reproach here from Bill? Was this discussion again exposing some of the complex power relationships of their friendship circle, akin to the fateful London trip where Hans and Bill were openly vying for Gregory's attention, a fight Bill had clearly won at the time? Gregory was not sure whether he wanted to go there, especially not after three or four pints. Could they, as mature and successful adults, not put behind them these petty power games from when they were kids? Would Bill's animosity and jealousy over Hans continue for the rest of their lives?

"No, I have not heard anything", Gregory replied meekly and slightly annoyed. "You seem to know much more than I do. In fact, I have not seen Hans since 1993 when I last visited him in the flat allocated to him by social services ... You know, in that awful area near the red-light district. It was a tough visit at the time, as Hans mentioned that he was suicidal. To be honest, I did not know how to react at the time … I have not seen him since." Gregory did not know why he was telling his friends about this meeting at this point in time, maybe the pints had loosened his tongue? If he remembered correctly, this was the first time he had mentioned that Hans had admitted that he thought about killing himself.

"Yeah, Hans was always pretty weird when he was young …", Bill replied, taking another swig from his *Andechser Weizen*, an especially strong and delicious dark yeast wheat beer brewed (since AD 1066) by one of the Bavarian monasteries on the basis of the German beer purity law (with only hops, barley, water and yeast allowed as basic ingredients). "Do you remember the time when he brought these two young tarts with him and started having sex with them right in front of us? We must have been about 14 or so at the time …"

Gregory was not sure whether Bill was referring to the strange occasion he still remembered so vividly when Martina and Ursula had joined Hans and him and Bill on the lawn outside their school. That was indeed strange behaviour, although Gregory was not sure how and whether it could be linked to Hans' latest escapade. And then there was Hans' strange behaviour when Gregory surprised him having sex back in Brittany, although his friends did not know about that episode. And, of course, there was also the sad story about Hans' 14th birthday present where he was forced to have sex with Elke Schmidt, which only Bill and Gregory knew about. *Could all these weird episodes explain why Hans continued to willy-nilly accost any beautiful woman he saw?*, Gregory wondered. *Were they the reason Hans had such strange attitudes and behaviour towards women he thought attractive?* But even in his progressively more inebriated state, Gregory was not willing to divulge these thoughts to his friends.

"I always thought that Hans was weird", Bill continued.

Here we go again, Gregory thought. *As I feared, this is beginning to turn into one of these evenings where Hans will be the centre of our discussions, the butt of jokes, exaggerated banter, the endless punchbag for desultory and derogatory comments. We have been here before, in this very same pub!* This was not where Gregory wanted to go, especially as he had enjoyed the evening before talk turned to Hans. But he also knew that he was in no position to change the course of the discussion at this point. What was going to happen now seemed inevitable.

"Yes, remember the time when Hans latched on to this weirdo … this peasant boy …what did we call him … 'Rucki' … that's it, 'Rucki' … because he always had this tick, jerking the right side his mouth upwards when he spoke", Rufus said, imitating Klaus Hintermaier's tick while jabbering, which elicited raucous laughter from Bill and Matthias.

"Yeah, they became almost inseparable", Matthias chipped in, "in fact so inseparable that some of us thought that Hans had gone over to the other side … you know … become a faggett!"

That was the first time Gregory had heard that theory. He was getting increasingly annoyed at the turn the discussion was taking, and he hated the arrogance and superiority evident in the comments of his three friends. How could they dare talk about Hans in this way, especially as they had been among those at school who admired Hans most for his way with girls and his debonair and flamboyant demeanour at the time? He almost felt as if he had to defend Hans, stand up for him in front of these three bullies.

"Yes, it's weird how Hans changed when we were in … hang on, which year would it have been when it all seemed to change for Hans?", Bill enquired.

"Year 12", both Rufus and Matthias replied in unison. To Gregory's increasing annoyance, they were evidently beginning to enjoy this discussion.

"Yes, Year 12 …", Bill continued. "He seemed to have completely lost it by then. All his womanising that had led to nothing. After all, it really transpired in Year 12 that Hans was really just hot air. And then this weird decision to repeat Year 12."

"Mmmmmh, that was very strange indeed", Matthias picked up the banter. "And it did not help him at all, as his A-level results at the end were pretty dismal. They guy was simply too thick for the *Gymnasium*. He should have realised that years earlier and gone to a *Realschule* or even a *Hauptschule*."

Gregory could now barely hide his anger at his friends' slanderous talk about Hans and their suggestion that Hans was only fit for the lower, more vocational, tier of German schools. After all, Hans had not been that bad at school, and there were several other pupils in their school class who had struggled even more. He clenched his fists in fury, but just managed to hold back telling off his friends. In the end, most of what they said was true, or at least chimed with what Gregory had thought over these past decades about Hans' last years at school.

"And all his talk at the time about what a great military career he would have after joining the military!", Bill said. "Remember when he came into this very pub just a few months after enrolling with the military, all dressed up in his stupid military uniform and greeting everybody with a soldier's salute. Totally weird!"

Gregory could not remember this specific episode with Hans greeting them with a military salute, but maybe Gregory had not been in the pub with them at the time. But he certainly remembered Bill's avowed pacifism and strong aversion of anything that had to do with the military, and he was also not surprised that Hans would flaunt his new military uniform and associated militaristic behaviour at the time.

"… and then he did not even complete his military service! Went to the loony bin at Bad Schlossenried instead", Bill continued, taking another sip of his *Andechser*, smiling back at his friends and evidently very pleased with himself about having dug out yet another dreadful episode in Hans' life.

And only I know the real reason why Hans had a mental breakdown at the time!, Gregory thought to himself, still unsure whether to chip into the conversation and to defend Hans' behaviour at the time.

"And how often has Hans now been at the loony bin in Schlossenried?", Rufus enquired. "Four or five times?"

There ensued a brief debate about how often Hans had been incarcerated in the mental asylum. Gregory himself was unsure how often Hans had been committed to spend time at Schlossenried. *Evidently the doctors there were not doing a great job at addressing Hans' mental problems!*, he thought not for the first time. *Poor guy!*

"My mum has mentioned several times that she's seen Hans roaming the streets of Heidenhausen, looking all filthy and dishevelled and mumbling to himself, completely oblivious to his surroundings", Matthias continued the tirade. Although Gregory was again appalled at the thought of his former idol having stooped so low, he could well believe that this story was true, judging from Hans' looks and demeanour during his last visit, the pile of junk he saw behind Hans' sofa at the time, and the fact that Hans seemed to completely lose the plot occasionally and hide from 'intruders' behind his sofa. Hans the flamboyant hunk and womaniser reduced to a mumbling, dirty beggar! How life's turns could be unpredictable!

Nonetheless, Gregory continued to be very annoyed at the turn the discussion had taken and at his friends who were lashing out against Hans who could not defend himself. Although inwardly he knew that most of the things that had been said about Hans were probably true, he also felt a constant urge to defend Hans, to dispel some of the myths surrounding him, to try and explain why Hans had acted the way he had since they left school. But somehow Gregory was too embroiled in this split allegiance between Hans and his friends. He simply did not have the energy, or the courage, to start a huge defence of Hans, to stand up for him, certainly not at this point and after four pints. He also felt too detached from Hans after having last seen him 17 years ago, too removed from the great, but short, time they had spent together when they were teenagers. But Gregory also felt sad that the evening had turned towards discussing Hans and bringing up all these former divides, jealousies, intrigues and nastiness that he thought they had all left behind now as adults with children of their own. The three or four pints had clearly loosened everybody's tongues, had allowed all of them to slip back into the roles they occupied when they were 17 or 18, with all the associated power games, vindictiveness and arrogance that Gregory thought they had all left behind a long time ago.

While his friends continued their tirades about Hans, digging up ever more dirt and ludicrous gossip, Gregory had increasingly withdrawn from the discussion, quietly sipping his fourth and last beer and feeling increasingly detached from his three friends. The others were so inebriated, or indeed drunk, by then that they had not realised that Gregory had withdrawn from the discussion. Matthias patted Rufus on the back for another ludicrous story about what Hans may or may not have done recently, while Bill continued to chatter away about how he had always hated Hans, never really looked up to him anyway, always saw Hans as a fraud, blah blah blah … Gregory just watched his friends but he no longer heard what they were saying. He saw their mouths move, but what they uttered no longer made sense to him. He saw their frowns, their laughs, their excitement at digging out ever more unbelievable gossip about Hans, but he now only saw their faces as nasty masks, their ugly wrinkles ever more evident, spittle coming out of Rufus' mouth as he shouted out another obscenity about Hans, the raucous laughter of Bill echoing across the entire pub after telling what he thought was another excellent joke about Hans' behaviour at school.

Gregory had had enough. Without saying a further word, he stood up unsteadily, mumbled some excuse that he was feeling tired, paid for his four pints at the bar, and swaggered outside without looking back at his friends who sat there perplexed at his sudden departure. Gregory stood outside the pub for a while, breathing in the fresh night air. He glanced at the closed shops, the few passers-by hurrying home or to nearby restaurants and bars, the cream-coloured taxis with their mainly Turkish drivers waiting for business, the late-night buses on their final rounds. This was not how he had imagined this evening to pan out. He had been looking forward to having a few pints with Bill, Rufus and Matthias, to talk about what they had been up to, how their kids were doing, their jobs and careers. But, instead, it had turned into a nasty mud-slinging match with regard to who could dig out the vilest stories about Hans. About a person they, at one point, had all claimed to be 'best friend' with!

Still utterly disgusted at the behaviour of his friends, a thought began to form in Gregory's mind. Although he had not planned this at all during this brief visit to see his dying mum, he would use his last day in Heidenhausen to see Hans again. Gregory felt that he owed this to his old friend after the dreadful scene in the pub. This, he felt, was the only way he could alleviate his bad conscience for not having stood up more for Hans in the pub in front of his friends. Yes! That was the right thing to do. He would visit Hans again! Walking briskly away from the pub towards his car, Gregory hoped that Hans still had the same phone number he had 17 years ago, and that he was at home and not on one of his spells back in Bad Schlossenried.

24

4th June 2010. Gregory was very unsure about whether this meeting with Hans was a good idea. All his resolve from the evening before seemed to have evaporated. But Gregory did not want to back down, not now after having taken 17 years to muster the courage to see his friend again.

Luckily Hans' phone number had not changed, and it had been no problem getting hold of Hans when Gregory made the call. But Hans' reaction on the phone had been very weird. At first, it took Hans a while to recognise who was at the other end of the phone, although Gregory did not blame him after 17 years of silence on his part. But once Hans had realised who Gregory was, the exuberance with which he greeted the possibility of a meeting had nonetheless taken

Gregory by surprise. Hans had said that he could not wait to see Gregory again, that he was available any time as it was Sunday, and that he had no other plans for the day. But Gregory could also clearly hear that Hans' speech was slow and slurred which, together with Hans' slowness of recognising at first who Gregory was, suggested that he was still under heavy medication and possibly not quite 'with it'.

Gregory replayed these thoughts in his mind as he stood in front of the squalid block of flats in this awful derelict part of Heidenhausen, the same flat where Gregory had visited Hans back in 1993. There were no begging kids this time, but to Gregory it seemed as if he had stood on that same spot just a short while ago. Was it really 17 years since he was last here? How could he let so much time elapse before seeing his old friend again? And yet, after his experience visiting Hans last time, there was this terrible nagging doubt as to whether this was the right thing to do. Based on the rumours flitting about during the awkward discussion with his friends in the pub the evening before, what had happened to Hans since their last meeting and how easy would it be to communicate with him this time?

After what was probably over a minute of hesitation, Gregory pressed the doorbell marked with a faded and yellowed name-tag that read 'H. Schlesier'. The buzzer activating the opening of the door could be heard almost instantaneously. Hans was evidently expecting him, maybe he had even watched him approach the flat from his balcony, Gregory wondered. He made his way up the stairs. Nothing much seemed to have changed in the block of flats, with strange unfamiliar noises emanating from the doors on each floor and echoing eerily around the staircase.

As last time, Hans stood on the fifth-floor landing in front of his flat. And, as last time, Gregory was shocked by how much Hans had changed. During all this time since he had last seen Hans, Gregory had a picture of Hans in his mind as he was during their last meeting: fat, ugly, dishevelled, but still with a semblance of the person he had been before all the problems had started. But the old man standing on the landing now was almost unrecognisable to Gregory. Hans had lost almost all his hair, only a few wild clumps of whitish hair remained above his ears and had been neglectfully shoved across his bald and shiny scalp. Hans' brown eyes had lost all their lustre, sheen and youthfulness, and although Hans was smiling broadly at seeing Gregory come up the last steps, his eyes remained dull and vacant as if Hans' mind was no longer connected to reality. There was, indeed, an immense sadness in Hans' eyes, amplified by deep wrinkles that spread out like crow's feet to the left and right of each eye. But it was not this stare of a person that was more a corpse than a living being that shocked Gregory most, but how much fatter Hans had grown since their last meeting. Hans had been very obese when he had last seen him back in 1993, but the person now in front of Gregory was morbidly obese, with flesh added everywhere, large chunks of which had slid down towards his waist like mud sliding down a hill. Hans' tummy was now so big and bulging and overhanging his trousers that Hans' hips were barely visible. The cumbersome way Hans heaved his heavy body around just to turn to face Gregory betrayed how much Hans was suffering from lugging this excess weight around. *He can barely move, he is so fat!*, Gregory thought, trying to hide his disgust. One of Hans' arms was in plaster which reached beyond his elbow and with metallic pins sticking out everywhere, suggesting that the cast was protecting multiple fractures from the fight Hans had recently had, and which had been mentioned with so much misplaced hilarity by Gregory's friends in the pub. As a result, Hans' plastered arm was sticking out in an unnatural and awkward angle making him look even more strange and unfamiliar. Hans held out his arms and they both awkwardly embraced, with Gregory trying to be as gentle as possible so as not to knock Hans' broken arm. Like last time, Gregory was repulsed by the smell of stale sweat emanating from Hans, but he nonetheless held the embrace for as long as Hans wanted to hold him.

"It is … so good … to see you … Greg", Hans slurred, the slowness and thickness of his voice confirming that he was still under the heavy influence of strong anti-depressants and tranquilizers. Gregory saw that Hans' hands were shaking and that his gait was very unsteady as they stepped into his flat, further supporting Gregory's suspicions about how the heavy medication was affecting Hans. Hans let out a hysteric laugh, just like last time when they had met. This reminded Gregory of how he had struggled at their last meeting to interpret what this laughter meant. Was it just nervousness on the part of Hans or was there something deeper, such as a medically-induced loss of emotional control, involved here?

"It is good to see you again, Hans", Gregory replied awkwardly, again lost for words in what he knew would be another very awkward encounter.

Hans laughed again hysterically and took Gregory through the narrow hallway into the living room and to the same chair Gregory still remembered from their last meeting. Gregory looked around him. Hans' flat did not seem to have changed much, the same mess lying everywhere, the kitchen a riot of dirty pans, pots and dishes. Possibly the walls looked a bit lighter, maybe social services had arranged the flat to be painted since last time? This time there was also no pile of bedding and discarded foot wrappers behind the sofa. Maybe Hans was on one of his better spells where he did not feel so scared of 'intruders', or maybe he was now on stronger medication that kept his paranoia better under control, Gregory wondered.

It took Hans a while to lower his heavy frame onto the sofa opposite Gregory. Hans had realised how Gregory was looking at him with a mixture of disgust and bemusement, and Hans was evidently embarrassed by how much he had changed since their last meeting.

"So, what happened to your arm?", Gregory asked in order to break the ice, although he knew the answer.

"I ... I had a little ... run-in with the boyfriend ... the boyfriend of a girl a while ago", Hans replied with the same slurred, slow and thick voice. He evidently had problems speaking and getting all his thoughts together, Gregory thought with sadness. *Or maybe he is no longer used to talking much?*, Gregory wondered.

"He … he hit me with a billiard queue … He would have killed me had other people nearby not intervened …", Hans continued. "It was … it was a multiple fracture, and the doctors had to put in several metal pins. It … it has taken forever to heal and I have been wearing this cast for months now. It … it still hurts like hell …"

Gregory was not sure whether he should probe Hans more about what happened. For fear of appearing impolite he did not want to seem too curious about Hans' most recent catastrophe.

"It was … it was totally stupid, really …", Hans carried on unprompted. "A misunderstanding really … I had seen that girl … this most beautiful girl in a shop … and I … I don't know what came over me … but I just gave her a rose out of a bunch I happened to have for my mum … not thinking much about it … you know … just telling the girl that I thought she looked lovely. Girls like that, you know …"

And here we are again!, Gregory thought, *Hans still trying to lecture me about what girls like! After all this, he thinks he still has a lesson to convey to somebody like me about how to treat girls. Unbelievable! And I slip yet again immediately back into my role of naïve and innocent friend of Hans who, even with his ugly looks and illness, wants to lecture me on how to handle girls. And look what it has done for him! Broken arm and nearly beaten to death, the stupid … stupid …!* But Gregory knew that it was dangerous to continue with this line of thought and that, after all this time, he should no longer see Hans' condescending comments about girls as a threat. After all, this was not a confrontation.

The times when Hans had heavily influenced Gregory's love life were long gone, and Hans was now a very ill person under heavy medication. *Give the guy a break!*, Gregory chided himself inwardly. He was here to see his friend, to find out how Hans had been over all these years since their last meeting, not to bring back memories about their former unequal power positions vis-à-vis each other.

But at the same time, Gregory's sub-conscience also reminded him that he was here because he felt guilty, especially after the nasty discussion about Hans with his friends in the pub the evening before had brought home to him how much he had neglected Hans over all these years. *Don't kid yourself!*, Gregory thought, trying to look back at Hans with as much sympathy as his struggling and confused mind could muster.

"This sounds pretty rough, Hans", was all Gregory could think of as a reply. "You need to be more careful". But he immediately realised that this sounded rather condescending and may be taken the wrong way by a person who was mentally unstable. But Hans seemed happy with Gregory's reply and smiled back at his friend.

"Since the incident about … being beaten up, I had to briefly go back to the clinic again", Hans continued his explanation. "You know … that dreadful place Bad Schlossenried. I think I have passed more time there than in this flat over the past … 25 years or so."

The attack by the girl's boyfriend must have triggered another psychotic shock, thought Gregory, remembering what Hans had told him last time about how the episode with

Monique had seemingly caused his first nervous breakdown. *Poor guy!*

Hans looked around him nervously and emitted his hysteric laughter again. "I thought we could … we could go for a drink somewhere", he said, looking expectantly at Gregory. "It would do me good to get out of here. I … I have not left the flat for a few days now, since I last went shopping."

This was rather unexpected and Gregory was not sure whether this was a good idea. First of all, in the absence of a lift how would Hans manage to get his heavy frame down five flights of stairs? And where would they go for a drink? The area nearby was so awful that it did not appeal much to Gregory.

"That sounds like a good idea", Gregory nonetheless replied meekly. Maybe talking to Hans outside of this oppressive flat would lighten his mood a bit and possibly make it easier to talk?

It took Hans an eternity to put on his coat, and Gregory had to help him put on his shoes and tie the shoelaces as Hans could no longer reach down to his feet. *How does he cope on his own?*, was Gregory's immediate thought. But once on the stairs Gregory was surprised at how nimbly Hans managed to descend each step at a time, carefully placing his fat legs in the right place and holding on tightly to the handrail. As they exited the building, Gregory asked where Hans wanted to go, hoping it would not be a pub or café where people would recognise him. He had to admit that he was embarrassed being seen with Hans outside, and, although he told himself repeatedly that this was silly, he nonetheless

238

scanned the street they walked down for people who may know him. *You stupid hypocrite!*, Gregory chided himself, *this shows again that you are first and foremost thinking about yourself and your reputation in Heidenhausen and not about Hans. You are only here to alleviate your bad conscience!*, he admitted to himself, hoping that Hans, slowly walking beside him, was not reading his mind. But inwardly Gregory also hoped that Hans would not emit his hysteric laughter again while they were surrounded by other people.

Hans led them towards a little café at the corner of the street where his flat was located. Gregory was surprised that the place actually looked nice and inviting, with a large outdoor terrace framed with short trees and bushes that sheltered it from the noise of a nearby bustling intersection. In early June it was pleasantly warm, not too hot but just right, with the odd cumulus clouds whizzing across the azure blue sky and occasionally blocking out the strong sunlight. It was certainly warm enough to sit outside and they chose one of the tables tucked away at the corner of the terrace. There were only two young couples eating ice cream and drinking coffee at tables at the other end of the terrace, and Gregory was relieved that he did not recognise them (or they him). Hans and Gregory sat down and ordered two soft drinks from the waitress.

"I can't drink any alcohol because of the medication…", Hans admitted with a shy smile, but he knew that Gregory understood. Gregory, in turn, did not feel like having another beer after the four pints he had had the evening before, the after-effects of which he was still feeling in the form of a persistent throbbing headache and a slight sluggishness characteristic for a hang-over.

"You know you were always my best friend …", Hans blurted out rather unexpectedly.

Gregory had not expected this kind of direct statement so soon after sitting down, and it took him a while to think about what to say.

"I know Hans", he eventually said, looking into Hans' eyes. Was there still a hint of emotion in Hans' extinguished, dull and lustreless eyes? Was the real Hans, the Hans from over 30 years ago when they were teenagers, still there, hidden behind this broken façade?

"And … you know … I always admired you, Greg."

This statement took Gregory even more by surprise. "That surprises me, Hans", Gregory replied sincerely. "As you know, you had always been the one we looked up to at school, our idol and the eternal womaniser with the good looks …", but Gregory immediately regretted his words, realising that it made Hans probably even more self-conscious about how negatively he had changed.

"Yeah, but you were the one with the brains … and all these talents … you know with music and singing … I could only dream of that …", Hans replied with a sullen voice.

While sipping his drink, Gregory thought for a while about what Hans had just said. All his life he had thought that his relationship with Hans was relatively one-sided, with him always looking up to Hans. But now Hans was saying that he also admired him. Was that really true, or was Hans' memory clouded by the distance of time or the medication he was taking.

Before Gregory could answer, Hans blurted out, staring straight at Gregory: "But you abandoned me … You suddenly spent all your time with Bill … with that band of yours … with that choir … You wanted nothing to do with me any more …"

This was not the discussion that Gregory had intended to have with his friend, especially after such a long time of not seeing each other. But what did he expect? Hans had not seen him for 17 years, and although for whatever reason this topic had not been broached during their last meeting so long ago, it was Hans' perfect right to bring up the topic of how their friendship had disintegrated. Why should Hans not mention it? But Gregory was unprepared for what could be a very difficult discussion. He closed his eyes for a moment and thought about how best to respond.

"Well, you know Hans", Gregory replied meekly, "a lot of things were going on at the time … you know when we were about 16 or 17 … It wasn't that I did no longer enjoy your company. We had such a great time together … But, as you know, other things began to interest me, music especially … and that was where Bill … and Matthias … became more important. You and I shared our moped outings and talking about girls together, but Bill and I shared music and other things … That was just a normal evolution … I think."

Gregory was not sure whether his answer was convincing. How could you, 30 years later, defend decisions made when you were teenagers? Maybe Hans was asking the impossible here?

"But it changed so quickly!", Hans replied, this time a bit more animated. His eyes had taken on a bit of an angry sheen, the discussion seemed to have taken Hans out of his medically-induced stupor. *Had Hans planned this ambush all along since I rang him earlier this morning?*, Gregory began to wonder. *But I guess he is just using the occasion to vent the anger that must have built up in him over so many years. Was the disruption of our friendship maybe one of the many factors that contributed to Hans' mental disintegration at the time?*, Gregory asked himself not for the first time.

"And on this awful trip to London you totally neglected me …", Hans continued, his voice almost rising to a shriek and ending with his tell-tale hysteric laugh. "You only did things with Bill … that … that bloody arrogant *Schweiss* kid …"

Here we go!, Gregory thought. *Every time we meet it comes back to these old stupid divisions! Schweiss-Kinder here, peasant kids there, stupid artificial divisions! But Hans has evidently thought about these issues in all these years. It's as if he has waited to see me again, so as to ambush me into this discussion! And now it is too late to get out of it. I am here, Hans is here, I need to explain what happened, even if it will hurt both of us. But will Hans' frail mental situation be able to stand up to a deep discussion about our friendship?,* Gregory nonetheless wondered as he pondered his answer.

"C'mon, Hans!", Gregory tried to defuse the tension. "I thought you and Bill had been friends? He wasn't that bad! Sure, he was pushy and I often felt torn between spending time with you or him, but, remember, we also did a lot of things together with Bill, especially when we all had girlfriends and often went to the disco with you and Bill in nearby Margelstetten."

As Gregory was talking, vivid memories about a very enjoyable trip to the Margelstetten disco with Hans, Bill, Evelyn, Monique and Bill's girlfriend at the time suddenly came to the surface. He had not thought about this for years! This had been one of the occasions when Bill and Hans had done something together and had, seemingly, enjoyed being in each other's company, even dancing together on the strobe-lit disco dancefloor to music by the Bee Gees, Wings and Van Halen.

But Hans only looked back glumly at Gregory. He was unwilling to take the bait.

"I could equally accuse you of abandoning our friendship by hanging out with Klaus Hintermaier all the time ...", Gregory continued, but he immediately regretted saying this. He knew deep inside that Hans had latched on to Klaus long after Gregory's friendship with Bill had become closer.

"Klaus was an asshole!", Hans replied defiantly. "I thought he was a good friend ... and for a while he helped me a bit at school ... But in the end I think he just used me. He never came to visit me after ... after I got ill."

This chimed with Gregory's impression of Klaus at the time, although he had never spoken to Hans about it.

"Yes, sure ... I was jealous of Bill", Hans admitted, "there was no doubt about that. But I also admit that Klaus played a role in wrenching you and me apart. He never liked you, you know ..."

Gregory was astonished how Hans' formerly slurred and slow speech had quickened and how lively he was defending his case. Maybe this discussion, although tough, was helping Hans? Gregory certainly had to admit that he also had never liked Klaus, that an element of jealousy probably also crept into his relationship with 'Jerky', and he vividly remembered the battles to death at the ping-pong table when he ended up playing the 'finals' against Klaus. In the end, they were both vying for Hans' attention at the time, but they were also trying to slaughter each other by winning at table tennis, by hitting ever more vicious shots that were aimed at 'annihilating' and 'killing' your opponent. *Sport as war!*, Gregory smiled inwardly.

"But I guess our friendship was already over by then anyway …", Hans said.

This statement deeply shocked Gregory. He had never thought about it that way, but maybe Hans was right? Maybe their friendship had already been on the brink, with or without Klaus Hintermaier. Maybe they had drifted apart so much already with regard to their interests, their school performance, their ambitions in life after school?

"Look Hans", Gregory replied with as conciliatory a voice as possible. "I am not sure this discussion is leading us anywhere. After all, we are talking about things that happened so long ago. We were just mere kids then! Is it really possible to criticise from our current vantage point what we may have, or may not have, done over 30 years ago? We were different people then. I can't remember why I took certain decisions one or two years ago, let alone over 30 years ago! It is hard for me to reconnect with the way I was feeling and thinking at the time, and probably this will be the same for you?"

But Hans did not appear to have heard Gregory's half-hearted excuse. He had talked himself into a rant now and stubbornly continued with his diatribe. "Did you know that Klaus was … was instrumental in my decision to repeat Year 12?"

Gregory had to recollect his thoughts. Evidently, Hans was not letting these old stories go. "But did you not tell me, when we were at Monique's place in Rennes, that it was mainly your father who pushed you to repeat Year 12?", Gregory replied surprised.

Hans looked deeply into Gregory's eyes. *Maybe he is impressed that I remember this detail from a discussion we had 30 years ago?*, Gregory wondered.

Hans averted his gaze again. "My father played an important role in that decision, but it was Klaus who ultimately persuaded me that repeating the year would be good for my final *Abitur* results. We all know now that this did not work out at all. On the contrary. I was very unhappy in my new year group as everybody was so much younger than I was, and I lost … I lost almost all contact with you and the other friends I had."

Gregory looked at Hans with immense sadness. He remembered very well that fateful decision of Hans to repeat Year 12 and how it had exacerbated the already existing rift in their friendship at the time. But he had no inkling that Klaus had played a part in this.

"In the end, all of this was part of Klaus' plan to separate me from you", Hans carried on his detailed dissection of what had happened at the time. "And he certainly managed that, as you and I barely saw each other after that. But Klaus … the bastard … also pretty much abandoned me then, and I barely saw him thereafter. That really hurt, as I thought he really cared about me. But in the end he was only interested in separating you and me. Once that was achieved he lost interest …"

At hearing all this, Gregory was clenching his fists. He had obviously not understood Klaus' role in all this at the time, and he felt deeply sorry for Hans. Hatred towards Klaus began welling up in Gregory. Klaus turned out to be yet another one of these key factors that had propelled Hans onto the pathway of mental breakdown. *And worst of all*, Gregory thought, *Klaus is probably even today not aware of the damage he caused! But then, who am I to talk? I abandoned Hans as much as Klaus did at the time. Maybe I was even happy that Hans was repeating the year, as it gave me a good excuse to spend even more time with Bill and the rock band and to neglect Hans.*

"After my first breakdown I never saw Klaus again", Hans continued his harangue. "In fact, I haven't got a clue what has become of him, whether he has had a successful life, career, kids … and, to be honest, I don't care …"

Gregory could understand how Hans felt, but he was also hoping that Hans would not break out in tears again like last time. *Please not here, not in this public space!*, Gregory thought selfishly while scrutinising Hans' face and sheepishly looking around him to see whether the other people in the café were watching them. But nobody stared back, they were all preoccupied with their own lives.

Hans' face had remained placid and stern, there were no signs of tears yet. "Although we have not seen each other a lot over the years", Hans continued, "you are the only one who has ever visited me … who has shown any interest in how I am … You are my only true friend … Bill doesn't give a shit … Sometimes I think that he is happy that I ended up … ended up in the loony bin … And people like Rufus and Matthias never cared about me anyway … And all my former girlfriends … Not one of them has come to see me all these years … They probably don't even know what has happened to me."

The discussion was taking the turn that Gregory had feared most, ending up in a self-pitying tirade by Hans. But, of course, Hans was right. It was indeed despicable how all Hans' former friends and girlfriends had avoided him as soon as he had his first psychotic break. And the dreadful discussion about Hans in the pub the evening before just confirmed what Hans' 'friends' were thinking about him. There was little sign of compassion, of understanding the difficult times Hans had gone through, indeed very little comprehension about mental illness and how debilitating it was. But Gregory also knew that he was in no position to criticise others. After all, his visits to see Hans had been very sporadic at best, and at worst sparked by feelings of guilt rather than a true interest to visit his friend. Gregory was as hypocritical as everybody else. Maybe even worse, because at least the others were showing their lack of caring and interest by not engaging with Hans at all, whereas Gregory's half-hearted attempts could easily be interpreted as hypocritical, shallow and insincere attempts to alleviate his own bad conscience.

"I know that my life has been rubbish …", Hans admitted, looking increasingly tearful. "The best time of my life was when we were 14 to 17 … when you and I were best friends. That was my golden time, when everything seemed possible, when I could get any girl I wanted … But look at me now …", and now tears began welling up in Hans' eyes as he looked down his morbidly obese body. "My life is a mess, not worth living any more … And I can't see any way out of this … It would best if I was dead …"

Gregory looked at his friend with as much compassion as he could muster. This was exactly the situation he had feared most. Another admission by Hans that he was feeling suicidal and that he was balanced on the edge of something that could snap at any moment! How Gregory hated this situation! But Hans' suicidal admission did not come as a surprise to Gregory after this very open but fierce dissection of their friendship and the challenges it had faced over time. Inevitably, dredging up all these deep memories from their pasts had, again, shown Hans how awful his current plight was. Surely his expression of suicidal thoughts was again a warning cry, but what could Gregory do? He could not stay in Heidenhausen to help Hans in his current depressive state, indeed Gregory's return flight from Stuttgart to London was leaving the next day. And he was not a psychiatrist. It had to be professional people who needed to deal with Hans. But why was the system failing? It was failing, Gregory suddenly realised, because all the problems Hans was facing could only be fully understood by someone who had been part of

Hans' life at the time all these problems were occurring: Hans' 14th birthday present (although Gregory had only heard from Hans about it much later); the beatings of Hans by his father; the pressure put on by his parents for Hans to excel at school; the rupture of their friendship; the sad role played by Klaus Hintermaier; the repeating of Year 12; Hans' time at military service; and his fateful episode with Monique. No shrink, no psychiatrist, no 'expert' could know and feel as much about Hans' desperate situation as somebody like Gregory could. Only Hans' former best friend was in a position to help him. Whether he wanted it or not, Gregory had to admit to himself that he was both a crucial part of Hans' problems but also a part of the solution. But what could somebody like Gregory, with a wife and kid, a job, a house, regular holidays, a good circle of friends ... what could somebody like him do? Like during their last meeting, all of Gregory's instincts were primed for flight, to get out of this situation, to escape, to leave as gracefully as possible.

"Look Hans ...", Gregory replied timidly, but Hans just stared at him with tearful eyes and made a gesture of waving him away with his good arm. *He probably remembers very well how weak my attempt was last time at consoling him*, Gregory wondered. *Maybe he knows that there is nothing I can do?*

Without saying a further word, Gregory waved to the waiter and paid the bill. They got up, Hans struggling to heave his heavy body from the tight chair, and they both walked slowly back towards the entrance of Hans' block of flats. Gregory looked worryingly towards his friend. This had again been a very tough visit, even tougher than the one 17 years ago. *No wonder I am so reluctant to see Hans often!*, Gregory thought with deep sadness. Hans walked very slowly, he seemed to have shrunk, diminished, as if this intense discussion about their friendship had sapped the last bit of energy out of his body. It looked as if he was utterly drained. Hans barely made it to the entrance door of his block of flats, and Gregory felt that he had to support Hans' heavy bulk, prevent this mass of human flesh from toppling over. Gregory wondered whether Hans needed help getting up the stairs, but Hans again just waved him aside with his good arm, saying that he would be alright. Hans looked Gregory deep in the eyes, but Gregory could not quite read in Hans' face what he was trying to say. *Just say something, damn it!*, Gregory thought trying to think of something, anything, appropriate to say. But he, yet again, knew that all had been said, that Hans understood that he could not expect any help from Gregory. Hans disappeared behind the closing entrance door, leaving Gregory standing on the front steps.

For a long time, Gregory just stood there, oblivious to his surroundings, wondering over and over again whether he had done and said the right things. Hans' mental state and depression had clearly been affected by Gregory's visit and their difficult discussion. But, Gregory thought, it was Hans, after all, who had steered their discussion towards these unsavoury reproaches and reprimands, it was Hans, not Gregory, who had opened again all these festering wounds of their troubled past. While Gregory was nonetheless happy that he had seen Hans again, he could also not deny that by seeing Hans he had again offered himself to be involved, to look after Hans, to have responsibility even if it was only remotely from the UK. But it was precisely this responsibility that made all the other friends, and former girlfriends, shy away from seeing Hans. Maybe they were right?

With a final look up towards Hans' flat, Gregory walked back towards his car. He was very unsure if and when he would ever see Hans again in person. As it turned out, he never would.

Part 4

Oblivion

25

29th October 2019. A damp mist had settled on the cemetery, casting gloomy shadows over the wet gravestones. Black crows, perched on branches of a beech tree, were cawing their eery chant, adding to the gloomy feeling of the place. Just an hour ago it had been a nice day, with autumn sunshine enhancing the orange, red and yellow colours of the deciduous trees fringing the cemetery, but the weather had gradually changed with a typical autumnal mist wafting in from the east.

Gregory stood among the small group of people lining the grave into which Hans' coffin was being cautiously eased by cemetery workers. Hans' mum, Sigrid, well into her 80s and in a wheelchair, tended by a person unknown to Gregory, stood a few metres away to his right. *Maybe a relative helping her with the wheelchair or a care worker?*, Gregory wondered. Sigrid had not recognised Gregory when they had met briefly earlier at the cemetery car park, and it took Gregory a while to remind her who he was. After all, the last time she had spoken to Gregory was on the phone, back in 1993 when she reluctantly had given him Hans' phone number. But Sigrid's mind also seemed clouded and she appeared not to be fully with it. She had only acknowledged Gregory's explanation that he had been Hans' best friend at school with a faint nod of the head. *Maybe Alzheimer's? Or maybe she just sees me as another one of Hans' acquaintances who abandoned him long ago?*, Gregory thought guiltily. Sigrid looked very old, with snow-white hair and a deeply wrinkled face that betrayed a life of hardship with a bastard of a husband and a mentally severely handicapped son. To Gregory's relief, Bernhard, Hans' dad, was nowhere to be seen. *Maybe he is dead?*, he thought. But during their brief greeting, Gregory had not dared asked Sigrid about her husband.

It was about two weeks earlier when Bill had rung Gregory out of the blue and had told him that Hans was dead. Although the rumours were again hazy, Bill had said, it appeared that Hans had spent another spell at the Bad Schlossenried psychiatric hospital, again in a confined ward, apparently to protect him from the paranoid delusions he continued to suffer. Somehow, and Bill did not have the full details, Hans had managed to escape from his room and go into the hospital gardens where he had hanged himself from a tree using the leather belt from his straightjacket. How Hans had managed to undo his straightjacket, and to heave his heavy bulk up a tree, Bill again did not know. Bill had been informed by his mother that the funeral was taking place on 29th October in the old Heidenhausen cemetery, not far from their old school.

Gregory had been utterly shattered by the news of Hans' suicide. While he was talking to Bill on the phone, his knees had given way and he had to sit down to steady himself. While talking to Bill, he could not hide his loud sobs and kept asking himself *'why, why, why?'* He felt particularly sad as he had started only a few months ago the whole painful process of engaging again with the painful story of his friendship with Hans, spurred on by memories rekindled through the old photos he had begun to scan. This in itself had been a rollercoaster ride of emotions, as, over the past few months, Gregory had reluctantly embarked on a self-critical dissection of what had gone wrong with his relationship with Hans, on analysing why Hans may have gone mad, and, most painfully, on whether Gregory himself had played a role in Hans' deteriorating mental state. And now this news that Hans had killed himself! Just at a time when Gregory had started contemplating whether to visit Hans again for a third time since Hans' mental breakdown, to make up for all his mistakes in the past, to atone for his bad conscience vis-à-vis Hans, and maybe even to continue their difficult discussion from 2010 about how and why their friendship had failed.

The news of Hans' death had exacerbated the guilt Gregory had already felt towards Hans since scanning the photos. It had rekindled memories of their last fateful and reluctant encounter in 2010 and how, yet again, he had not only failed to help his friend at the time, but how he had also cowardly escaped as soon as Hans had mentioned suicidal thoughts. *I am such a coward!*, Gregory had thought upon receiving the news of Hans' death. *I never took responsibility for looking after Hans. As soon as there were any signs of suicidal thoughts I just left him. I never rang him, never passed him my phone number so that Hans could contact me in the UK when he was feeling down, I just didn't want anything to do with him. And my last visit to see Hans in 2010 was spurred on more by my reaction towards the slanderous*

talk and gossip about Hans by my friends, than from a true
desire to actually see and help Hans!

These thoughts, and the regret that he would never be able to visit his friend again, had gone through Gregory's mind over and over after hearing about Hans' suicide. These thoughts also came out repeatedly in lengthy discussions with Gregory's wife Amelia as to whether he should go to Hans' funeral or not. Amelia had been very helpful in this situation. Not only had she reminded Gregory that of all of Hans' friends he was the only one who had at least seen Hans a few times since his breakdown, that he was the only one who had thought about Hans and his condition, especially over the past few months, and that he was the only one who ever cared about Hans after he had lost his position as flamboyant teenage school idol and a person they had all looked up to. Seeing Gregory's turmoil and sadness, Amelia had also encouraged Gregory to go to the funeral. Although he would have wished her to be there with him and to be at his side during this difficult visit, Amelia also rightly persuaded Gregory that it would be best if he went on his own. After all, his friendship with Hans belonged to another life, long before Gregory had met Amelia. It was part of Gregory's past, of his youth, of a time when he was somebody different from the person he was now. Gregory fully understood Amelia's position. He made up his mind to attend the funeral on his own, bought his plane tickets and booked himself into one of the Heidenhausen hotels for a few days. He was going to use the opportunity to spend a few days in Heidenhausen and to look around his old hometown he had not seen for a while. As his mother had died soon after he had last visited Hans in 2010, it had been over nine years since he had last been there. Had the place improved since, or was it still the rural backwater it had always been, leaking population and seemingly unaffected by the enthusiasm of reunification that had swept through most other parts of Germany? Was his old school still the way he remembered it?

Standing by Hans' grave, Gregory took another look at the people around him. Apart from Sigrid he did not recognise anyone. There was the priest, standing to the right of Gregory at the top of the grave and mumbling the usual religious rubbish that unfortunately had to accompany any burials in this Christian, conservative and backward part of Germany. Gregory did not even know whether the priest was Protestant or Catholic, and he did not care. *Had Hans been religious at all?*, Gregory wondered. He could not remember having talked much about religion with Hans, although he supposed that his parents, who had come from Silesia, were Catholic. But Gregory was not here to listen to some religious mumbo-jumbo but to pay his last respects to his friend, so he did not pay any attention to the priest's vacuous utterances. Opposite Gregory on the other side of the grave stood an old man accompanied by a younger woman. There was some vague resemblance to Bernhard, Hans' father, so was this possibly Hans' uncle, the one who had kindly lent Hans his van back in 1978 for their trip to Brittany, possibly with his daughter who would have been Hans' cousin? But Hans had never talked much about his uncle and had never mentioned a cousin, so Gregory was unsure. *When we were at school, Hans had only frequently mentioned his*

257

grandparents whom he felt quite close to, but they were obviously long dead, Gregory thought.

To Gregory's left, at the other end of the grave, stood another woman. Her face was covered in a black veil and Gregory could not fully make out her features, but he guessed she was about his age, i.e. late 50s. Was this one of Hans' former girlfriends? If yes, which one? Ursula? Martina? *Could it even be Monique?*, Gregory wondered, but he thought it unlikely as Monique had cut off all contact to Hans since their last fateful encounter and abortion of their child back in the early 1980s. If it was indeed Monique, then in another life, on another one of life's tree branches, on another life pathway, Hans and her could have been married with a child and may have lived a happy life together. *Or at least happier than Hans' life had been since they separated!*, Gregory thought mournfully. *How life may have been different for Hans if he had taken different decisions at this specific turn of his life branch!*, Gregory thought with great sadness about Hans' fateful decision at the time of telling Monique about his visit to a hooker. Gregory thought that he should maybe introduce himself to the woman after the ceremony was over and find out who she was.

But this bunch of people is all that remains of Hans' sad life!, Gregory thought with a sigh. Including Gregory, the priest and the person tending Sigrid's wheelchair there were only seven people standing at Hans' grave. *Is this really the sum of Hans' life?*, Gregory thought disgusted. *What about all the people from school who knew Hans well. Bill, Rufus, Matthias and especially bloody Klaus Hintermaier? And all of Hans' former girlfriends? Why are none of them here?*

From their phone conversation Gregory knew that Bill would not be there. Although he felt grateful to Bill for telling him about Hans' funeral, Gregory was also, yet again, angry at Bill for caring so little about Hans. Sure, Bill and Hans had had their run-ins and disagreements over the years, and their friendship had been marred by petty jealousy over who would spend more time with Gregory. *Pretty childish, really!*, Gregory mused, *and certainly not enough of an excuse to completely shun Hans, especially at times of desperate need when he had been so down mentally.* Surely, Hans' former friends could have mustered the courage to at least see their old friend off one last time, to acknowledge that he had at least been a little bit important at one point in their lives. *Ok, but maybe, apart from Bill, they did not know that Hans was dead?*, Gregory tried to find excuses for the absence of their friends.

Sigrid was quietly crying, shyly dabbing her wrinkled face with a handkerchief. The woman to the left of Gregory just stood there stoically, no emotion visible on her veiled face. Gregory had felt a heavy lump in his throat ever since entering the cemetery and walking with the small congregation towards Hans' grave, and he could no longer hold back the tears. Past memories about him and Hans were again flooding in, the many good times they had when they were teenagers, Hans looking at him with his full shock of brown hair and tanned from his last game of tennis, with his brown eyes and this heart-warming smile that made all these young girls and everybody he encountered melt away. What had happened to that person? Why had life turned out so badly for Hans Schlesier, why had it made him so desperate that he had sought the worst of all possible exits from life – suicide? Gregory let out loud sobs, his whole body shaking, which even made the priest look up and briefly pause his dull harangue. But Gregory was not embarrassed at all by his open show of grief. *Let them know that there is at least one person who cared about Hans, who was a good friend after all, who will miss him immensely!* As if on cue, Sigrid looked up and straight into Gregory's eyes. *Is there a hint of gratitude in her eyes?*, Gregory wondered looking back at her through misty eyes, *an almost imperceptible thank you that at least somebody cared about her son?*

Thankfully, the priest had by now stopped his dull religious dribble. After each of the attendees threw a small spade of earth onto Hans' coffin – a ritual Gregory found rather weird – the congregation began to move away from the grave. Sigrid held Gregory's gaze for one last moment, she was evidently thankful that at least one of Hans' former friends had turned up. But Gregory was too slow to catch up with the mysterious woman who had stood by the grave to his left. By the time he had made up his mind to accost her, to catch up with her, and to tell her who he was, she had already reached her car and driven off without a look back. *Maybe it was not Monique but simply Hans' carer or one of the health workers from Bad Schlossenried who had looked after Hans?*, Gregory wondered. He would never know.

26

29th October 2019. For a long time, Gregory sat in his rental car with a vacant stare, impervious to the gravestones shrouded in mist lining the parking space. *Maybe it had not been such a great idea to come to this funeral after all?*, he thought. It had not been a very pleasant experience, very drab and sullen, with no words spoken, no embraces, no speeches recounting some of the good times Hans had had in his life, no post-funeral dinner where members of the congregation would have had a chance to at least exchange a few words. The dank mist shrouding the cemetery had not helped either. *Only seven people!*, Gregory thought again. That's all that was left of Hans' formerly rich life! Seven people who turned up for his burial and probably only three or four of them who were there out of compassion and not because they had to, like the priest or Sigrid's care worker. *What a dreadful end to someone's life!*, Gregory thought with a shudder and a brief dystopian vision of his own funeral, hopefully years away, and a question mark about how many people would attend his ultimate demise. *Maybe we all do not leave much of a trace behind after all, irrespective of whether we have remained healthy or whether we have become severely mentally ill or incapacitated?*, he mused philosophically.

He turned the ignition key and drove slowly out of the cemetery, surprised that his dazed mind remembered to drive on the right side of the road. Without thinking where he was going, his mind still embroiled in acrimonious thoughts about how the whole world had abandoned Hans Schlesier, the road took him directly to *Franz-Bosch-Gymnasium*, their former school located just around the corner from the cemetery. *I must have subconsciously chosen this route*, Gregory thought, surprised at himself. It was a Saturday and the school was empty, the eery mist still shrouding everything in a hazy and indistinct blur. Gregory parked his car and walked towards the school's main entrance. To his surprise, the front door was open. *Maybe there is a function on somewhere in the school?*, Gregory thought absent-mindedly. Again, he did not know what he was doing here and where he was going, but his subconscious seemed to guide him. It had been nearly 40 years since he had last been here, but the building still looked the same as when he had last seen it after his A-levels, although everything seemed to be much smaller, distances between corridors and classrooms shrunk compared to when he was young and smaller. Here was the corner where they had usually met during breaks, here was the spot where Gregory had first kissed Evelyn in front of his friends, eliciting embarrassed smiles from Bill and Matthias at the time. Here was the corridor where Herr Möller had had his heart attack and lay there for minutes, surrounded by gaping students who did not know what to do.

Gregory's body seemed to be on remote control, taking him towards their last classroom. Not once did Gregory hesitate or lose his way, it was as if he was on remote control, as if he had only been there recently. He still knew every nook and cranny of his school and he suddenly felt like being

17 again. He was surprised again that the door to their classroom was unlocked but, so far, he had not seen anyone else in the building. He was amazed at how lax security seemed to be, or was he just dreaming all this? But no, it was all real standing here in their former classroom, the stage of so many intrigues, plotting, laughter, reluctant learning, pleasure, tears, fights, joke-telling, teasing, disrupting teachers, and small personal tragedies that seemed so all-important at the time. The ping pong table was no longer at the back of the classroom, and the space was used instead as a repository for discarded chairs and desks. Visions of table tennis battles with Klaus Hintermaier flashed up in Gregory's mind, two sweaty, gritty, stern kids fighting to death over who would win the 'finals'. It had seemed so crucial at the time and appeared so trivial now! And yet, these battles were all-important then, as they were instrumental for establishing and consolidating the school class power hierarchy, and, most importantly, for getting Hans' attention. Their ping pong fights were much more than just sport events and kids letting out steam between lessons. They were fights for the heart and soul of Hans' friendship. *And now Hans is dead and all of this was for nothing!*, Gregory nudged himself back from past to present, *and none of the kids who had been in our school class care about what has happened to Hans!* Somewhere they are out there, with their pathetic little lives, going about their business and not realising that life for Hans had become so difficult, so burdensome, that the only option he had seen was to kill himself. Hans was dead, while most of the others were still alive. How unfair was this?

Gregory could no longer stand the flood of past memories associated with his former classroom overwhelming him. He was angry, angry at himself for not having prevented Hans' suicide, angry for not having found the courage of visiting Hans again or at least for keeping in touch with Hans by phone or mail, angry at his former classmates who did not care, angry at the world for having abandoned Hans. Without a further glance back, Gregory stormed out of the classroom, rushed through the empty school corridors, through the main entrance hall, and back to his car. Only when he was cocooned in the confined safety of his car bubble – a space not linked to his past which did not bring back uncomfortable memories – did Gregory allow himself a deep breath. Maybe it was a deep sigh of relief?

Again, Gregory sat there for several minutes, staring into the misty void ahead of him. He was still not sure why he had come to Heidenhausen. Was it just to say goodbye to his old friend or was it also that he was forcing himself to conjure up these old memories, to visit places that had some association with Hans? He started the engine and drove slowly past the school and down the hill, a route he had often walked with Hans after school when they were 14 and 15. After a few minutes he had reached the quiet cul-de-sac in which Hans' parents' house was located. Again, not much seemed to have changed. A few houses had a new lick of paint, the odd loft extensions were evident, but the row of houses seemed pretty much unchanged, an almost fossilised vision of the past, with the juniper heath visible at the end of the street, surviving probably thanks to strict planning restrictions that prevented the heath from being swallowed up by new housing developments.

Gregory drove past Hans' house slowly. He did not want to be spotted by anyone, especially not by Hans' mum who must have been on her way back from the funeral or already at home. But did she still live here or was she in an old people's home? Gregory opened the driver's window and leaned out, glancing up towards the window of Hans' former room. Here they had spent both good and bad times together. Good times listening to music, drinking alcohol from Hans' parents' garish 70s-style bar, and chatting about girls. Bad times sitting over intractable Maths problems, for which no solutions could be found in their pea-sized brains, and having to deal with Bernhard's unpredictable tantrums and Hans' mum's strange demure behaviour. All these memories were intermixed with the pungent scents of Sigrid's disinfectant and cleaning liquids that lingered infinitely both in Gregory's mind and the immaculately cleaned and sterile staircase and which, Gregory imagined, were now wafting towards his open car window.

Sitting in his car and looking up at Hans' room, Gregory felt like he was pushing against something, some invisible barrier in his head, like opening a door against a storm. He felt trapped back in time when he was 13, 14 or 15, at the mercy of memories about Hans from which he may never be able to escape. Was this the place where Hans had developed his first mental problems – problems that at the time were impossible to spot by Gregory? Could he have done more to help his friend then, to pay more attention to the subtle changes that were evidently occurring in his friend? But no,

Gregory had become so absorbed with their rock band, the choir, with Evelyn, with having fun, with life itself, that he had begun to neglect his best friend. Eventually, he had left Hans to rot in his miserable room up there, at the mercy of stupid decisions taken by both his domineering father and jealous friend Klaus. Again, Gregory was overwhelmed by emotions and tears rolled down his cheeks.

He did not want to linger and swiftly turned his car around. He drove slowly further down the hill towards the centre of town located in the valley below. Yet, although Gregory wanted to stop thinking about the past, he could not prevent the emergence of visions of him and Hans speeding along these roads with their mopeds. These were maybe the best times he had when he was young, zooming along with Hans on their mopeds down these very roads, along adjoining narrow alleyways, and over unpaved tracks on the edge of Heidenhausen, mud and stones flung in the air by their screeching tires. How carefree they had been then, and how free they felt! This freedom of being able to drive your own two wheels, away from the confines of your parents and home, the fact that you could go anywhere you wanted for the first time in your life, it was great! And all this spiced up by the fact that they were zooming through the streets of Heidenhausen at night, in the gloomy and mysterious dark, pretending to chase girls, whistling at good-looking ones, and Gregory shyly turning away when the girls happened to respond. All this had raised the allure of what they were doing a thousand-fold. Even now, in the present, Gregory's old body could feel a pleasant tingling down his spine, all the small hairs of his body standing up at the thought of the pleasure he had felt at the time, driving behind Hans and thinking that the whole world and their whole lives lay there ahead of them – an unopened book full of promises and opportunities.

And now this!, Gregory brought himself crashing back to reality again, gripping the steering wheel of his rental car more tightly. Only a few years after their moped outings Hans would have his first nervous breakdown, never to be the same person again he had been when they were zooming along on their mopeds. Why had he not visited Hans more in recent times and talked about these good times they had together? Why did their last discussion in 2010 have to veer towards incriminations about who had abandoned who, with whom, and for what reason? Why could they not have simply enjoyed each other's company more, make the most of the great times they had together when they were young? And even just the odd phone calls would have helped, chatting with Hans about the past and how he was feeling, reminding Hans that everybody had problems in their lives, that nobody was immune to depression, sadness, self-doubts, insecurities … not even bloody Klaus Hintermaier. Maybe this could have prevented Hans' suicide?

Of course, Gregory had thought to himself after his last visit to Hans in 2010 that Hans would be alright, that *Heidenhausen Social Services* would look after Hans, that the German support system was good and robust, possibly more so than the system in the UK. But, at the same time, Gregory knew that these thoughts were just an excuse to placate his guilt. After all, he did not have more courage than any of their other friends who had all abandoned Hans. But

Gregory also knew that 'ifs' and 'buts' could not change the brutal truth about reality. Hans was dead and there was nothing he could do about it now! He had missed so many opportunities to make up for his mistakes with Hans, he had not been a good friend after all. *But maybe that was just how life was meant to be?*, Gregory thought, his eyes misting up again with tears as he drove slowly through the deserted streets of Heidenhausen's centre. Maybe there was no fairness in life after all, maybe you could only do so much, maybe it was futile to constantly feel guilty about what you could have, or should have, done in the past? *Looking at your behaviour in hindsight is always open to criticism and fraught with intractable problems*, Gregory thought, knowing that he should not be too hard on himself. He had been at least partly there for his friend, and nobody could have foreseen what would happen.

Gregory clutched the steering wheel more firmly while driving through the almost deserted streets betraying Heidenhausen's continuing economic decline. The best he could take away from all this was that in future he should be even more considerate to the people close to him, his wife, his son, his friends. You never knew what life could throw at you, the vicissitudes of one's pathway along your chosen, or not so chosen, life branch. *Make the most of it while you can ...*

Printed in Great Britain
by Amazon